THE SERGEANT'S CAT

THE

SERGEANT'S CAT

AND OTHER STORIES

JANWILLEM VAN DE WETERING

PANTHEON BOOKS, NEW YORK

First American Edition

Library of Congress Cataloging-in-Publication Data

Van de Wetering, Janwillem, 1931–
The sergeant's cat and other stories.
1. Detective and mystery stories, Dutch.
I. Title.
PS3572.A4292S4   1987   813'.54   87-2411
ISBN 0-394-54925-2

Book design by Guenet Abraham

Manufactured in the United States of America

CONTENTS

To the seals on Tupper Ledge

THE SERGEANT'S CAT

THERE GOES RAVELAAR

It was a late-summer day, crisp under a pale sun suspended within a circle of lifting fog. An old-model Volkswagen, fat and round, purred happily through the Amstel Dike's curves, headed for the city's limits. The driver, a tall, lean man with an angular face adorned by curly hair and a huge handlebar mustache, admired a flock of ducks, coming in low above the river. As the car accelerated, the passenger, an older, heavy man, flapped his large hands while he woke up.

"Are we going anywhere?"

"Radio is talking about a fire and a corpse."

"Way out?"

"Close-by."

Sergeant de Gier, assigned to the Homicide Department of the Amsterdam Municipal Police,* slowed the car and pointed. A wild goose floated quietly between the cattails, its neck bent back sleepily, about to insert itself between warm wings. "Look, Adjutant, isn't that a nice inspiration for you? That bird has swum right out of one of your favorite Hondecoeter paintings."

"Not now," Detective Adjutant Grijpstra said. "My mind is on duty." The adjutant stared ahead, focused on a large, spheric pitch-black cloud, billowing slowly from behind tall trees. "You say that pollution ahead hides a corpse?"

De Gier swerved abruptly to the right. A fire truck, clanging and hooting, passed them rudely. The Volkswagen maneuvered around a sloppily parked patrol car. It stopped. A constable, legs wide apart, had posted himself in front of imposing cast-iron gates. The sergeant got out. "It's us, your very own detectives. What's up?"

The constable scowled.

"Accident?" the sergeant asked kindly.

"Murder!" the constable shouted.

"Hear, hear," Grijpstra said, treading heavily on the driveway's gravel. "I urge you to keep calm, colleague." The adjutant beheld the large flames ahead with awe. "A most stately mansion."

"Not for much longer," the constable said.

"It'll be magnificently restored," de Gier said. "The city's architects are good at that sort of thing now; ancient square sixteenth-century merchants' palaces are all in vogue."

"Hop along," a fireman's bullhorn roared, "there are more fire engines on the way. Be off with your rust bucket, at once, you hear?"

De Gier drove the car through the gates that the constable

---

* The ranks of the Amsterdam Municipal Police are, in descending order, chief constable, commissaris, chief inspector, inspector, adjutant, sergeant, constable first class, constable.

was now willing to open. Two big red trucks thundered by on either side. Firemen, red-faced under gleaming helmets, unrolled hoses.

"Why murder?" the adjutant asked, pulling the constable to the side.

"*Whammo!*" the constable shouted. "That's what we heard, me and my mate. Over there we were driving, quietly on patrol on the dike, and all of a sudden, *kerboom*, all the windows popped out, flashing sparks, flames, what have you. We shot right down the drive, looking for what's what. Got into the place to see if anyone could be saved but the little lady was quite done for—bits of her all over the place . . ."

"In the kitchen?" Grijpstra asked.

The constable's arms pointed vaguely. "Over there. In the house. Disgusting, I tell you."

"The gas range," the adjutant said. "Seen it many times before. Missus tries to light the stove, but the pilots are off. She never notices, the kitchen fills up with gas, she's doing something else now, comes back, lights a cigarette and . . ." The adjutant nodded at the flames licking out of the mansion's windows, mocking the pressurized water aimed at them from three trucks at once.

"Faulty pilots," de Gier said, shaking his head. "I'm changing over to electric."

"No, no, no," the constable shouted. "She was in a room, over there, up front. A bomb exploded. I heard it myself."

"You heard a bang," the adjutant corrected. "What else did you notice?"

"A bomb," the constable said. "Aren't people *bad*?"

"Oh, *there* I agree," Grijpstra said. "But all we have here is a bang that disturbs and an innocent corpse to follow. Anything else to report?"

"A fat, furry, short-tailed cat," the constable said. "The fire was getting worse but we could still be heroic, so me and my mate rushed about for a bit. There was a fireplace with a cat up the chimney, blown right out of its basket. We heard him holler. I pulled his bit of a tail, but he was stuck in too far."

Another constable became visible. He was talking to a lady. The lady ran along. De Gier ran along, too.

"Who was that?" Grijpstra asked, grabbing hold of the other constable. "The neighbor woman," the policeman said. "She was alerted by the bang. She's going home now to phone Mr. Ravelaar. The corpse inside would be Mr. Ravelaar's wife."

"A bomb," the first constable said. "Bad people killing good ones. How can they do it, Adjutant? Won't it come back to them in dreams?"

Grijpstra wandered off, away from the smoke and into the park. De Gier came running back. "Got any wiser, Sergeant?" Grijpstra asked.

"The cat blown up the chimney was called Max," de Gier panted. "Tubby little fellow, well equipped with brains. Sense of humor, philosophically gifted, like all good felines. Mr. Ravelaar, the fellow who lives here, has been contacted and is on his way in a two-horse Citroën. He's a lawyer."

"A baby Citroën goes with this opulent elegance?" Grijpstra asked.

"According to the lady next door, Adjutant, we're dealing with crazy folks again. Missus inhabited the mansion while estranged Mister had to live in the servants' quarters. Missus is qualified as 'disturbed,' Mister as 'most definitely rather odd.' "

"A leisurely walk," Grijpstra suggested, "will provide clarity of mind."

The wind was pushing most of the smoke toward the river. De Gier stroked the bark of a huge tree. "This poplar must date back a hundred years, and those oaks over there could be older still; imagine dwelling in the midst of all this ancient splendor. What is that graceful little building ahead? The servants' villa?"

Grijpstra opened a door. "One garage—contents: one late-model Mercedes-Benz."

De Gier opened another door. "One steep staircase with a

mahogany railing. Leads to an apartment? Maybe Mister's digs?"

They were walking again. "Artful arrangements of rocks overgrown with assorted mosses," de Gier said. "A rose garden, a greenhouse filled with a complete collection of orchids; more wealth, more beauty. Over there—an antique gazebo with a mushroom roof topped by a giant hardwood cherry. Our couple would take tea there, with cream cakes on the side."

"Cream cakes," Grijpstra said, "turn sour when harmony is lacking. However"—his arm swept around—"someone took loving good care of all this. Acres of high-class lawn. All sorts of herbs in splendid condition. Greek statues surrounded by neatly clipped hedges. No weeds."

"Wah," de Gier said.

"Wah what?"

De Gier frowned. "Filth ahead. *Yagh.* One muddy pond under a broken-down bridge." He held his nose. "Extreme decay."

Grijpstra rubbed his chin.

"Thinking?" de Gier asked.

Grijpstra smiled. "I often do."

"In the car you often sleep."

"Deep concentration is often mistaken for slumber." Grijpstra looked around. "Why this contrasting mess all of a sudden? A forgotten and dying nook in an immaculately kept park? Nobody has been near this filth in years. But why, eh, Sergeant? Ponds go very well with parks. If this were mine, I'd keep rare fowl."

"There were birds here once," de Gier said. "Over there: rotten coops and cages, and broken little ducks' houses on posts." He moved his hand dreamily. "Scarlet-beaked Mongolian geese, long-legged whooping cranes, multicolored gooney birds, a flamingo here and there." He slapped Grijpstra's shoulder. "The magnificence of our national Golden Age preserved in the here-and-now. Here is where your cherished Hondecoeter pulls up his silk stockings above his silver-clipped boots before knocking together another of those priceless pictures of his. Just like you pull up your sixty-five percent polyester socks before getting into the acrylic paints."

"Please," Grijpstra said.

De Gier patted his superior's ample back. "I'm serious, Hank. Your talent leaves me breathless. Remember the coot-cock look-alike you whipped up on your last day off?"

The first constable came running. "The fire chief wants to see you two."

The constable brought along the stench of thick smoke, and flakes of ashes that attached themselves to Grijpstra's dark blue suit. He rubbed them into stains.

"Report on proceedings," Grijpstra ordered.

"The fire is under control. Limited damage. But the lady is still dead."

"How's Max doing?" de Gier asked.

The constable shivered. "He finally popped out of the chimney."

"He's okay?"

"Not okay." The constable dropped his half-smoked cigarette and stamped it into the path. "They sprayed him full of foam, but the poor fur ball was fried solid." The constable snarled. "You better get the perpetrator. The neighbor lady showed again and analyzed what must have been going on here for years and years." The constable held up both hands. He shook one. "I now know *what*"—he shook the other hand—"is *what*."

"You do, eh?" Grijpstra asked. "That's not your business. Now refer your knowledge to proper quarters. Describe both sides of this equation."

The constable talked. De Gier summed up. "Prolonged domestic conflict on the left—premeditated violent death on the right."

"It's the prolonging that always does it," Grijpstra said. "I was married myself. Couldn't I imagine what would have happened if the connection hadn't been cut?" He mopped his cheeks.

"Could be self-defense?" de Gier suggested. "Missus pushes Mister into poverty, the servants' quarters. He has to do all the hard work. She lords it in the castle. He drives the second car."

The constable was observing another half-smoked cigarette. "I see," he mumbled.

"Changing sides?" de Gier asked. "What about the cat?"

The constable stamped on the stub. "Right. *Right*. So what does the despicable demon of a husband come up with? With a bomb. Planted inside. We saw the windows blown out. What did he care? There must be insurance."

"A bomb with a long fuse?" Grijpstra asked. "All the way to his city office?"

"Please," the constable said. "We have technology now. A mechanism?"

De Gier's head swayed rhythmically. "Ticktock, ticktock, ticktock."

"Or a radio device?" the constable asked, imitating an antenna with his raised arm. "Can't you see it? *I* see pure premeditation. Ravelaar must have listened to the weather forecast, too. Today the wind changed. It has been blowing the other way for weeks. With the wind the wrong way, he would have killed some good trees maybe, and had the fire going into his own quarters."

De Gier pointed at something dark and dirty left out on the lawn.

"Yeh. Max." The constable nodded. "Wow, did that animal ever howl!"

De Gier leaned against a fence.

Grijpstra looked away. "A lawyer?" he asked. "An attorney? A master of our people-pleasing laws? A gentleman playing perverted criminal?"

"Gents are the worst," the constable whispered loudly. "They got to be real bad to stay on top. For us it's different; we've learned to be comfortable down below."

"Easy now," Grijpstra said. "As a noncommissioned officer,

I'm half a gent myself, and the sergeant here is an auto-didact intellectually inclined. Asphalt bunnies like you should not try to understand their betters."

The constable apologized. De Gier let go of the fence.

Adjutant and sergeant walked into the ravaged house.

"So what kept you?" the fire chief asked. "I come up with something interesting at long last and there's nobody around to see it. Oops. Bah."

Grijpstra stepped aside from something moist that had dropped from the room's high ceiling.

"Bit of Missus," the fire chief said. "The larger part has been scraped into the ambulance just now."

De Gier stumbled away.

"Can't stand it?" the fire chief asked.

"Tags along anyway," Grijpstra said. "I don't like to be lonely."

The fire chief displayed a small object.

Grijpstra peered. "Shard of gray metal?"

"Also known as a bit of deadly shrapnel," the fire chief said. "You have no idea how hard it is to prove intent when there's a fire. This may be my first chance."

"Shrapnel," Grijpstra said. "What does that call to mind? War? Grenades?"

De Gier came in again, holding a hand on his mouth.

The fire chief picked up another small object and gave it to de Gier. De Gier dropped it. The fire chief picked it up. "Too hot for you? It's just mildly warm."

"What is?" de Gier asked.

"Bit of brass, from the shrapnel's shell. A brass shell casing designed for a cannon. Brass is close to copper. Missus here must have been a great copper collector, for there are torn-up plates, jugs, pails all over the place. Came off those ripped-out shelves there."

"A shell casing?" de Gier asked. "From a big gun?"

"*Now* I see," Grijpstra said. "Someone shot up the house with a fully automatic cannon."

"Close," the fire chief said, "but not quite. The shell *casing* exploded, meaning the whole thing blew up, not in a gun's chamber, more like on a shelf."

"How?" de Gier asked.

"Dunno," the fire chief said.

"By accident?" Grijpstra asked.

"Of course," the number one constable said. "An accident, what else? I'll tell you what happened. Missus sort of accidentally hit the shell with a hammer. No, listen here: she happened to find a nail, tucked it into the shell's detonator cap, *then* got it with the hammer. All by accident, like, just to see what would happen."

Grijpstra applauded.

"It's my hobby," the constable explained. "I sometimes like to figure things out a bit, when I have an odd moment."

"And would anyone by any chance know what sort of shell we are dealing with here?" Grijpstra asked.

"I'm not sure, of course," the fire chief said, "for I'm never sure of anything ever, but I'm somewhat sure that this here was part of an Oerlikon shell, for I was a soldier once and carried cannon shells around in cases."

De Gier nodded. "I found some once, in a terrorist's apartment. This long? This thick?" He made indications.

The constable nodded too. "About my size. No wonder it caused utter devastation."

"And why did this phallic object explode?" Grijpstra asked. "Did the fire set it off? So what set off the fire? Which chicken? Which egg? Or shall we never know the sequence of either?"

"There he is," the constable said. "That must be Ravelaar, the suspect, who just sneaked from the compact Citroën that just sneaked in."

"You take him, Chief," Grijpstra said. "When he has seen the victims, you can pass him along. We'll be in the gazebo."

"Mr. Ravelaar," Grijpstra said twenty minutes later, "meet Sergeant de Gier. I'm Adjutant Grijpstra."

"Ha-ha."

"Beg pardon?" De Gier asked.

"I laughed," Ravelaar said. "Very sorry. Delighted to meet you both." He laughed louder. *"There goes Max!"*

"You're saying?"

Tears of joy ran down Ravelaar's puffy cheeks. He clapped himself on the polished skull. He leaned against the gazebo's wall and patted his round belly. The detectives waited. Ravelaar managed to master his emotions. "I do beg your pardon, but this is really very funny. Would you care for a drink? Follow me to my humble quarters?"

"Are you suffering from shock?" De Gier asked.

"Not at all," Ravelaar said, "but a pick-me-up will do us all good."

De Gier sat on a wobbly Gothic stool, Grijpstra rocked in the remains of a Victorian armchair, Ravelaar's weight made the springs of a reject Empire couch creak. "Throw-outs from the mansion's life-style," Ravelaar said. "Alicia kindly let me have them. Now they can be sent to the dump."

Grijpstra chose a lemon soda; de Gier selected a glass of water. Ravelaar poured into chipped mustard jars, filling his own with cheap jenever. "To an end," Ravelaar said, raising his drink, "to a beginning."

"There goes Max?" De Gier asked.

"Ho-ho," Ravelaar laughed. "Oh, dear. Not again."

"I don't quite believe we fully follow your line of reasoning," Grijpstra said.

"Alice in Wonderland," Ravelaar said. "English literature, an obscure quote."

"Tell us more?" Grijpstra asked.

Ravelaar smiled. "My wife, Alicia, also lived in a most different world."

His audience smiled, too. There was a long silence. Ravelaar got up and pulled a book off a shelf. "Here, let me find the passage." He flipped pages. "Alice is growing quickly and becomes stuck in a house. Curious animals come along; they're outside. A lizard is nominated as their scout, and the poor fellow is pushed down the house's chimney. Alicia kicks it up again." Ravelaar wiped his eyes with a large handkerchief, "Oh, dear. Hee-hee. Here we are. The animals outside see Bill rocket into the sky and shout: *'There goes Bill!'*" He dropped the book. "Hyee-hyee!"

Grijpstra picked up the book and put it back on the shelf. "You like that passage?"

"Adjutant," Ravelaar said, exercising supreme effort to become calm. "Adjutant, you will agree that this is a comical moment. To me it is the best scene in my most favorite tale."

"Not funny," de Gier said, "not in this context."

"Not even," Ravelaar asked, "when a real little devil flies into the sky, straight from Alicia's house of horror?"

"No," Grijpstra said.

Ravelaar's thin eyebrows danced in indignation. "Please. Don't tell me you don't appreciate what went on here. It all fits in nicely. Alicia's threatening presence becoming larger and larger, her kicking *me* out first. *There goes Ravelaar*, and all her subconscious animals laughed, and then her own wickedness took over, in the shape of Mighty Max, and then justice came about, and then, ha-ha . . . excuse me . . . *there goes Max?*" Ravelaar tittered expectantly. "No . . . ?"

"No," de Gier said. "Are you crazy?"

Ravelaar sat down. "No." He grabbed the bottle and refilled his jar. He drank.

De Gier checked the books on the shelf. His forefinger followed an orderly row of leather-bound volumes that contained a complete series of articles on the application of tax laws. "Your specialty, I presume?"

"Yes," Ravelaar said. "My profession. I deal in justice."

"So you aren't crazy?" Grijpstra asked.

Ravelaar massaged the smile off his face. "No. Not normally, and circumstances will excuse my present state of mind. You can forget that line of thought. Madness presupposes being able to prove that subject is a danger to others or himself. There are other conditions, too. An irregular life? I'm as regular as they come. Irresponsible behavior? I've always been known to pay my bills."

"Max died painfully," de Gier said.

"Good." Ravelaar grinned. "That hairy horror has pestered me for years. You try and prune roses when a snarling and clawing varmint prepares his attack behind a bush. You take pleasure in neatly raked gravel when Misery Max translates your labors into the preparation of a giant litterbox. I ate stale bread; Mouthy Max lived on salmon and smoked eel." The jenever bottle gurgled angrily.

"So much for Max," Grijpstra said. "Your wife was blasted into death by an exploding cannon shell. Parts of her are still stuck to the mansion's living-room ceiling. How about that, sir? Are we having justice again?"

Ravelaar's fingertips tried to knead his drink's container.

"We could become technical," Grijpstra said. "A cannon shell in a magnificent mansion?"

Ravelaar smiled stiffly. "Good question. I've been asking that myself. I came up with an answer. Alicia was neurotic. She collected like a magpie. There was no end to her greed for gleaming objects. She haunted the fleamarkets and secondhand stores. She was particularly fond of brass. Some hooligan sold her a live cannon-shell casing. She happily displayed it on the mantelpiece."

"Where it exploded?" Grijpstra asked.

Ravelaar waved impatiently. "Wait. I am not done yet. Alicia liked to polish her wonderful possessions. She bought polish by the drum. Polish, polish, polish." He laughed, while both his hands rubbed air.

Everyone stared at each other.

"I see," Grijpstra said.

"But do you understand what you see?"

"Not quite," Grijpstra said. "Maybe it'll come to me after a while. Could you meanwhile tell me how old you would be?"

Ravelaar got up. "Sixty-four springs have passed me by."

"Can you explain to me what you do for a living?"

Ravelaar bowed. "With pleasure. The office that will retire

me next week fights the Tax Audit Bureau on behalf of clients. I am their most respected and underpaid slave. Senior inspectors, however, tend to accept my suggestions. If not, they know they'll be cruelly defeated. I prepare my cases carefully, approach slyly, my attack is lethal. I will miss making mincemeat out of them."

"Try us," Grijpstra said.

Ravelaar rubbed his hands, then winked.

"Let's go," de Gier said.

"One more little question," Grijpstra said at the door.

"I knew you would do that," Ravelaar said. "All authorities are trained the same way. Cajole suspect into dropping his defense, then strike." He caressed Grijpstra's arm. "Go on, Adjutant, let's have your unexpected sudden trip-up."

Grijpstra led the way down the little building's steep stairs. Outside, he looked around. "You take care of the park yourself?"

Ravelaar bowed. "Alicia wouldn't spend money on upkeep. This is a perfect example of the garden art of yesteryear, conceived by masters, kept up by humble me."

"So why," Grijpstra asked, "stop short of the pond?"

"That dirty swamp?"

"Yes, now maybe," de Gier said, "because you paid no attention. If you had, you could be keeping great crested grebes, cormorants, swans—growing water lilies in between the waving reeds."

Ravelaar looked unhappy. "Don't care for water."

The three of them stepped back as an ambulance, the patrol car, and fire trucks drove past them toward the gates.

"The property borders the river," de Gier said.

"The river can't reach me," Ravelaar said, "and the pond I will fill in. Never mind the hellish dreams . . ."

"Drowning dreams?" Grijpstra asked kindly.

Ravelaar shivered.

"Chilly?" de Gier asked. "Better get back inside. We will be seeing you again, no doubt."

■　■　■

"Here you are again," Ravelaar said, "two disturbers of the Sunday peace." He held up a crystal flask, pointed at long-stemmed goblets.

The detectives declined.

"It's all yours now?" Grijpstra asked.

"There were never any children," Ravelaar said.

"All yours," de Gier said. "The mansion is being worked on already; then there's the park, the Mercedes, a million guilders* invested by your wife in a mutual fund."

"Another half million," Grijpstra said, "in life insurance. Unusual, rather. Husband collects on dead wife?"

"I had the mutual clause inserted," Ravelaar said, "to raise the policy's sense of justice. In my modern view both marriage partners have equal emotional worth. In case of death the surviving party has her or his anguish tempered with cash."

"You've manipulated yourself into a position of perfect freedom," Grijpstra said, looking out of the apartment's window. He smiled. "Luxury, beauty, solitude, no low-level worries."

Ravelaar smiled, too. "I like you, sir. You may not be too far removed from my level of perception. There's still a bit of a gap, but I see a willingness to breach it. Can't say as much for your uncouth friend."

"You're my top suspect," de Gier said sharply.

"See?" Ravelaar shouted. He leered at Grijpstra. "I've met your henchman's type before, in the Audit Bureau. Eager nincompoops who never fail to come in from the wrong angle." He glared at de Gier. "You really see a chance to blame me for that mishap? You can't even *think* of charging me with murder here. Facts and circumstances do not add up to a criminal situation. I'll review your so-called case for you, once and for all. My deceased wife, Alicia, unwittingly purchases a live cannon shell in another hopeless attempt to complete her magpie's collection of gleaming objects. The shell somehow

---

* 1 guilder = 48 cents (1987).

16

explodes. All by itself. I wasn't even anywhere close. My visits to the main house were both rare and brief. How could I have noticed a live shell among all those shiny whatevers?"

"Watch this," de Gier said. He held an invisible object between his legs and moved his free hand in a rubbing manner.

"Are you masturbating?" Ravelaar asked.

"The sergeant is polishing an Oerlikon shell," Grijpstra said. "The faster and the longer he rubs, the more heat is generated. The temperature within the shell rises to danger point."

De Gier stopped smiling. *"Kaboom?"* he asked softly. "A neurotic lady venting her frustrated energy on an explosive phallic object?"

Ravelaar studied the glowing fluid in his goblet.

"Polish, polish, polish," de Gier said.

Ravelaar nodded. "Yes. You may have something there, Sergeant." He smiled forgivingly. "Alicia was rather a frustrated woman. That activity you demonstrated could be sexual, yes; why not? She didn't have any normal sexual outlets, of course." He gestured. "Not much of a looker, you know. Short. Chubby. Thick spectacles, not much nose. Rather looked like an owl, I thought."

Grijpstra grimaced. "Don't miss her much, do you now?" He opened his notebook. "We did our homework. Your retirement income is less than half of your salary." He flicked a page. "Your marriage contract held you liable for half the estate's upkeep." He put the notebook away. "Character witnesses define you as extremely stubborn, quite incapable of negotiating a better agreement with your estranged wife. You were a soldier during the war; you would know about shells."

"You found one at the fleamarket?" de Gier asked.

"Yes?" Grijpstra asked.

"Proof?" Ravelaar asked.

"Arrest him, I say," de Gier said in the car. Grijpstra grunted while admiring a flock of ducks, coming in low from across the river. A wild goose floated slowly forward between the cattails at the water's near side. "Look," Grijpstra said. "I think I can use that bird. Good model for my next Sunday painting."

"Not now," de Gier said. "I'm working."

Grijpstra grinned grimly. "Work audibly, Sergeant."

"I say, harass the cat-killer," de Gier said gruffly. "Keep dropping in on him from time to time. Send him official little letters, ordering him to Headquarters at a few days' notice. Steam his brain, I say, rattle his conscience. I'll record my cat and have a tape meow in the bushes. Loud Siamese yells? A full moon? I can get a raccoon's tail at a furrier's. Attach it to a line? Dangle it through the mansion's chimney?"

"Suspect killed his wife mostly," Grijpstra admonished.

"I'm too tall," de Gier said. "You could dress up like her, wait for a foggy night? Dance in the park? On one of those lawns?"

Grijpstra pondered. "Nah."

"Got to do something."

"Yes," Grijpstra said. "But your ice is too thin. Let's stay on decent ground."

"Then do what?"

"Wait," Grijpstra said, rapping his knuckles against the Volkswagen's roof. "Wait for nice justice."

Autumn came and went. Rain became sleet; sleet changed into snow. The Volkswagen's windshield wipers protested squeakily.

"Where?" de Gier asked.

"Amstel Dike," the radio answered. "Just this side of the city limits. A car slipped into the river and broke through the ice. Our wrecker hauled it out, but the driver seems to be missing. Try to assist."

"Will go," de Gier said. He pushed the microphone back into its clip and shook Grijpstra's shoulder. "Are you there, Adjutant?"

"Tell us?" Grijpstra asked a constable directing traffic on the dike.

"Over there," the constable said. "A large Mercedes skidded off the curve in front of that stately mansion, slithered onto the river's ice, and sank, but we managed to retrieve it. The driver must have freed himself, but the body is still missing. See my mate walking on the ice? He could use some help."

Grijpstra moved along slowly, anxious not to slip. De Gier shuffled along. "Thin ice?" de Gier asked. "Last time *you* said it."

"Your turn," the constable on the river said. "Take my broom. Sweep off the snow so that we can look through the ice."

De Gier swept with broad strokes.

"There," Grijpstra gasped.

Ravelaar floated on his back an inch under the ice, arms spread, legs stretched out; his eyes protruded, his mouth hung open.

"Looks crucified," de Gier said softly. "Let's get him out."

The constable had fetched a sledgehammer and was banging on the ice. Each bang produced a jerky movement in the corpse, moving it closer to the area of open water. Grijpstra and de Gier followed slowly. Grijpstra sighed. "I told you we had only to wait."

De Gier nodded, then stepped back as the body suddenly bobbed up, half jumped, and slid up onto the far side of the ice.

"There goes Ravelaar," Grijpstra said.

Six this, Six that

Quite a pleasant summer morning, Adjutant Grijpstra thought, with nothing amiss, except that wasp. The outsize bug hums in an irritating manner and is armed with a poisonous sting. What do I know about wasps? Do they attack without warning? Maybe not; maybe they only go for you when you bother them. How do I not bother the opponent? By sitting quietly. While observing, I will see the connection of cause and effect. How the wasp got here in the first place, and how he will leave again, maybe, because the window is open.

In the same room, on the third floor of Police

Headquarters in Amsterdam, opposite the adjutant, sat Sergeant de Gier, feet on his desk, head against the wall. He also observed the wasp. The sergeant's hands were out and ready. De Gier waited. The wasp dove, straight at the sergeant.

Whap.

"There you are," de Gier said. "One enemy removed." He flicked the striped corpse into the wastepaper basket. "At your service. You're welcome."

"Is that the way we're going now?" Grijpstra asked. "Violence in the early morning? Would that be the solution? Does the opponent have to be flattened? Without the slightest consideration?"

"Indeed," de Gier said. "I analyzed the situation and acted at once. Ever been stung by a wasp? This morning that didn't happen. No painful swelling, no throbbing. On the contrary, you're now experiencing a continuing feeling of peace of body. Be happy and thankful."

There was a knock on the door. A well-dressed middle-aged man entered. The detectives got up and shook the man's hand. De Gier found a chair for the client. Grijpstra found paper and ballpoint. "Yes, sir, what can we do for you?"

The man dried his skull with a silk handkerchief. An expensive watch glittered on his hairy wrist. "My name is Vries; I have a complaint."

"Go ahead," Grijpstra said.

The man talked with authority and confusion, in a civilized but nervous manner. Grijpstra wrote; de Gier listened. "That's it?" Grijpstra asked five minutes later. The man nodded. Grijpstra cleared his throat. "Allow me to tell you what I think I've understood. You work for the supermarket chain Zwart Incorporated. You're the chief accountant. Your company has profitable outlets all over the country. Your number one store is right here in Amsterdam, in New South, our fanciest suburb, where the well-heeled live on choice and rare foods only. Before your last check the store did well, but now it doesn't. Money seems to have disappeared."

"Millions, Adjutant."

"How much exactly?"

"Two-point-eight million, Adjutant."

"How did you get to that figure?"

"Look here," Vries said. "We know what we're buying, right? We know what overall profit percentage we're making, right? So we know what our sales should be, right? Sixteen-point-eight million."

"And the actual sales were?"

"Fourteen million."

"A small mistake perhaps?" de Gier asked. "Accountancy involves bookkeeping, does it not? Did you check the books properly this time? Did you look at the right side of the page? Administration is always off. Have you been reading the paper lately? Take the government's budget for instance—billions come and billions go. A billion is a thousand million and you're talking about a mere two-point-eight."

"Do me a favor, Constable," Vries said. "Save me your amateurish gibberish. Every figure has been chewed and digested. Don't tell me how to look at figures. My computers don't make mistakes and my deduction is correct. Theft is a crime, and you work for the police."

"Theft means a hand reaching in from outside," de Gier said, "and the hand is connected to a masked face under a cap. What we have here is something else—embezzlement, I would say. An employee makes off with money that has been entrusted to him. Embezzlement is worse than theft, for it's nasty and sneaky. It therefore ranks higher on our list."

"I didn't know," Vries said.

"But you do know that your complaint is not related to violence," Grijpstra said. "Who sent you to us? We're Murder and Manslaughter. You're in the wrong room."

"Never mind," Vries said. "I was in the right room before and waited an hour. I demand prompt action. Zwart Incorporated is a pillar of our society. We provide work and feed the people. You're just sitting here. Do something, Adjutant."

"One moment." Grijpstra lifted his phone and dialed a number. "Is that you, Inspector?"

"Yes?" shouted the inspector. "Yes? Yes? *Yes?*"

"Your client strayed into our room, sir. Some lost millions. Do you have a minute? Can I bring him in?"

"A minute?" shouted the inspector. "Minute what? Minute where? Nothing but fraudulence in the land and we're short-staffed. The tax department has lost its safes, the rent-a-cars their cars, the building companies their building materials, and the pension funds their pensions. Railways just phoned; they've lost ten miles of track. My files are stacked to the ceiling. Yesyes. *Yesyes.*"

"A bit busy, sir?"

The telephone cackled and coughed.

"Put the phone down," de Gier said. "I saw the inspector in the canteen just now. He was pouring coffee on his trousers, for he had dropped and broken his cup. He'll be taken away soon and will have leave for the duration."

Vries got up and looked out of the window. "Are you doing something or not? If not, I'll be going, but not through the door." He looked down. "It's high enough." He lifted his leg and rested it on the windowsill. "Please give me a push."

"Are you all right, sir?" Grijpstra asked.

"Isn't suicide within your duties, Adjutant? Will my death instigate your investigation?"

"Sit down," Grijpstra said. "Tell me what you have done about this case so far."

Vries ticked off his fingers. "Checked programs. Compared results with other stores. Completed stocktaking. Followed flow of incoming goods. Checked cash registers. Screened all members of staff. Worked in the store myself."

"Found nothing?" de Gier asked.

"Found something, a difference of two-point-eight million guilders." Vries produced a calculator from his pocket and placed it on Grijpstra's desk. He pressed its keys. "See how much two-point-eight million is? Lost in a year. You know how much that is in a day? Divided by three hundred? Sundays and holidays discounted?"

De Gier read the result. "Nine three three three three point three three three three."

"A hundred thousand a day," Vries said. "Bit of a leak, I would say."

"Illegal," Grijpstra said, "but rather abstract, don't you think?"

"A mere falsification," de Gier said. "Not our field, Mr. Vries. We'll pass your complaint if you can't find the time to wait, and I can promise you that a colleague will take your case. A specialist, I'm sure. We're all specialists here. How can we be of use to you if your complaint isn't our specialization? I assure you, sir, we know nothing about groceries."

Vries pushed the sergeant aside and replaced his leg on the windowsill.

"Please," Grijpstra said. "Give this another thought. Perhaps it's unnecessary to inflict violence on yourself. You sure there is no violence in this complaint?"

"Yes," de Gier said. "Any fights in your office? Someone disappeared perhaps? A secretary maybe? Left an incomprehensible note and never showed her pretty face again?"

Vries thought. "Gennep never showed again."

"Murdered?" Grijpstra asked. "The name means nothing to me and I do have a memory for the lost and unfound."

"Accident," Vries said. "May this year, on Mallorca. We didn't even know he was vacationing out there. A bachelor, in charge of buying machines for the administration. Slipped off a cliff."

"Were we informed?" Grijpstra asked. "I assume we weren't. Did the Spanish police issue some statement?"

"*Accidente*, Adjutant, that's what we were told."

"Tell us about this Gennep," de Gier said.

"These things shouldn't be said," Vries said, "but I can do without Gennep. He was a maker of messes. He also bought too much. I picked up after him, as far as I could. Gennep didn't know the alphabet. His files were a disaster."

"Purchasing invoices referring to computers and such?"

Vries nodded.

Grijpstra studied his notes. He tore a fresh sheet from his notebook and wrote down in an artistic hand the figures $16.8 - 14 = 2.8$. He held up the sheet. "Like this or not like this?"

"Like that," Vries said.

"I suggest you leave us now," Grijpstra said. "You may hear from us soon. We'll take on your case."

"Catch the embezzler," Vries said, and walked toward the door. "Please. My boss is a devil who haunts all my moves. He breathes on me during the day and telephones at night. I can't go on like this. I'm going crazy."

De Gier closed the door. "He's crazy now, don't you think? Even so, accountants seem to have a way with figures. My brother-in-law is an accountant, and he can add a page of telephone numbers, in his head, straight from the book. What do we make of this tale? A mistake after all? The electrons got stuck in the conduits so that the profit evaporated in a loose condenser in an odd nook of a computer? How can a deli-supermarket in New South not make a profit?" The telephone rang. The sergeant listened and spoke. He put the phone back and put on his jacket. "Something to do. Drowned bum in the inner harbor. Man is known to us and to most local bars. Coming to have a look?"

"No," Grijpstra said. He glanced at his watch. "Ten in the morning—there's still some working day left. I'm going to sniff about and will meet you at the supermarket's office at three in the afternoon."

De Gier left. Grijpstra contemplated. Meanwhile, he looked at his equation: $16.8 - 14 = 2.8$. Figures. Who would know about figures? What do figures show? Aren't they mathematical symbols? Symbols that can be rubbed off a piece of paper? Who rubbed out two-point-eight million guilders? Who blew away a sum of money sufficient, if conservatively invested, to last a luxurious lifetime? And who was still blowing, rubbing, hiding, embezzling?

Who knows about figures? He opened the telephone book and found the Free University's number. "The chief of the

Mathematics Department, please." A female voice answered. "Hello?"

"This is the police, ma'am. Are you a professor?"

"I am."

"Adjutant Grijpstra, Murder Brigade. I would like to speak to you. What would be a good time?"

"Two o'clock," the lady said. "Elize Schoor is the name, the room is 212."

"Professor Schoor," Grijpstra said. "Here is a store with a yearly turnover of fourteen million, but it should be sixteen-point-eight million, as total purchases and profit margin are known. What does that mean to you?"

She's attractive, Grijpstra thought. She has a lovely face. A professor in her early thirties. Step right up, step right up. And while you get closer, listen to her voice. Isn't it pleasantly low, warm, and sympathetic?

"It means," Elize Schoor said, "something. You may call me Elize. I'm rather fond of dignified, heavy-set, old-fashioned-looking gents. Are you married?"

"Yes, Elize."

"Happily?"

"No, Elize."

"I wasn't either, but I'm bored with celebrating celibacy now." She wrote. "Look here. Do you see the equation? There is an unfavorable difference, of two-point-eight million."

"Elize," Grijpstra said heavily, "I had reached that point myself. Please move on a little."

"You see the factor?"

"Factor, Elize?"

"Agent," Elize said. "There's a fixed agent at work here, who's unmasked by the equation. Isn't logic wonderful? Six-teen-point-eight divided by two-point-eight is six. Six times the difference equals the original amount. The factor is now known—six. Are you following me?"

"Six times this?" Grijpstra asked slowly. "Six times that?"

She frowned and wrinkled her dainty nose. "The layman's vagueness, the amateur's vagary. Logic is hard, since Newton, although since Einstein it has softened a great deal." She bent toward him. Grijpstra inhaled her perfume. "Do you know, Adjutant, that the connection between cause and effect may no longer be valid?"

"So where does that take us?" the adjutant asked.

"Where we were in the beginning." She smiled. "Nowhere, Adjutant."

"Can you calculate nowhere?"

"Hardly." She smiled. "But isn't it better not to pinpoint the illusion? Didn't logic limit us too much?"

Grijpstra flapped his hands gently.

"You don't believe me, Adjutant?"

"But Elize? Common sense?"

She laughed softly. "Do you know how Einstein defined common sense? The conglomeration of prejudice formed before the student's eighteenth year?"

Grijpstra got up.

"You must leave so soon?"

"I move on a flat surface," Grijpstra said. "Within limited time. When the agent is caught, I would be honored to have dinner with you. Would that be possible?"

"Time," Elize said, "in a flat space. That's how hurry is created. From the Past through Now to Later. While Nowhere is timeless." She raised her voice a little. "I cannot stop you. I have no better advice. *Six*, Adjutant; the key is the figure six. Maybe you shouldn't multiply, you might also divide."

"Six," Grijpstra said. "Right. I thank you, Elize."

She walked him to the door. "And when you have your answer, we'll share dinner; that's fine. My place will do?"

"I'll phone," Grijpstra said. He hesitated at the door.

"Six," the professor said. "That's one plus two plus three. Or one times two times three. A holy figure in the kabbala. The Star of David has six points. Kepler thought that six was the essential figure. Ever heard of Johann Kepler?"

"No, Elize."

"Sixteenth century. A mathematician. We thought then that there were only six planets, and Kepler thought that the relation of their various distances from the sun would hide the key to the universe. He kept calculating with six, and not quite in vain, although his supposition was false."

"Is that right?" Grijpstra asked.

"You know nothing about mathematics?"

"Two parallel lines," Grijpstra said heavily, "cut each other in the infinite."

"Your line and mine," Elize said, "and all the others, too. You do have something there. Many a mathematician started with less."

"Bye," Grijpstra said, kneading the door handle.

He walked along a long corridor. "The incalculable," Grijpstra said to the emptiness that surrounded him, "is the enemy that I despise. There has to be clarity, especially at the end."

"And there *is*," Grijpstra said as he drove to the supermarket, "even before the end. We can rely on facts; if we couldn't, our very existence would be at stake."

Grijpstra parked. "It's three o'clock. De Gier is here. The splendid fellow. When de Gier says he'll be somewhere at three, he'll be somewhere at three."

De Gier wasn't there.

"Twice three is six," Grijpstra said, entered the supermarket, and asked a clerk to take him to the manager's office.

"Jansen," the manager said. "At your service. I was expecting you. The administration telephoned this morning. The police would arrive to have a look. You came alone?"

Grijpstra nodded.

"You heard about the missing difference? There is no difference and nothing is amiss. This store flourishes and makes a sizable daily profit. The administration has gone mad. Please sit down, Adjutant."

This is a suspect? Grijpstra thought. This kindly fellow with the name of the company embroidered on his uniform? This friendly compatriot with his open face? His close-cropped hair? His blushing cheeks? His clear blue eyes? This trustworthy soul running a spic-and-span store? Why am I wasting my time?

"Mr. Vries says . . ." Grijpstra said coolly.

"I know, I know." Jansen pointed at his forehead. "An idiot, with permission. I make profit and he makes trouble. It's been like that for months. But there's nothing wrong. The goods come into the store, in trailers, and the goods leave the store, in brown paper bags. The money the clients give us flows into the registers, and the total is banked at the end of each day. Whatever the computer says is checked by me. Okay, there may be a difference, the ladies who work the registers are human. Half a percent too little today, half a percent too much tomorrow."

"Two-point-eight million," Grijpstra said coolly, "is not half a percent this way or that."

"Nah," Jansen said cheerfully.

"You've worked here long?"

"Thirty years."

"Five times six?"

"Beg pardon?" Jansen asked.

"The figure six? Does *six* mean anything to you?"

"What?"

"A sixth of your turnover is lost, it seems."

"Nah," Jansen said. "Is craziness catching? Mr. Vries is nuts, but you still seem sane."

"Can I look around?" Grijpstra asked.

The adjutant counted the girls who arranged packages on shelves. There were six girls, but they were joined by a seventh. He counted the boys who were opening cartons. Three boys. He counted the shelves and the counters, the tables and the cupboards. Too many. The store was busy and getting busier. He counted, pressed by customers from all sides, the registers. There were five registers. Ladies pushed carts against his shins, toddlers climbed over his feet, a passing baby drooled on his sleeve. He looked down into the blouse of a bending-down lady. Two. He was stabbed by a loaf of French bread. One. A lady grabbed eight bottles of hot sauce. A fat gent swept two candy bars off a shelf. Whoever buys three cans of bean soup gets a fourth as a present. What am I counting here? the adjutant thought. I'm too stupid for this type of job. I have never been able to solve puzzles with figures. Six this, six that? There are no sixes in this store.

Mr. Jansen came by. "Found anything, Adjutant?"

"I'm leaving," Grijpstra said.

"I'll take you through the back way," Jansen said. "Too much of a crowd up front today. Can't get through in a hurry. Only one set of doors and six streams of clients converge at that point."

"Whoa," Grijpstra shouted.

Jansen stopped in his tracks.

"Six?" Grijpstra asked.

"Sure, Adjutant, look for yourself—six registers, right?"

"I just counted five," Grijpstra said. "I didn't see the sixth because it was blocked by that stack of cartons."

"We've got six registers," Jansen said.

"Can I have a minute with you, in your office?"

Adjutant and store manager faced each other in the office. "You know," Grijpstra said, "I do believe you were lying to me just now."

"Me?"

"You." Grijpstra tore a cigar from its plastic envelope. He tried to blow a ring, in vain. The ragged cloud made Jansen cough.

"Me? Why should I lie?"

"I may seem clever," Grijpstra said cheerfully, "but I had help, professional help from a professor. Did you tell me just now that nothing could be wrong?"

"Nothing is wrong," said Jansen.

"Five times right, once wrong," Grijpstra said triumphantly. "Ha-ha. How simple."

"I don't follow, Adjutant."

Grijpstra observed the moist end of his cigar. "Yes."

"You claim I'm a crook, Adjutant?"

"Only a suspicion," Grijpstra said. "I suspect you of murder.

You're under arrest. Don't say anything from here on if you don't want to say anything from here on. Whatever you say now may be used as evidence against you. You can phone your lawyer, later on, from my office. Take off your dustcoat and put on your jacket. We'll be going."

"Murder?" Jansen whispered.

"I'm sorry," Grijpstra said. "I suspect you of embezzlement, too, of course. I forgot that for a moment because embezzlement is something else. I work for Murder. You see, there are six registers here, but only five connect to your computer. That will be proved in due course, by an expert, an electrician, I suppose."

Jansen smiled. "What nonsense, Adjutant."

"You have another solution?" Grijpstra asked. "One sixth of your turnover never reaches the terminal. What does it reach, if not your pocket? It has to go somewhere and you're in charge."

"And the murder?" Jansen asked.

"In May," Grijpstra said, "you were on holiday."

"Correct."

"Mallorca?"

"No," Jansen said, "hiking, here in Holland."

"Alone?" Grijpstra asked. "With a backpack? Surrounded by nature? You slept in a tent? A trip we can't check on?"

"Indeed."

"You were in Mallorca," Grijpstra said, "with your accomplice, man by the name of Gennep. The very same Gennep who didn't file his invoices properly. The very same Gennep who bought too many registers for this store. He bought six, connected five."

Jansen was silent.

"Just a minute," Grijpstra said. "*You* were the accomplice. Gennep invented the trick. You were a mere pawn. But he needed you, of course, for you had to empty out that sixth register at the end of every working day. Without you the plan couldn't work. So you got your share. Half, isn't that right?"

"Really," Jansen said.

"Are you married?"

"No."

"Neither was Mr. Gennep," Grijpstra said.

"So?"

"I can see it clearly now," Grijpstra said. "Two bachelors, unfettered by family chains, stealing together. And one glorious day you would both take off. Each with half the loot. Wasn't enough for you, was it now? So you kicked your friend Gennep off that cliff. Pointed out the view, Gennep turned away, and you actually kicked his ass."

"Homemade riddles," Jansen said, "homemade answers."

Grijpstra got up. "Not at all. The Spanish police made an accident report. I plan to go to Mallorca myself. You two must have been camping somewhere; there'll be a record. Camps keep names. I'll prove you and Gennep were there together. What did you do with the money?"

"What money?"

"Two-point-eight million guilders," Grijpstra said patiently, "and a lot more has been added to that meanwhile. Three million by now? There'll be papers in your home. You must have bought dollar checks and made transfers to foreign banks. There'll be receipts. Maybe you keep accounts on tax-free islands."

"Sit down," Jansen said.

Wasn't he quick, Grijpstra thought. Never saw him take that gun from his drawer. "Put that down," Grijpstra said firmly. "You're making things worse. Threatening a police officer who's exercising his duty."

Jansen got up and locked the door. The lower part of the door was plywood, the upper part glass. Jansen's pistol was still aimed at Grijpstra. "Into the cupboard, Adjutant. I'm going to bind and gag you now. We'll be closing soon, and you won't be found until the cleaners arrive tomorrow morning. Can I have your gun and handcuffs, please?"

"You cannot," Grijpstra said. "You're under arrest and you stay under arrest. Are you quite right in the head?"

Jansen tapped his temple. "Quite sane, thank you. People do underestimate me, however. Take Gennep now, he wanted to go on until we had a total of five million, but that would take too long. I have more than half that now, for we both paid into the same account. I can sign alone and I'll be doing that tomorrow. The true criminal works alone. Once I'm across the border, which will take a few hours, I'm as free as a bird. Let's have your pistol and your handcuffs now."

"Shall I tell you something?" Grijpstra asked. "You may pretend what you like, but you really wanted to be arrested."

Jansen stared.

"Don't even know that yourself, do you now?"

Jansen kept staring.

"Listen. Didn't you draw my attention to the sixth register yourself? Hadn't I told you already that I was fascinated by the figure six?"

Jansen gaped.

"Subconscious guilt feelings," Grijpstra said. "We see it all the time. Suspects move themselves straight into our hands. Now put that pistol down and follow me."

"I'll have to kill you," Jansen whispered. "You leave me no choice. I'd rather not, but if I do, there's no risk. The pistol doesn't make too much of a bang and it's noisy in the store now; no one will notice. Last chance, Adjutant. Your weapon and your cuffs. I'm not going to fight you; I can kill you from behind my desk."

"No," Grijpstra said.

Jansen charged his pistol and closed one eye.

There was a knock on the door.

"Not now," Jansen shouted.

Someone rattled the handle of the door.

"Go away," Jansen shouted.

De Gier came through the door, following his raised foot that had splintered glass and plywood.

"Careful," Grijpstra shouted.

De Gier wasn't careful. He jumped on top of Jansen. The

sergeant's left arm knocked up Jansen's right. The pistol fired at the ceiling. De Gier grabbed Jansen's arms and twisted them together. Handcuffs clicked. "You're under arrest."

"He's been under arrest for a while now," Grijpstra said. "What kept you so long?"

De Gier picked up the gun, shook out the clip, and dropped both parts into his pocket. He picked up the suspect and put him on a chair. "Complications delayed me. The bum in the harbor had been beaten up by other bums. I had to find the others. There were witnesses, but they kept wandering off. All tied up and taken care of now. Sorry, Adjutant."

"Bah," Grijpstra said. "I counted on you."

"You can't count on anything," de Gier said. "You should know that by now."

"Aren't we great?" de Gier asked, leaning against the counter of a bar in the inner city. "Complaint received in the morning, suspect arrested in the late afternoon. Unheard of these days, but we took it in our stride."

"No," Grijpstra said. "That'll be two more jenevers, bartender, please."

"I'm closing," the bartender said, "and as you're what you are, you'll be taking your time. Two more and that's it."

"How do you mean, 'no'?" asked de Gier.

Grijpstra drank and ordered two more. "Armed and threatening suspects should be talked at, not jumped. A quiet conversation usually leads to a complete confession."

"I was just in time," de Gier said.

"They never shoot at me," Grijpstra said. "I'm too nice. The professor thought so, too—I'll be having dinner with her tomorrow."

"Tell me about the professor."

Grijpstra explained.

"Wow," de Gier said sadly. "Then what will you do? After dinner, I mean."

"Coffee?" Grijpstra asked. "Cognac perhaps? Help her wash up? Help her keep her distance?"

"You'll be chaotic again," de Gier said enviously, later that night. "You can do that so well. If you keep that up, you'll dance away from your own fate. True existence is true illusion, and you're the only one I know who has learned to ignore what circumstances seem to be offering for free, or am I idealizing you again?"

"You better not drive home," the bartender said.

"But don't you *see*?" the drunken sergeant asked. "If we can undo logic, like the adjutant will do when he refuses the beautiful professor, we free ourselves from self-inflicted chains and . . ."

"I'll have one, too," the bartender said, checking his watch, "just let me lock the door."

"The wise," the sergeant said, "only *seem* to behave unwisely, but . . ."

"I'm truly unwise," Grijpstra said sadly. "We'll have three more."

De Gier was mumbling. "To undo logic . . . to refuse fate's gifts . . . to accept chance . . . if only we dared . . ."

"Three more," the bartender said.

"Common sense," Grijpstra said, "is my only motivation. To see what's what. The professor is so beautiful. I will not drag her down to my level."

"Poor Grijpstra."

"No, no, you see that wrong. On the contrary. When I'm alone, I'm safe. Strengthened by common sense, following the line of logic, adhering to the law, reasoning clearly, moving in a straight direction reaching B from A . . ."

"You really think you're doing that?"

"I do." Grijpstra smiled modestly. "But I do need help from time to time, by people with more sense, like that graceful professor—by you even, for you're so quick." Grijpstra sighed. "She presented me with the figure six."

They stumbled home together. It was early in the morning.

There was no one about. "To be certain is good," Grijpstra said. "I'm certain at times. Like now. Nothing can happen to us now. When emptiness surrounds me, there can be no threat. I so like to be sure. To go home in a void. Can you follow me so far?"

"No," de Gier said. "And I don't agree either. The chaos is all around us. Anything can happen and it will, as you'll see."

Grijpstra pulled his arm out of de Gier's. It was time to say good-bye. He stumbled and embraced a lamppost. His feet slid away and he pulled the lamppost toward him. The lamppost fell, on top of Grijpstra.

"What?" the commissaris asked the next morning.

"The lamppost fell on top of Grijpstra, sir," de Gier said. "The adjutant was drunk and failed to step aside. The lamppost was quite heavy. Grijpstra suffered three bruised ribs. The ambulance picked him up."

"And?"

"He's in the hospital, sir, doing fairly well."

"Lampposts don't fall over," the commissaris said.

"This one did, sir. Dogs, you know?"

"Hm?" the commissaris asked.

"Urinated," de Gier said.

"Are you withholding information?" the commissaris asked.

"I do believe in the unexpected," the sergeant said, "although there's always a reason afterward. Factors combine in an unpredictable pattern, but there will be a connection if you follow the pattern in reverse. There are a lot of dogs in that particular part of the city and they all seem to prefer that particular post. Urine contains acid, and enough acid will eat through the heaviest metal. It can take a while, in this case a hundred years perhaps, but once the adjutant grabbed that particular post at that particular moment, he had to bruise three ribs."

"So?" the commissaris asked.

De Gier spread his hands.

The commissaris began to smile. "I see your point. Our very own Grijpstra comes along, believing only in the obvious, but behind the obvious hides the nonobvious, and it's just as true?"

The commissaris laughed.

De Gier frowned furiously.

"Poor Grijpstra," the commissaris said, "but he did solve his case."

"By chance," de Gier said.

"And choice," said the commissaris. "But what else can we choose but chance?"

THE

DEADLY EGG

T he siren of the tiny dented Volkswagen shrieked forlornly between the naked trees of the Amsterdam Forest, the city's largest park, set on its southern edge: several square miles of willows, poplars, and wild-growing alders, surrounding ponds and lining paths. The paths were restricted to pedestrians and cyclists, but the Volkswagen had ignored the many no-entry signs, quite legally, for the vehicle belonged to the Municipal Police and more especially to its Criminal Investigation Department, or Murder Brigade. Even so, it looked lost and its howl seemed defensive.

It was Easter Sunday and it rained, and the car's two occupants, Detective Adjutant Grijpstra and Detective Sergeant de Gier, sat hunched in their overcoats, watching the squeaky, rusted wipers trying to deal with the steady drizzle. The car should have been junked some years before, but the adjutant had lost the form that would have done away with his aging transport, lost it on purpose and with the sergeant's consent. They had grown fond of the Volkswagen, of its shabbiness and its ability to melt away in traffic.

But they weren't fond of the car now. The heater didn't work, it was cold, and it was early. Not yet nine o'clock on a Sunday is early, especially when the Sunday is Easter. Technically, they were both off duty, but they had been telephoned out of warm beds by Headquarters' radio room. A dead man dangling from a branch in the forest; please, would they care to have a look at the dead man?

Grijpstra's stubby index finger silenced the siren. They had followed several miles of winding paths so far and hadn't come across anything alive except tall blue herons, fishing in the ponds and moats and flapping away slowly when the car came too close for their comfort.

"You know who reported the corpse? I wasn't awake when the radio room talked to me."

De Gier had been smoking silently. His handsome head with the perfect curls turned obediently to face his superior. "Yes, a gentleman jogger. He said he jogged right into the body's feet. Gave him a start. He ran all the way to the nearest telephone booth, phoned Headquarters, then Headquarters phoned us, and that's why we are here, I suppose. I am a little asleep myself—we are here, aren't we?"

They could hear another siren, and another. Two limousines came roaring toward the Volkswagen, and Grijpstra cursed and made the little car turn off the path and slide into a soggy lawn; they could feel its wheels sink into the mud.

The limousines stopped and men poured out of them; the men pushed the Volkswagen back on the path.

"Morning, Adjutant; morning, Sergeant. Where is the corpse?"

"Shouldn't you know, too?"

"No, Adjutant," several men said simultaneously, "but we thought maybe you knew. All we know is that the corpse is in the Amsterdam Forest and that this is the Amsterdam Forest."

Grijpstra addressed the sergeant. "You know?"

De Gier's well-modulated baritone chanted the instructions. "Turn right after the big pond, right again, then left. Or the other way round. I think I have it right; we should be close."

The three cars drove about for a few minutes more until they were waved down by a man dressed in what seemed to be long blue underwear. The jogger ran ahead, bouncing energetically, and led them to their destination. The men from the limousines brought out their boxes and suitcases, then cameras clicked and a videorecorder hummed. The corpse hung on and the two detectives watched it hang.

"Neat," Grijpstra said, "very neat. Don't you think it is neat?"

The sergeant grunted.

"Here. Brought a folding campstool and some nice new rope, made a perfect noose, slipped it around his neck, kicked the stool. Anything suspicious, gentlemen?"

The men from the limousines said there was not. They had found footprints—the prints of the corpse's boots. There were no other prints, except the jogger's. The jogger's statement was taken; he was thanked and sent on his sporting way. A police ambulance arrived and the corpse was cut loose, examined by doctor and detectives, and carried off. The detectives saluted the corpse quietly by inclining their heads.

"In his sixties," the sergeant said, "well dressed in old but expensive clothes. Clean shirt. Tie. Short gray beard, clipped. Man who took care of himself. A faint smell of liquor—he must have had a few to give him courage. Absolutely nothing in his pockets. I looked in the collar of his shirt—no laundry mark. He went to some trouble to be nameless. Maybe something will turn up when they strip him at the mortuary; we should phone in an hour's time."

Grijpstra looked hopeful. "Suicide?"

"I would think so. Came here by himself, no traces of

anybody else. No signs of a struggle. The man knew what he wanted to do, and did it, all by himself. But he didn't leave a note; that wasn't very thoughtful."

"Right," Grijpstra said. "Time for breakfast, Sergeant! We'll have it at the airport—that's close and convenient. We can show our police cards and get through the customs barrier; the restaurant on the far side is better than the coffee shop on the near side."

De Gier activated the radio when they got back to the car.

"Male corpse, balding but with short gray beard. Dentures. Blue eyes. Sixty-odd years old. Three-piece blue suit, elegant dark gray overcoat, no hat. No identification."

"Thank you," the radio said.

"Looks very much like suicide. Do you have any missing persons of that description in your files?"

"No, not so far."

"We'll be off for breakfast and will call in again on our way back."

"Echrem," the radio said sadly, "there's something else. Sorry."

De Gier stared at a duck waddling across the path and trailing seven furry ducklings. He began to mumble. Adjutant Grijpstra mumbled with him. The mumbled four-letter words interspersed with mild curses formed a background for the radio's well-articulated message. They were given an address on the other side of the city. "The lady was poisoned, presumably by a chocolate Easter egg. The ambulance that answered the distress call just radioed in. They are taking her to the hospital. The ambulance driver thought the poison was either parathion, something used in agriculture, or arsenic. His assistant is pumping out the patient's stomach. She is in a bad way but not dead yet."

Grijpstra grabbed the microphone from de Gier's limp hand. "So if the lady is on her way to the hospital, who is left in the house you want us to go to?"

"Her husband, man by the name of Moozen—a lawyer, I believe."

"What hospital is Mrs. Moozen being taken to?"

"The Wilhelmina."

"And you have no one else on call? Sergeant de Gier and I are supposed to be off duty for Easter, you know!"

"No," the radio's female voice said, "no, Adjutant. We never have much crime on Easter Day, especially not in the morning. There are only two detectives on duty and they are out on a case, too—some boys have derailed a streetcar with matches."

"Right," Grijpstra said coldly, "we are on our way."

The old Volkswagen made an effort to jump away, protesting feebly. De Gier was still muttering but had stopped cursing. "Streetcar? Matches?"

"Yes. They take an empty cartridge, fill it with match heads, then close the open end with a hammer. Very simple. All you have to do is insert the cartridge into the streetcar's rail, and when the old tram comes clanging along, the sudden impact makes the cartridge explode. If you use two or three cartridges, the explosion may be strong enough to lift the wheel out of the rail. Didn't you ever try that? I used to do it as a boy. The only problem was to get the cartridges. We had to sneak around on the rifle range with the chance of getting shot at."

"No," de Gier said. "Pity. Never thought of it, and it sounds like a good game."

He looked out of the window. The car had left the park and was racing toward the city's center through long empty avenues. There was no life in the huge apartment buildings lining the old city—nobody had bothered to get up yet. Ten o'clock and the citizenry wasn't even considering the possibility of slouching into the kitchen for a first cup of coffee.

But one man had bothered to get up early and had strolled into the park, carrying his folding chair and a piece of rope to break off the painful course of his life, once and for all. An elderly man in good but old clothes. De Gier saw the man's beard again, a nicely cared-for growth. The police doctor had said that he hadn't been dead long. A man alone in the night that would have led him to Easter, a man by himself in a deserted park, testing the strength of his rope, fitting his head into the noose, kicking the campstool.

"Bah!" he said aloud.

Grijpstra had steered the car through a red light and was turning the wheel.

"What's that?"

"Nothing. Just bah."

"Bah is right," Grijpstra said.

They found the house, a bungalow, on the luxurious extreme north side of the city. Spring was trying to revive the small lawn and a magnolia tree was in hesitant bloom. Bright yellow crocuses set off the path. Grijpstra looked at the crocuses. He didn't seem pleased.

"Crocuses," de Gier said, "very nice. Jolly little flowers."

"No. Unimaginative plants, manufactured, not grown. Computer plants. They make the bulbs in a machine and program them to look stupid. Go ahead, Sergeant, press the bell."

"Really?" the sergeant asked.

Grijpstra's jowls sagged. "Yes. They are like mass-manufactured cheese, tasteless; cheese is probably made with the same machines."

"Cheese," de Gier said moistly. "There's nothing wrong with cheese either, apart from not having any right now. Breakfast has slipped by, you know." He glanced at his watch.

They read the nameplate while the bell rang: H. F. MOOZEN, ATTORNEY AT LAW. The door opened. A man in a bathrobe made out of brightly striped towel material said good morning. The detectives showed their identifications. The man nodded and stepped back. A pleasant man, still young, thirty years or a bit more. The ideal model for an ad in a ladies' magazine. A background man, showing off a modern house, or a minicar, or expensive furniture. The sort of man ladies would like to have around. Quiet, secure, mildly good-looking. Not a passionate man, but lawyers seldom are. Lawyers practice detachment; they identify with their clients, but only up to a point.

"You won't take long, I hope," Mr. Moozen said. "I wanted to go with the ambulance, but the driver said you were on the way, and that I wouldn't be of any help if I stayed with my wife."

"Was your wife conscious when she left here, sir?"

"Barely. She couldn't speak."

"She ate an egg, a chocolate egg?"

"Yes. I don't care for chocolate myself. It was a gift, we thought, from friends. I had to let the dog out early this morning, an hour ago, and there was an Easter bunny sitting on the path. He held an egg wrapped up in silver paper. I took him in, woke up my wife, and showed the bunny to her, and she took the egg and ate it, then became ill. I telephoned for the ambulance and they came almost immediately. I would like to go to the hospital now."

"Come in our car, sir. Can I see the bunny?"

Mr. Moozen took off the bathrobe and put on a jacket. He opened the door leading to the kitchen, and a small dog jumped around the detectives, yapping greetings. The bunny stood on the kitchen counter; it was almost a foot high. Grijpstra tapped its back with his knuckles; it sounded solid.

"Hey," de Gier said. He turned the bunny around and showed it to Grijpstra.

"Brwah!" Grijpstra said.

The rabbit's toothless mouth gaped. The beast's eyes were close together and deeply sunk into the skull. Its ears stood up aggressively. The bunny leered at them, its torso crouched; the paws that had held the deadly egg seemed ready to punch.

"It's roaring," de Gier said. "See? A roaring rabbit. Easter bunnies are supposed to smile."

"Shall we go?" Mr. Moozen asked.

They used the siren, and the trip to the hospital didn't take ten minutes. The city was still quiet. But there proved to be no hurry. An energetic bright young nurse led them to a waiting room. Mrs. Moozen was being worked on; her condition was still critical. The nurse would let them know if there was any change.

"Can we smoke?" Grijpstra asked.

"If you must." The nurse smiled coldly, appraised de Gier's tall, wide-shouldered body with a possessive feminist glance, swung her hips, and turned to the door.

"Any coffee?"

"There's a machine in the hall. Don't smoke in the hall, please."

There were several posters in the waiting room. A picture of a cigarette pointing to a skull with crossed bones. A picture of a happy child biting into an apple. A picture of a drunken driver (bubbles surrounding his head proved he was drunk) followed by an ambulance. The caption read, "Not *if* you have an accident, but *when* you have an accident."

De Gier fetched coffee and Grijpstra offered cigars. Mr. Moozen said he didn't smoke.

"Well," Grijpstra said patiently and puffed out a ragged dark cloud, "now who would want to poison your wife, sir? Has there been any recent trouble in her life?"

The question hung in the small white room while Moozen thought. The detectives waited. De Gier stared at the floor, Grijpstra observed the ceiling. A full minute passed.

"Yes," Mr. Moozen said, "some trouble. With me. We contemplated a divorce."

"I see."

"But then we decided to stay together. The trouble passed."

"Any particular reason why you considered a divorce, sir?"

"My wife had a lover." Mr. Moozen's words were clipped and precise.

"Had," de Gier said. "The affair came to an end?"

"Yes. We had some problems with our central heating, something the mechanics couldn't fix. An engineer came out and my wife fell in love with him. She told me—she doesn't like to be secretive. They met each other in motels for a while."

"You were upset?"

"Yes. It was a serious affair. The engineer's wife is a mental patient; he divorced her and was awarded custody of his two children. I thought he was looking for a new wife. My wife has no children of her own—we have been married some six years and would like to have children. My wife and the engineer seemed well matched. I waited a month and then told her to make up her mind—either him or me, not both; I couldn't stand it."

"And she chose you?"

"Yes."

"Do you know the engineer?"

A vague pained smile floated briefly on Moozen's face. "Not personally. We did meet once and discussed central heating systems. Any further contact with him was through my wife."

"And when did all this happen, sir?"

"Recently. She only made her decision a week ago. I don't think she has met him since. She told me it was all over."

"His name and address, please, sir."

De Gier closed his notebook and got up. "Shall we go, Adjutant?"

Grijpstra sighed and got up too. They shook hands with Moozen and wished him luck. Grijpstra stopped at the desk. The nurse wasn't helpful, but Grijpstra insisted and de Gier smiled and eventually they were taken to a doctor who accompanied them to the next floor. Mrs. Moozen seemed comfortable. Her arms were stretched out on the blanket. The face was calm. The detectives were led out of the room again.

"Bad," the doctor said. "Parathion is a strong poison. Her stomach is ripped to shreds. We'll have to operate and remove part of it, but I think she will live. The silly woman ate the whole egg, a normal-sized egg. Perhaps she was still too sleepy to notice the taste."

"Her husband is downstairs. Perhaps you should call him up, especially if you think she will live." Grijpstra sounded concerned. He probably was, de Gier thought. He felt concerned himself. The woman was beautiful, with a finely curved nose, very thin in the bridge, and large eyes and a soft and sensitive mouth. He had noted her long delicate hands.

"Husbands," the doctor said. "Prime suspects in my experience. Husbands are supposed to love their wives, but usually they don't. It's the same the other way round. Marriage seems to breed violence—it's one of the impossible situations we humans have to put up with."

Grijpstra's pale blue eyes twinkled. "Are you married, Doctor?"

The doctor grinned back. "Very. Oh, yes."

"A long time?"

"Long enough."

Grijpstra's grin faded. "So am I. Too long. But poison is nasty. Thank you, Doctor."

There wasn't much conversation in the car when they drove to the engineer's address. The city's streets had filled up. People were stirring about on the sidewalks and cars crowded each other, honking occasionally. The engineer lived in a block of apartments, and Grijpstra switched off the engine and lit another small black cigar.

"A family drama. What do you think, Sergeant?"

"I don't think. But that rabbit was most extraordinary. Not bought in a shop. A specially made rabbit, and well made, not by an amateur."

"Are we looking for a sculptor? Some arty person? Would Mr. Moozen or the engineer be an artist in his spare time? How does one make a chocolate rabbit, anyway?"

De Gier tried to stretch, but didn't succeed in his cramped quarters. He yawned instead. "You make a mold, I suppose, out of plaster of Paris or something, and then you pour hot chocolate into the mold and wait for it to harden. That rabbit was solid chocolate, several kilos of it. Our artistic friend went to a lot of trouble."

"A baker? A pastry man?"

"Or an engineer—engineers design forms sometimes, I believe. Let's meet this lover man."

The engineer was a small nimble man with a shock of black hair and dark lively eyes, a nervous man, nervous in a pleasant, childlike manner. De Gier remembered that Mrs. Moozen was a small woman, too. They were ushered into a four-room apartment. They had to be careful not to step on a large number of toys, spread about evenly. Two little boys played on the floor; the eldest ran out of the room to fetch his Easter present to show it to the uncles. It was a basketful of eggs, homemade, out of chocolate. The other boy came to show his basket, identical but a size smaller.

"My sister and I made them last night," the engineer said. "She came to live here after my wife left, and she looks after the kids, but she is spending the Easter weekend with my parents in the country. We couldn't go because Tom here had measles, hadn't you, Tom?"

"Yes," Tom said. "Big measles. Little Klaas here hasn't had them yet."

Klaas looked sorry. Grijpstra took a plastic truck off a chair and sat down heavily after having looked at the engineer, who waved him on. "Please, make yourself at home." De Gier had found himself a chair, too, and was rolling a cigarette. The engineer provided coffee and shooed the children into another room.

"Any trouble?"

"Yes," Grijpstra said. "I am afraid we usually bring trouble. A Mrs. Moozen has been taken to the hospital. An attempt was made on her life. I believe you are acquainted with Mrs. Moozen?"

"Anne," the engineer said. "My God! Is she all right?"

De Gier had stopped rolling his cigarette. He was watching the man carefully; his large brown eyes gleamed, but not with pleasure or anticipation. The sergeant felt sorrow, a feeling that often accompanied his intrusions into the private lives of his fellow citizens. He shifted, and the automatic pistol in his shoulder holster nuzzled into his armpit. He impatiently pushed the weapon back. This was no time to be reminded that he carried death with him, legal death.

"What happened?" the engineer was asking. "Did anybody hurt her?"

"A question," Grijpstra said gently. "A question first, sir. You said your sister and you were making chocolate Easter eggs last night. Did you happen to make any bunnies, too?"

The engineer sucked noisily on his cigarette. Grijpstra repeated his question.

"Bunnies? Yes, or no. We tried, but it was too much for us. The eggs were easy—my sister is good at that. We have a pudding form for a bunny, but all we could manage was a pudding. It is still in the kitchen, a surprise for the kids later on today. Chocolate pudding—they like it."

"Can we see the kitchen, please?"

The engineer didn't get up. "My God," he said again, "so she was poisoned, was she? How horrible! Where is she now?"

"In the hospital, sir."

"Bad?"

Grijpstra nodded. "The doctor said she will live. Some sort of pesticide was mixed into chocolate, which she ate."

The engineer got up; he seemed dazed. They found the kitchen. Leftover chocolate mix was still on the counter. Grijpstra brought out an envelope and scooped some of the hardened chips into it.

"Do you know that Ann and I had an affair?"

"Yes, sir."

"Were you told that she finished the affair, that she decided to stay with her husband?"

"Yes, sir."

The engineer was tidying up the counter mechanically. "I see. So I could be a suspect. Tried to get at her out of spite or something. But I am not a spiteful man. You wouldn't know that. I don't mind being a suspect, but I would like to see Ann. She is in the hospital, you said. What hospital?"

"The Wilhelmina, sir."

"Can't leave the kids here, can I? Maybe the neighbors will take them for an hour or so . . . yes. I'll go and see Ann. This is terrible."

Grijpstra marched to the front door with de Gier trailing behind him. "Don't move from the house today, if you please, sir, not until we telephone or come again. We'll try and be as quick as we can."

"Nice chap," de Gier said when the car found its parking place in the vast courtyard of Headquarters. "That engineer, I mean. I rather liked Mr. Moozen, too, and Mrs. Moozen is a lovely lady. Now what?"

"Go back to the Moozen house, Sergeant, and get a sample of the roaring bunny. Bring it to the laboratory together with this envelope. If they check, we have a heavy point against the engineer."

De Gier restarted the engine. "Maybe he is not so nice, eh? He could have driven his wife crazy and now he tries to murder his girlfriend, his ex-girlfriend. Lovely Ann Moozen, who dared to stand him up. Could be. Do you think so?"

Grijpstra leaned his bulk against the car and addressed his words to the emptiness of the yard. "No. But that could be the obvious solution. He was distressed, genuinely distressed, I would say. If he hadn't been and if he hadn't had those kids in the house, I might have brought him in for further questioning."

"And Mr. Moozen?"

"Could be. Maybe he didn't find the bunny on the garden path; maybe he put it there, or maybe he had it ready in the cupboard and brought it to his wandering wife. He is a lawyer—lawyers can be devious at times. True?"

De Gier said, "Yes, yes, yes . . ." and kept on saying so until Grijpstra squeezed the elbow sticking out of the car's window. "You are saying yes, but you don't sound convinced."

"I thought Moozen was suffering, too."

"Murderers usually suffer, don't they?"

De Gier started his "Yes, yes," and Grijpstra marched off.

They met an hour later, in the canteen in headquarters. They munched rolls stuffed with sliced liver and roast beef and muttered diligently at each other.

"So it is the same chocolate?"

"Yes, but that doesn't mean much. One of the lab's assistants has a father who owns a pastry shop. He said that there are only three mixes on the market and our stuff is the most popular make. No, not much of a clue there."

"So?"

"We may have a full case on our hands. We should go back to Mr. Moozen, I think, and find out about friends and relatives. Perhaps his wife had other lovers, or jealous lady friends."

"Why her?"

Grijpstra munched on. "Hmm?"

"Why *her*?" de Gier repeated. "Why not him?"

Grijpstra swallowed. "Him? What about him?"

De Gier reached for the plate, but Grijpstra restrained the sergeant's hand. "Wait, you are hard to understand when you have your mouth full. What about him?"

De Gier looked at the roll. Grijpstra picked it up and ate it.

"Him," de Gier said unhappily. "He found the bunny on the garden path, the ferocious bunny holding the pernicious egg. A gift, how nice. But he doesn't eat chocolate, so he runs inside and shows the gift to his wife, and his wife grabs the egg and eats it. She may have thought *he* was giving it to her; she was still half asleep. Maybe she noticed the taste, but she ate on to please her husband. She became ill at once and he telephoned for an ambulance. Now, if he had wanted to kill her, he might have waited an hour or so, to give the poison a chance to do its job. But he grabbed his phone, fortunately. What I am trying to say is, the egg may have been intended for him, from an enemy who didn't even know Moozen had a wife, who didn't care about killing the wife."

"Ah," Grijpstra said, and swallowed the last of the roll. "Could be. We'll ask Mr. Moozen about his enemies. But not just now. There is the dead man we found in the park—a message came in while you were away. A missing person has been reported and the description fits our corpse. According to the radio room, a woman phoned to say that a man who is renting a room in her house has been behaving strangely lately and has now disappeared. She traced him to the corner bar where he spent last evening, until two A.M., when they closed.

"He was a little drunk, according to the barkeeper, but not blind drunk. She always takes him tea in the morning, but this morning he wasn't there and the bed was still made. But she does think he's been home, for she heard the front door at a little after two A.M. opening and closing twice. He probably fetched the rope and his campstool then."

"And the man was fairly old and had a short gray beard?"

"Right."

"So we go and see the landlady. I'll get a photograph—they

took dozens this morning and they should be developed by now. Was anything found in his clothes?"

"Nothing." Grijpstra looked guiltily at the empty plate. "Want another roll?"

"You ate it."

"That's true, and the canteen is out of rolls; we got the last batch. Never mind, Sergeant. Let's go out and do some work. Work will take your mind off food."

"That's him," the landlady with the plastic curlers said. Her glasses had slipped to the tip of her blunt nose while she studied the photograph. "Oh, how horrible! His tongue is sticking out. Poor Mr. Marchant. Is he dead?"

"Yes, ma'am."

"For shame, and such a nice gentleman. He has been staying here for nearly five years now and he was always so polite."

Grijpstra tried to look away from the glaring pink curlers, pointing at his forehead from the woman's thinning hair.

"Did he have any troubles, ma'am? Anything that may have led him to take his own life?"

The curlers bobbed frantically. "Yes. Money troubles. Nothing to pay the tax man with. He always paid the rent, but he hadn't been paying his taxes. And his business wasn't doing well. He has a shop in the next street; he makes things—ornaments, he calls them—out of brass. But there was some trouble with the neighbors. Too much noise, and something about the zoning, too; this is a residential area now, they say. The neighbors wanted him to move, but he had nowhere to move to, and he was getting nasty letters, lawyers' letters. He would have had to close down, and he had to make money to pay the tax man. It was driving him crazy. I could hear him walk around in his room at night, round and round, until I had to switch off my hearing aid."

"Thank you, ma'am."

"He was alone," the woman said, and shuffled with them to the door. "All alone, like me. And he was always so nice." She was crying.

"Happy Easter," de Gier said, and opened the Volkswagen's door for the adjutant.

"The same to you. Back to Mr. Moozen again—we *are* driving about this morning. I could use some coffee again. Maybe Mr. Moozen will oblige."

"He won't be so happy either. We aren't making anybody happy today," the sergeant said, and tried to put the Volkswagen into first gear. The gear slipped and the car took off in second.

They found Mr. Moozen in his garden. It had begun to rain again, but the lawyer didn't seem to notice that he was getting wet. He was staring at the bright yellow crocuses, touching them with his foot. He had trampled a few of them into the grass.

"How is your wife, sir?"

"Conscious and in pain. The doctors think they can save her, but she will have to be on a stringent diet for years and she'll be very weak for months. I won't have her back for a while."

Grijpstra coughed. "We visited your wife's, ah, previous lover, sir." The word "previous" came out awkwardly and he coughed again to take away the bad taste.

"Did you arrest him?"

"No, sir."

"Any strong reasons to suspect the man?"

"Are you a criminal lawyer, sir?"

Moozen kicked the last surviving crocus, turned on his heels, and led his visitors to the house. "No, I specialize in civil cases. Sometimes I do divorces, but I don't have enough experience to point a finger in this personal case. Divorce is a messy business, but with a little tact and patience reason usually prevails. To try and poison somebody is unreasonable behavior. I can't visualize Ann provoking that type of action—she is a gentle woman, sensual but gentle. If she did break her relationship with the engineer, she would have done it diplomatically."

"He seemed upset, sir, genuinely upset."

"Quite. I had hoped as much. So where are we now?"

"With you, sir. Do *you* have any enemies? Anybody who hated you so badly that he wanted you to die a grotesque death, handed to you by a roaring rabbit? You did find the rabbit on the garden path this morning, didn't you, sir?"

Moozen pointed. "Yes, out there, sitting in between the crocuses, leering, and as you say, roaring. Giving me the egg."

"Now, which demented mind might have thought of shaping that apparition, sir? Are you dealing with any particularly unpleasant cases at this moment? Any cases that have a badly twisted undercurrent? Is anyone blaming you for something bad that is happening to them?"

Moozen brushed his hair with both hands. "No. I am working on a bad case having to do with a truckdriver who got involved in a complicated accident; his truck caught fire and it was loaded with expensive cargo. Both his legs were crushed. His firm is suing the firm that owned the other truck. A lot of money in claims is involved and the parties are becoming impatient, with me mostly. The case is dragging on and on. But if they kill me, the case will become even more complicated, with no hope of settlement in sight."

"Anything else, sir?"

"The usual. I collect bad debts, so sometimes I have to get nasty. I write threatening letters; sometimes I telephone people or even visit them. I act tough—it's got to be done in my profession. Usually they pay, but they don't like me for bothering them."

"Any pastry shops?"

"I beg your pardon?"

"Pastry shops," Grijpstra said. "People who make and sell confectionery. The rabbit was a work of art in a way, made by a professional. Are you suing anybody who would have the ability to create the roaring rabbit?"

"*Ornaments!*" de Gier shouted. His shout tore at the quiet room. Moozen and Grijpstra looked up, startled.

"Ornaments! Brass ornaments. Ornaments are made from molds. We've got to check his shop."

"Whose shop?" Grijpstra frowned irritably. "Keep your voice down, Sergeant. What shop? What ornaments?"

"Marchant!" de Gier shouted. "Marchant's shop."

"Marchant?" Moozen was shouting too. "Where did you get that name? *Emil* Marchant?"

Grijpstra's cigar fell on the carpet. He tried to pick it up and it burned his hand, sparks finding their way into the carpet's strands. He stamped them out roughly.

"You know a Mr. Marchant, sir?" de Gier asked quietly.

"No, I haven't met him. But I have written several letters to a man named Emil Marchant. On behalf of clients who are hindered by the noise he makes in his shop. He works with brass, and it isn't only the noise, but there seems to be a stink as well. My clients want him to move out and are prepared to take him to court if necessary. Mr. Marchant telephoned me a few times, pleading for mercy. He said he owed money to the tax department and wanted time to make the money, that he would move out later; but my clients have lost patience. I didn't give in to him—in fact, I just pushed harder. He will have to go to court next week and he is sure to lose out."

"Do you know what line of business he is in, sir?"

"Doorknobs, I believe, and knockers for doors, in the shape of lions' heads—that sort of thing. And weathervanes. He told me on the phone. All handmade. He is a craftsman."

Grijpstra got up. "We'll be on our way, sir. We found Mr. Marchant this morning, dead, hanging from a tree in the Amsterdam Forest. He probably hanged himself early this morning, and at some time before, he must have delivered the rabbit and its egg. According to his landlady, he has been behaving strangely lately. He must have blamed you for his troubles and tried to take his revenge. He didn't mean to kill your wife; he meant to kill you. He didn't know that you don't eat chocolate, and he probably didn't even know you were married. We'll check further and make a report. The rabbit's mold is probably still in his shop, and if not, we'll find traces of the chocolate. We'll have the rabbit checked for fingerprints.

It won't be difficult to come up with irrefutable proof. If we do, we'll let you know, sir, a little later today. I am very sorry all this has happened."

"Nothing ever happens in Amsterdam," de Gier said as he yanked the door of the Volkswagen open, "and when it does, it all fits in immediately."

But Grijpstra didn't agree.

"We would never have solved the case, or rather *I* wouldn't have, if you hadn't thought of the rabbit as an ornament."

"No, Grijpstra, we would have found Marchant's name in Moozen's files."

The adjutant shook his heavy, grizzled head. "No, we wouldn't have checked the files. If he had kept on saying that he wasn't working on any bad cases, I wouldn't have pursued that line of thought. I'd have reverted to trying to find an enemy of his wife. We might have worked for weeks and called in all sorts of help and wasted everybody's time. You are clever, Sergeant."

De Gier was studying a redheaded girl waiting for a streetcar.

"Am I?"

"Yes. But not as clever as I am," Grijpstra said, and grinned. "You work for me. I personally selected you as my assistant. You are a tool in my expert hands."

De Gier winked at the redheaded girl and the girl smiled back. The traffic had jammed up ahead and the car was blocked. De Gier opened his door.

"Hey! Where are you going?"

"It's a holiday, Adjutant, and you can drive this wreck for a change. I am going home. That girl is waiting for a streetcar that goes to my side of the city. Maybe she hasn't had lunch yet. I am going to invite her to go to a Chinese restaurant."

"But we have reports to make, and we've got to check out Marchant's shop. It'll be locked; we have to find the key in his room; and we have to telephone the engineer to let him off the hook."

"I am taking the streetcar," de Gier said. "You do all that. You ate my roll."

SURE, BLUE, AND DEAD, TOO

The evening had passed and night was due, but it wasn't quite dark yet. Sergeant de Gier had noticed the mysterious moment of change and passed the information on to Adjutant Grijpstra. "Evening gone, night not quite come." He went further and drew the adjutant's attention to the faint coloring of the sky that curved like a tight metallic-blue sheet above the city of Amsterdam, iridescent in its entirety, intensified by the first pulsating stars.

"Quite," Grijpstra answered.

"Blue," Sergeant de Gier said, "but not your

everyday blue. A most noteworthy shade of blue, don't you think?"

"So what are we doing here again?" Grijpstra asked.

"We're police detectives," de Gier explained, caressing his full mustache and delicately curved nose. "We're waiting for the heroin dealers about to meet and exchange merchandise for money."

"And when are they due?"

"We don't know."

"And what do they look like?"

"We don't know that either."

Adjutant and sergeant, members of the Amsterdam Murder Brigade, were assisting—because no murders had been reported recently—the Dangerous Drugs Department. They were doing so quietly, dressed like innocent civilians, comfortably reclining in their unmarked blue Volkswagen, parked on Brewers' Square, opposite the Concert Building, pointed at Museum Square. They had been reclining for a while now.

"And how do we know that the dealers will meet?"

"Because," the sergeant answered, "Detection passed on the message. Our very own Detection, with the whispering voice of a handsome man like me, who in turn had heard another whispering voice—in the restroom of a better brothel, perhaps. A large quantity of the evil drug will pass hands tonight. For us to see. For us to apprehend, together with the hands that pass it."

Grijpstra spilled cigar-ash on his neat pin-striped waistcoat. He also arranged his bristly gray hair. "Bah."

"Bah how?"

"Both in general," the adjutant explained, "and in particular. What can we see? The sky. Numberless passersby. Do you honestly think that we would be able to spot a suspect popping up, parcel in hand, to greet and do business with another?"

"The sky is lovely," said de Gier. "Do look before the blue becomes black. Now is the time to be impressed."

Grijpstra looked up, grunted, and looked down. He grunted again, more emotionally.

"Nice woman," de Gier agreed. "Same color as the sky. Blue summer coat, blue scarf, blue high heels. I can't see her face, but from her general bearing I would deduce she is crying. Why is she crying?"

The woman's hands dropped away from her face. "She's only crying a little," Grijpstra said. "We could investigate the mystery, but we don't want to push our duty. A crying woman hardly disturbs the peace of our city."

De Gier sat up. "I feel like working. We were sent on a fool's errand. We aren't fools. I suspect the subject of being a prostitute and want to question her. Are you coming, Adjutant?"

"Prostitution isn't illegal."

"It is, too," de Gier said. "*Here* it is. We are within two hundred feet of the Concert Building, which contains a bar. Prostitution within two hundred feet of a public place where alcoholic beverages are sold is illegal."

"Leave the woman in peace," Grijpstra said gently. "We're after heroin."

"Very well, Adjutant. But now look at that. What do you see? A handcart loaded with rags. Parked under a no-parking sign. And a subject climbing into it. A most suspicious agglomeration of events." He put his hand on the handle of his door. "May I?"

"You may not. Leave Blue Pete alone."

"You know the subject?"

"An old acquaintance."

"Tell me about him," the sergeant said. "I feel a trifle restless. Your tale will calm me down."

"Anything to keep your youthful enthusiasm within suitable bounds.

"Some years ago," Adjutant Grijpstra intoned pleasantly, "when the local station here hadn't been computerized away, I happened to be behind the counter and Blue Pete came in, accompanied by his dear wife, a fat woman, just like mine. Maybe even fatter, if that could be possible. She pushed Blue Pete aside and lodged a complaint. He was part of the complaint, so she had brought him along."

"Yes?" de Gier prodded.

"If you interrupt me, I won't tell the tale."

"Right. But over there goes a gentleman carrying a parcel. Does it contain heroin? No, it's a present for a loved one, adorned with a ribbon. Perhaps his wife has her birthday. Go on, Adjutant."

"Her name was Anne, Blue Pete's wife's was, and probably still is, and she was suffering from a venereal disease at the time."

"That was the complaint?"

"Part of it. She had contracted it from her neighbor and passed it on to Blue Pete."

"Shall I inquire about the nature of the contents of the parcel the gent is carrying? Now look at that, will you? A well-dressed, well-educated gentleman, probably holding an important position in our society, on his way home, where his wife awaits him, is bothering our blue lady. Just because she is crying. Let me arrest the scoundrel."

"He has stopped bothering her," Grijpstra said. "He's still carrying the parcel. Has he perhaps exchanged it for a similar parcel the lady was hiding under her coat?"

"No, I had a full view from here. Nothing passed hands."

"I never have a full view of anything," Grijpstra complained mildly. "Very well, Anne's charge was that her neighbor presented her with a venereal disease. She carried proof."

"She showed you her microbes?"

"Her pills. And a prescription for more, signed by her physician. Proof of her affliction."

"The complaint is not clear to me."

"Because you're too young," Grijpstra explained. "You're not familiar with yesteryear's laws. Whippersnappers like your good self gambol about while totally unaware of the great happenings. The present connects with the past. You have no past yet."

"Since when is the spreading of venereal disease prohibited?"

"It was during the war. A German Occupation law, to protect the Nazi soldiery."

"And Blue Pete?"

"A detached personality. Blue Pete drinks methyl alcohol, a well-known killer of microbes, and he only came along to support his wife in her struggle with the paramour next door."

The sergeant looked at the ragman, now settled comfortably on his cart. "You have a marvelous memory, Adjutant."

"Blue Pete showed up again that very same night, the night of the complaint. I was driving a patrol car through an alley and nearly ran into the blighter's cart. No lights. I was going to fine him, but he did have a light, he said. He showed me a candle that he hadn't lit. There was a bit of a breeze, you see, and the light might have been blown out."

"Did you fine him?"

"Nah," Grijpstra said. "Mustn't bother the poor too much."

The sergeant looked out of the window again. "Not even when they keep breaking the law? Parking under no-parking signs? How sad it all is. And the blue lady is still crying. What could be the matter with her?"

"The fourteen-six?" the radio under the blue Volkswagen's dashboard asked.

Grijpstra grabbed the microphone. "Go ahead. This is the fourteen-six."

"Not correct," the radio said. "Even the Murder Brigade has to adhere to the rules. First you have to confirm your number and then you should ask me for orders."

"Yes, ducks. Sorry, ducks."

"Ducks?"

De Gier took over the microphone. "The fourteen-six here, Marie. Sergeant de Gier. What can we do for you?"

"Darling," the radio purred. "Do go to Headquarters. The constables guarding the building are being bothered by a man."

"We're on our way."

The Volkswagen veered away from the curb.

"And our heroin?" Grijpstra asked.

"Will wait for us," de Gier said. "The radio room is at Headquarters, too, and who knows what will happen if that terrible man penetrates to Marie's whereabouts. She's a constable, of course, but rather vulnerable because of her beauty. Onward at once."

Grijpstra clutched the dashboard. "Please, Sergeant, this is an unmarked car. Nobody knows we're the police. Oh, Sweet Savior—"

"That pedestrian got away, didn't he?" de Gier asked, glancing at his rearview mirror. "Sporty type, climbing a tree now."

"Whoa!"

"I can't slow down for joyriding cyclists. Assistance to endangered colleagues is our most prized emergency."

"Red light ahead."

"Not anymore."

"The streetcar!"

"Police always have the right of way and streetcars have powerful brakes. Ha-ha, look at all those people sliding off their seats. Right, here we are. Headquarters."

"What's happening here?" Grijpstra asked.

"Well," the constable coming from the doorman's lobby said, "we're supposed to guard this building, right? This is no police station, this is Headquarters itself, but this subject walks straight in, drunk and all, and bothers us. What can we do? We can't guard the building and arrest him at the same time."

"But aren't there two of you?" de Gier asked. "You could arrest the subject while your colleague guards the building."

"The subject wants to be violated," the constable whispered.

"Violence," de Gier whispered, "is lawfully permitted under special circumstances. Didn't they teach you that at police school?"

"The subject is somewhat big," the constable whispered.

The subject was in the lobby, well over six feet, barrel-chested, and waving large fists. He was dressed neatly and swayed slowly. He smiled. "You're a cop, too?" he asked the sergeant.

"Sergeant de Gier, at your service entirely."

"Serve me," the subject said. "If you don't, I'll kill you. I've already killed tonight—an innocent bystander. I deserve to suffer suitable punishment. I wish to wither away in a dank cell."

Grijpstra moved forward and addressed the other constable.

"Tell your side of it," Grijpstra said.

The constable backed out of the drunk's earshot. "He didn't kill anyone, Adjutant, he just happens to have been indulging. He says he knocked someone down with his car on Brewers' Square, but we have our radio here and no accident has been reported in that area."

"When would the mishap have occurred?"

"An hour ago, and he has been here ever since, yelling at us. How can we guard the building with the subject distracting us?"

Grijpstra breathed deeply. He reshaped his smile. "Constable, we're of the Criminal Investigation Department. We are highly trained. We learned how to count, for instance. Am I mistaken if I count two of you?"

"I'm not familiar with the ways of the supercops, Adjutant," the constable said pleasantly, "but we regular officers work in couples. My mate and I form just one couple—and couples, we were taught at police school, may never be split. The subject is big. It will need a complete couple to arrest him. If we arrest him, we cannot guard the building."

Grijpstra faced the drunk. "Sir."

The subject continued to sway and to smile.

"You're under arrest. Follow me."

The subject balled his hands into fists.

"Let's go," Grijpstra bellowed.

The subject hit Grijpstra. Grijpstra fell down. De Gier jumped forward. The subject's arm flew up and turned behind his back, yanked expertly by de Gier's arms. Handcuffs clicked.

"The subject is now a suspect," de Gier told the constables. "I suspect him of harassing the police. Watch him." He squatted next to Grijpstra. "How are you doing?"

Grijpstra groaned.

"Ambulance," de Gier said. A constable picked up a phone.

The suspect kicked. De Gier, still squatting, bent sideways and clutched the suspect's leg. The suspect fell over backward and hit the floor with the full impact of his own strength and weight.

"Take him to a cell," de Gier said. The constables dragged the suspect away.

A siren howled in the street. De Gier opened the door.

"Evening," the ambulance driver said. "You guys damaged a subject again?"

"A colleague is hurt," de Gier said. "Be careful with him; he's my friend."

"We're always careful." The driver turned to his assistant. "Ready? Let's pick him up."

Grijpstra opened his eyes.

"Don't relax too much," the driver said. "Otherwise we can't get you on the stretcher. You're a bit heavy, you know."

"I'm not heavy," Grijpstra said, "and I have no intention of cooperating. I was out for a moment, but I'm back again. Where's the suspect, Sergeant?"

"He's in his cell and you're on your way to the doctor."

"No." Grijpstra started to his feet.

"Grab him," de Gier said to the driver.

The driver shook his head. "Not if the patient refuses."

De Gier held his fist under the driver's nose. "Take him along."

He held his fist under Grijpstra's nose. "Be taken along. Your skull hit the stone floor, and I want to know whether it's cracked or not. You can come back if the doctor releases you."

"Who outranks who?" the driver asked.

"I'm outranked," de Gier said, "but I happen to be more aggressive than he is and I'm good at judo."

"Let's pick him up and get out of here," the driver's assistant said.

"I'll be on my way, too," de Gier said to the constables. "Have a good night now, the two of you."

. . .

The blue Volkswagen was parked on Brewers' Square again, opposite the Concert Building, pointed at Museum Square. De Gier was at the wheel. He picked up the microphone. "The fourteen-six."

"Darling."

"I'm back doing what I was doing," de Gier said, "and I have a request."

"Yes?"

"Please ask one of the constables guarding your building to speak to me on the radio."

"Sergeant?" one of the constables asked a few moments later.

"Listen," de Gier said. "The situation was somewhat bewildering just now. What exactly was bothering your suspect when he first approached you?"

"An excess of alcohol," the constable said.

"Anything else?"

"He said he had run someone down on Brewers' Square."

"Details?"

The constable grinned noisily. "He ran down a blue one."

"What does that mean?"

"I wouldn't know, Sergeant."

"Thanks." De Gier pushed the microphone back into its clip.

Over there, de Gier observed, the blue lady is still crying. Patiently. Into her handkerchief. Seeing that no one is restraining me now, I'll go and find out what causes her lengthy grief. He got out and walked over.

"Good evening."

"Please leave me alone."

"I only wanted to ask you something," de Gier said. "I am a—"

A patrol car stopped next to the conversing couple. Two constables got out. They had left their caps in the car. "What's going on here?" one of them asked.

"This man is annoying me," the lady said.

The constables turned to de Gier. "We've been watching

you for a while, sir. You were ogling the lady and now you're actually waylaying her. Move along—and be glad that we don't intend, for the moment, to pursue the misdemeanor."

De Gier showed his police card.

The constables edged him along the sidewalk. "Look here," the older of the two said, "even we aren't allowed to bother crying females. It's tempting to do it anyway, I will admit, for when they're in tears, they're easy to push over, but we shouldn't, don't you agree?"

De Gier showed his watch. "You see the seconds change numbers?"

"Yes?"

"Five more numbers and the two of you are back in your car and driving away. I have to talk to the lady. Make yourselves scarce. All right?"

"I don't know whether you recognize the sergeant," the younger constable advised his partner, "but Rinus de Gier has just been declared judo and karate champion of Amsterdam. Let's go. Good evening, Sergeant Champion."

The patrol car drove off. De Gier walked back to the lady. He showed her his police card. "Miss," he said in a low and pleasant voice, "you seem to be unhappy. Did a car run into you a while ago?"

The lady sobbed.

"Let's have nothing but the truth," de Gier said. "Crying only makes your eyes bulge. You have been run into by a car and you had a bad fright. Share your misery."

"No," the lady said. . . . "Do my eyes really bulge?"

"Not really. Would you like a cigarette?"

"I never smoke in the street."

"Smoke in my car."

The lady adjusted her skirt and drew on her cigarette.

"Well?" de Gier asked.

"I'll tell you. I'm having an affair with a certain Mr. Dams and he promised to marry me."

"He did?" de Gier said.

"So he would have to divorce his wife."

"He would."

"But he didn't. And I had enough of waiting. Tonight I decided to go to his house."

De Gier waited.

"His wife opened the door. I said, 'I'm your husband's girlfriend and I want to know about the divorce.' She let me in and he switched off the TV and looked at both of us. His wife said, 'What's this about a divorce?' He got up and went to the kitchen and came back with a bottle of gin and drank it all."

De Gier waited.

"And then he left the house and his wife said it was all my fault. I ran out of the house and followed his car, in my own."

De Gier waited.

"He could hardly drive, but he managed to get as far as here and to park it. He walked off before I could park."

"Mr. Dams is a big man?"

"Oh, yes." She blew her nose.

"Three-piece suit? Wide-shouldered?"

"Yes."

"Where's his car?"

"The big Chevrolet over there."

"You saw him park. Did he hit anyone?"

"He drove over the island, where the pedestrians wait for the streetcar."

"Your friend, Mr. Dams," de Gier said, "has been arrested. He hit an officer. He won't be released until tomorrow morning. I would advise you to go home and sleep well."

De Gier unclipped the microphone. "Headquarters? The fourteen-six."

"Darling?"

"Could I speak to that constable again?"

"Sergeant?" the constable asked.

"Go to the suspect's cell and ask him about his accident. Then come back and tell me exactly what he answers."

Heroin, de Gier thought, brought me here, and I haven't seen any trace of it yet and never will, I'm sure, for soon the Concert Building will empty and there will be thousands of people on the square and they can give each other parcels forever without me seeing any of it. Let's solve puzzles that can be solved. Like what's with the blue lady and her Mr. Dams?

"The fourteen-six?" the radio asked.

"Right here."

"Sergeant," the constable said. "Sure, blue, and dead, too."

"What?"

"That's what the suspect said just now."

"That's all?"

"All."

If there's anything, de Gier thought, that really annoys me, it's a simple situation I can't comprehend. Blue. What blue? Blue what? The lady was blue, but the suspect didn't hit the lady. The sergeant looked out of the car. The cart loaded with rags was still parked under the no-parking sign. The rags were moving. De Gier got out.

"Is this where you sleep?" de Gier asked.

"I have a bed at home," Blue Pete said, "but my wife is in it and she's watching TV. I'd rather be here. Resting. Drinking a little." He held up a bottle. "Care for a sip?"

"Methylated spirits?" de Gier asked.

"The best Dutch gin," Blue Pete said. "What with welfare on the up again, methyl alcohol has become too cheap for me. Pity in a way. I really prefer methylated spirits—the taste is a bit sharper."

"But you're still blue," de Gier said.

"That'll never wear off. Sure you don't want a nip?"

De Gier pushed the bottle away. "Tell me, Pete, did anyone happen to run into you tonight with his car?"

"No."

"Are you sure?"

"Yes!" shouted Blue Pete. "Do you think I need to lie to anyone? With my welfare going up and up and up?"

"Pete," de Gier said. "Relax, it's a beautiful night. But someone drove into 'a blue one' tonight, and you are blue."

"If I'd been involved in an accident," Blue Pete said, "I would have made a fuss. Maybe I'm just a simple textile dealer, but nobody drives over *me*, not even if the millionaire drives a brand-new Chevrolet!"

"Aha," said de Gier. "A Chevrolet, eh? The one over there, perhaps?"

"But it never drove into me," Blue Pete said. "It drove across the traffic island over there. It was stopped by the little pillar with the blue light in it." He laughed raucously. "And it had just been fixed. I watched a uniformed chap fussing with it with a screwdriver and pliers. Fixed it finally and bang, there comes the millionaire with the Chevrolet and bends it all out of shape again. Ho-ho."

De Gier walked back to his car. He thought as he walked. He changed his direction and investigated the pillar. It was bending over a few degrees and scratched, but the light still burned. He walked over to the Chevrolet. Its bumper was dented a little and some of the paint from the pillar was stuck in the dent. The sergeant slid back into the Volkswagen, sighing contentedly. Facts fitted once again. Here was Mr. Dams, an upright citizen trapped by another woman. Temporarily insane, Mr. Dams got himself drunk and hit a pillar. How easy everything was once seen from the correct angle.

He released the microphone. "The fourteen-six."

"Darling?"

"Hello, Marie," de Gier said. "Please don't call me darling. The channel is open—any police car can listen in."

"Yes, my beloved."

"Any news about the adjutant's condition?"

"A sore chin. He's on his way to you."

■ ■ ■

Grijpstra tapped on the window. De Gier opened the door for him.

"Nothing the matter with me," the adjutant said. "You forced me to make a spectacle of myself."

"I'm sorry," de Gier said. "I'll never do it again. Next time you're out cold on the floor, I will stand on your head."

"Thanks," Grijpstra said. "How's our heroin deal?"

"What heroin?"

"Our original assignment."

"Ah, that." De Gier cursed. "I thought I had it all figured out—and now this." He pointed.

"Are you pointing at the man in the blue uniform opening the little door in the pillar with the blue light in it?"

"I am."

"What could be wrong with that? The man is employed by the electric company and he's checking the pillar."

"I just found out," the sergeant said, "that the light was checked a little while ago. Besides, it's burning. What's he fiddling with the insides of the pillar for?"

"Replacing a fuse?" Grijpstra asked lazily. "Dusting connections? Scraping the socket? Should we care?"

"I think so," de Gier said. "Because he's doing none of that. He's removing some small cellophane packages. You go right; I'll take the left. Pull your gun."

The man in the uniform also pulled a gun. There were two shots. De Gier dropped when the shots went off and kicked the suspect's legs from under him. Grijpstra caught the falling suspect. Handcuffs clicked.

"He didn't hit you, did he?" de Gier asked.

"No," Grijpstra said. "But I hit him. He's bleeding from the chest. I don't think the cuffs were necessary."

"Come right in," the commissaris said. "The chief is waiting for you. Good work—but it's a pity the suspect didn't survive his arrest."

The chief got up from behind his desk and smiled at his

visitors. "Adjutant. Sergeant. My congratulations. The suspect has been identified and important clues have been found in his home that will lead to further arrests. What brilliant reasoning led you to believe that the man masquerading as an electric company worker was your man?"

Grijpstra didn't say anything. De Gier was quiet.

"Well?"

"No brilliant reasoning, sir," de Gier said. "A melody perhaps—one blue note leading to another."

The chief smiled patiently. "Tell me about it."

Grijpstra reported.

"I see," the chief said. "Who put the heroin *into* the pillar?"

Grijpstra shrugged. "We didn't see that. The big dealer presumably."

"And the small dealer took it out?"

"So it seems."

"The pillar merely served as a third party? The dealers didn't want to meet?"

Grijpstra nodded. "The less they know, the less they can tell."

"And the lady in blue?"

"No connection, sir. Neither was Blue Pete."

"Yet the *events* connected," the chief said. "A typical example of proper police work. What do you think, Commissaris? These men are from your department. Don't you agree that they did well?"

The commissaris was standing near the door. He came forward and studied his assistants. His eyes rested on de Gier's brow. "You're pale, Sergeant."

"Blue," de Gier mumbled. "It's such a beautiful shade. It's pursued us all night, leading to death."

The commissaris led the sergeant to the door. Grijpstra followed.

"What was that?" the chief asked when the commissaris returned.

"An erratic statement," the commissaris said. "It's a while since you and I were assigned to street duty. After a violent death a colleague may tend toward erratic behavior." He looked out the window. The sky curved like a tight metallic-blue sheet above the city of Amsterdam, iridescent in its entirety, intensified by the first pulsating stars. "It's the blue hour again," he said to the chief. "Let's go across the street. You may allow me to buy you a drink."

THE
SERGEANT'S
CAT

"**A** shot in the night," Sergeant de Gier of the Amsterdam Municipal Police was saying as he put on his jacket, "does break the routine rather pleasantly." He faced the mirror next to the door and arranged his silk scarf. Adjutant Grijpstra agreed and pushed the sergeant aside. The adjutant held up his left arm and attempted to smooth the fold under his armpit. De Gier raised his arm as well. "My bulge is worse. The new gun is too large."

Grijpstra smiled in the elevator. It had been a quiet evening, with coffee in the canteen and friendly conversation with colleagues. De Gier complained contentedly next to him, still on the subject of the new oversize gun. Grijpstra acknowledged his assistant's objections, repeating them in part. The new service handgun was the Walther P-5, and although it was lightweight and aimed well—very well, up to two hundred meters, so Grijpstra stated—the weapon served the plainclothes detective badly, for it was too long.

"And too wide," said de Gier. "All right for the uniformed branch—they show the gun—but we're supposed to hide it."

The elevator door opened, offering a view of a sterile corridor wherein neatly dressed constables marched to and fro. Their clear blue tunics contrasted sharply with the light gray corridors. A lady cop came along on long slender legs, her bosom gently bouncing. Her hair was long and blond, curling from under her small round hat. Grijpstra observed her approvingly. He was working on a painting at home in his spare time. The painting had been set up in outline and now needed color. The policewoman had lilac-colored lips. Grijpstra chose the shade for one of the flowers in the foreground of the painting.

She nodded at Grijpstra and greeted de Gier. "Hi, Rinus."

"Hi, Jane," said the sergeant.

"Jane?" Grijpstra asked when they crossed the inner courtyard of Police Headquarters. "Isn't Jane somewhat prosaic for such a luscious woman? Where are we going?"

De Gier got into the unmarked car and opened Grijpstra's door. He waited until Grijpstra had forced his bulk into the car's interior. "What's wrong with Jane? It's a good name. She's a good woman, too. We're headed for the southern suburbs."

The car stopped at the first set of traffic lights. Grijpstra tore at the cellophane cover of a cigar. His eyebrows were still up as he looked at the sergeant again.

De Gier made the car surge forward, following bicycles whose riders were impatient and wouldn't wait for the lights to change. "The shot in the night was fired in Ouborg, an exclusive area for the well-heeled."

"And Jane?"

The car was half on the sidewalk, speeding to pass clogged traffic, and de Gier had to pay attention. Finally he reached a square offering more space. "Jane?"

"You said she's a good woman," Grijpstra said patiently. "How do you know? Did you try? With success?"

"Not yet." De Gier avoided more traffic lights by crossing over to the part of the boulevard reserved for streetcars, ambulances, and patrol cars. "I think she's good, but it might just be that she's not prepared to prove my point." He looked at Grijpstra triumphantly. "A shot in the night." He hunched his shoulders and lowered his chin so that he could look up and admire tree branches adorning a starry sky. "It's a lovely night, but ripped apart by a shot. That's what the lady on the phone said. She lives next door, in another small palace. She also said that a car drove away after the shot had been fired— an expensive car, silver-shaded. She didn't note the number." He made the car increase speed again. "And she heard a woman scream."

"What do you know," Grijpstra said, and glanced over his shoulder. "And look at that."

De Gier looked into his rear mirror. A patrol car had loosened itself from the parking lot in front of a suburban police station and was following them, flashing its lights, howling its siren.

"Ignore them," Grijpstra said, sucking his cigar. He checked the speedometer. A hundred kilometers an hour. He listened to the scream of tires. He nodded.

"You're nodding," de Gier said. "You usually complain when I drive too fast. Are you changing?"

"Everything changes," shouted Grijpstra. He had to shout because the patrol car was now riding next to them.

De Gier braked.

"Why?" Grijpstra wondered aloud. The patrol car stopped ahead and two cops tumbled onto the pavement.

"Because their car is brand-new and ours is falling apart," de Gier said. "Old cars don't drive very fast. They were cutting me off."

"Ho-ho-ho!" the cops shouted. "Speeding, dear sir? And failing to stop when followed by a patrol car flashing its lights and howling its siren. Are you blind? Are you deaf?"

De Gier showed his police card. Grijpstra loosened the microphone from under the dashboard and held it up by way of proof.

"Detectives, eh?" the cop on the left said.

"Can we come, too?" asked the cop on the right.

"Something nice?" the cop on the left asked.

"Be our guests," de Gier said, "as long as you don't make so much noise. It's close. Ouborg. Do you happen to know where that may be?"

The patrol car guided the way. The address was in a lane overshadowed by plane trees, with spacious bungalows on each side. A windmill stood behind the trees, artistically cutting the night sky with its sails.

A lady came running toward them, waving her arms.

"I don't think that's legal," one of the cops said a little later.

"That's breaking and entering," the other cop said. "You need a permit, signed by a commissaris."

"The hell," de Gier said, hammering on a window with the butt of his gun. "I've looked through the side window and I've seen a lady on a bed. She has no clothes on and she's bleeding from the head."

"That won't work," Grijpstra said, "the new gun is mostly made of light plastic. It won't break glass. Use this rock."

"Jane," Grijpstra said.

"I beg your pardon?" asked de Gier.

"She looks like Jane," Grijpstra said. "Very much like Jane, and she's dead. Sit down, Sergeant. You always faint when in the presence of a corpse. Ah, it's suicide, see? She's still holding the gun. There's a glass. She had a drink first and then she shot herself through the temple. But why is she naked?"

"Can I phone?" one of the policemen asked. "I know Headquarters' secret number."

The other cop wandered about the room. "Posh," he commented. "That painting is by Edward Hopper, a famous American, worth a year's wages—two maybe. Look at the books. The collected works of a number of geniuses, at fifty guilders a volume. What would that antique couch cost?"

"The house alone costs a million," Grijpstra said. "Yes? What is it, Sergeant?"

De Gier stood in the open door to the garden, nicely silhouetted against the dark, clear sky, flanked by small poplars. He was a tall man, narrow-waisted, wide-shouldered. His mustache was modeled on those of high-ranking cavalry officers a hundred years back. His eyes were large, brown, softly pleading. His cheekbones were pronounced, his hair thick and curly. He looked good in the open garden door until he staggered and grabbed a post.

"Don't look at the lady," Grijpstra said. She had been attractive, but she was bleeding now and her eyes stared strangely. "Did you see anything worth noting?"

"Yes," de Gier said. "There's a car in the garage and it's burned out. It was a Camaro, I think, or a Corvette, resembling a fish of prey. Chevrolet makes those cars, for the rich and happy people."

"So what do we know?" Grijpstra asked three hours later in the car on the way back to the inner city, driving quietly through empty streets, silent but for the chirruping of birds and the squeak of a paperboy's roller skates.

"That the lady is dead," de Gier said, "and that the doctor isn't pleased. The fingerprint gentlemen aren't pleased either." He held up a finger. "The doctor seems to think she was drugged." He held up a second finger. "The fingerprint gentlemen checked her hand. They think she didn't fire the gun. If she had, the porridge they smeared on her palm would have discolored—because of the fumes of the exploding cartridge, mixed with her sweat and the oil of the gun."

"Modern methods," Grijpstra said unhappily. Grijpstra was an older man, in a forbidding three-piece dark blue suit softened a little by thin white stripes.

"Adjutant," de Gier said, "we do have modern methods and they're sometimes known to work. If the corpse didn't kill herself, then somebody else did. The murderer shot her and took her hand afterward and inserted the gun."

"Why did she take her clothes off?" Grijpstra asked. "Did she make love to the killer? The doctor wasn't sure."

"He used modern methods, too, our killer," de Gier mused, "and then he drove away in his silver-shaded car. But we have found that the lady's lover is also the owner of the house. He's a man by the name of Wever and he doesn't drive a silver car. He hasn't been home for a few days. And we know the lady's name, which is Cora Fischer."

"Drive on," Grijpstra said. "I don't want to go to Headquarters. The building is bleak at this time of the early morning."

"Where would sir like to be driven to?"

"To an all-night café on a picturesque canal where we can drink gin and beer and smoke black cigars. If we get drunk, we'll leave the car and stagger home."

"Right," de Gier said. "Here's your beer and here's your gin and here's my coffee."

"Is there cognac in your coffee?" Grijpstra asked. "What a lovely café this is. Behold the heavy rotten beams supporting a smoky ceiling. Take a look at that criminal-looking bartender and that small crowd of hopeless alcoholics. Isn't Amsterdam a beautiful city?"

"There's cognac in my coffee," de Gier said. "Let me wish you good health. Cora Fischer. First she was loved and later killed. This is a choice crime and I'm glad I work for the police. And you know, she looked rather relaxed. I hardly think there was a fight. Was she drugged or not?"

. . .

"I'm not quite sure," the pathologist said some six hours later. "Sit down over there, Sergeant. The autopsy will supply us with tangible information. I haven't seen you here before. Are you sure you can take it? I'll have to cut and saw."

"He can't take it," Grijpstra said, "and I don't think I can either, but the law says there should be some officer of the law here to watch you. But the inspector is otherwise engaged, and the commissaris has been told to rest in the morning. Please go ahead."

"I'm going out for a walk," said de Gier. "It's a nice day and I hardly ever visit cemeteries. I'll walk about for a while and study flower arrangements on tombstones. I'll be back when you're done."

Grijpstra watched how the pathologist, in a white coat and a plastic apron, made the incision: two long cuts from the shoulders to the navel and a shorter one from the lower belly to the pubic area. Another doctor, a clone of the first, cut the head skin in order to bare the skull. The one doctor cut while the other sawed with an electric gadget that sprayed sawdust against his mask. Why don't I rather think something? Grijpstra thought. This is not appetizing. They are damaging her, as if she isn't damaged enough already.

The lady's consort, Grijpstra thought, is called Wever, and he owns the villa, worth a million, which is about as much as I can make in twenty years. The man is extraordinarily wealthy, although he isn't an attorney, or a dentist, or even a registered accountant. He's rich because he owns illegal gambling houses and a drugs-and-sex joint in the fashionable little seaport of Noordwijk close by. His name is known to us, but we haven't been able to arrest him so far. He doesn't pay taxes because he fiddles his books. He's a gangster, an evil spirit from the underworld. With the old police gun we couldn't shoot him because the bullets would have been stopped in his fat. With the new gun we could kill him easily, but we don't because that would be illegal. He's known to us because our secret detectives visit brothels and are equipped with large ears.

We've heard that about a year ago he took a new mistress, a certain Cora Fischer, the ex-model of a famous painter, the ex-star of the art-loving society.

The pathologists handled their knives like indifferent but knowledgeable butchers. As they cleaned the parts taken from the body with fresh water bubbling from a hand shower and dumped them in dishes and bottles, one of them spoke in a loud, monotonous voice, reporting his observations to a clerk, positioned at a safe distance. "Liver," the pathologist said, "slightly enlarged and discolored." He weighed the liver and announced the figure. The clerk wrote the figure down.

Where was I? Grijpstra thought. Right. Cora impressed the arty and the affluent. But the famous painter tired of her and removed her from his turn-of-the-century loft. She was without employ, but she was still attractive. Wever welcomed her, and Cora became the hostess of his club in Noordwijk and sometimes of his illegal blackjack joints. Or so said the secret detectives who live in the underworld and whisper through telephones and slip letters under Headquarters' doors.

"Well?" Grijpstra asked.

"We still can't be sure," the second pathologist said. "We'll have to do some tests. She didn't inject, that's for sure, but she did sniff cocaine. She drank a bit too much and she smoked."

"Can I smoke?" Grijpstra asked.

"I'd rather you didn't."

"I think I will all the same," Grijpstra said. "This is a good cigar and I'm a bit nervous."

"I'll open a window," the doctor said, doing so. "Smoking can kill you, you know."

"Is that right?" Grijpstra said. "So what killed her?"

The doctor smiled. "A bullet through the head. No doubt about it. And her vanity. She was a lovely dame."

"Well?" de Gier asked.

"They're still not sure," Grijpstra said, "but there was alcohol in her stomach, mixed with a sleeping draught. It's very pleasant out here."

"I saw three thrushes," de Dier said, "and a crow. Some chickadees, too, and a magpie. Some of the tombstones carry impressive poetry. And I saw a gent with a motor helmet under his arm hiding behind sunglasses. He must have been a boxer, in view of his flattened nose, and is still a sporting type, in view of his bouncy gait. Look, there he is, riding away on a four-cylinder motorcycle."

Grijpstra looked. "That's a very large gent. Six foot six, I would think. What was he doing here?"

"I'm beginning to think I know," de Gier said. "He looked at me for quite a while with much interest. . . . Does she still look like Jane?"

"*Mister* Wever," de Gier said four hours later, "listen, and listen good. There are some facts. One of the facts is that your reputation stinks. Your gambling joints and your brothel are no good. You're a pimp and a drug dealer."

"Facts," Wever said, sitting uncomfortably on a straight-backed chair in Grijpstra's office, holding his hands on his knees so that the middle fingers rested on the immaculate creases of his tailor-made sharkskin pants, "should be proved. You've never proved anything regarding me. You haven't done that because no drugs have ever been found in the establishments I own. So what's all this empty talk, eh?"

"I'm telling you," de Gier said, "that you're a curse on our society. There's another fact." The sergeant held up a finger. "Your girl friend was murdered—in your house, on your bed."

Wever showed the gold stuck in his whitish gums. "So what?"

De Gier said, "She didn't shoot herself—our modern methods say so."

Grijpstra nodded. "And someone had mixed a sleeping pill into her drink."

Wever adjusted his hairpiece. "So you claim. But why should

I believe you? Why should the judge believe you? So Cora took a tranquilizer—she often did, she was a highstrung woman, you know. She worried a lot, whether I loved her or if I didn't. And I didn't, of course, because I have this other lady, in my club in Noordwijk, who is younger and more appetizing. I was spending nights with Yvette, so Cora shot herself."

De Gier had become angry. He was hitting his desktop with the flat of his hand. "And burned her own car? No, sir, *you* burned her car and later you had her killed. Now listen to me—"

"But what if I don't want to listen to you?" Wever asked. "You're impolite and I'm a gentleman of sorts. I wasn't home. Alibi, don't you know? Are you familiar with the word? She shot herself." Wever got up. He was a big man; he kept getting up.

"Sit down, Mister Pimp," de Gier said. "If you leave this office, you'll be arrested in the corridor, for not paying traffic tickets. And we'll close your joints."

Wever sat down. "What's wrong with my gambling? Blackjack's okay. The court says so and the Supreme Court is about to confirm it. Blackjack has to be played with intelligence; that's why you could never play it. I wasn't home; I can prove I wasn't home. It ain't me."

Grijpstra looked up. "Can't you conjugate verbs correctly? Can't you do anything right?"

Wever got angry, too. Sweat trickled down his cheeks on its way to his many chins.

"What happened was this," de Gier said. "First you were proud of Cora. Because she was so lovely, and so famous. You put her in your palace and she was the queen in your club—people pointed her out to each other. You bought her a car worth forty thousand. Clothes. Jewelry. She was a *nouveauté*. But after a while she wasn't anymore. But she was still around, costing money. You're a businessman in a way and like balancing things out. If you lose money you have to gain it back again. So—"

Wever put up his hands. Sunlight reflected from his varnished nails. "That's enough."

"Not at all," de Gier said. "We're after the truth. So what was Cora to do? She had to smuggle dope. The Camaro nosed into Paris and back again, once a week. Cora carried cocaine and heroin in her pants, in her cleavage. She slipped easily back and forth through the checkpoints, the customs smiling at her. But then she wouldn't go anymore."

"No?" Wever asked. "Changed her mind, did she? Whatever for?"

"Let's not be funny," de Gier said. "She stopped smuggling your drugs because she realized drugs are bad for people. Cora was never a bad girl. You made her bad, but she wanted to be good again."

Wever sighed. "*Good?* That phony, hysterical broad?"

De Gier stirred his coffee. The room became quiet.

"Hello?" Grijpstra asked.

"Yes," de Gier said. "Then you destroyed her car a few nights back. The fire department came, but they couldn't save the Camaro—that classy car she liked so much, gone forever. Insured, but that didn't help her since you weren't planning on replacing it. You threatened her, right?"

"Right," Wever said softly. "Suppose, as long as we're playing this game together, that what you say is true. It isn't, but okay. Even if it were true, you can't prove I killed her. You can't because I didn't kill her. I wasn't home."

"*You* weren't," de Gier said, "but you sent your right hand— a gent by the name of Freddie. A big gent—bigger than you, but with a good build. You're horribly fat, you know. Freddie isn't, but he does have a fat head, and the chips in it aren't very complicated. Kill, you say, and Freddie kills. He gets into a silver car and shoots the lady. He also drives a motorbike, by the way."

"I'm going," Wever said. "You're not only wasting my time, you're spoiling it. I'll pay my traffic tickets on the way down. Good-bye."

●　●　●

"You weren't really angry?" Grijpstra asked.

"*He* was," de Gier said.

"Yes," Grijpstra agreed. "And I believe you're right. I don't particularly care for bluffing, but we sometimes have to do it. How could you know that Freddie is the motorbike rider."

De Gier shrugged. "I sensed evil in the man and checked our files. The secret branch sent in a snapshot of Freddie once. We've got nothing on him, but we know he works for Wever. He doesn't go to cemeteries because he likes watching tombs. He's an artist in a way. He follows up on his work. Or maybe he's horribly crazy. Perhaps this was a special job for him, because Cora was such a beautiful woman. She was naked, remember? He had her, then he killed her. He felt a link that pulled him right to the cemetery—to me, the avenger. I'm an angel of light; he's a demon of darkness."

"A farfetched conclusion."

"Wasn't I right?" de Gier said. "Didn't you say so just now?"

Grijpstra murdered his half-smoked cigar with a spark-whirling stump in the ashtray. "I never went in for mysticism. It doesn't get anybody anywhere. You were right, certainly; but we're where we've been so often—nowhere. Wever wasn't home, he really wasn't. And Freddie will say that he wasn't in Ouborg either. There'll be witnesses in Noordwijk claiming that they were playing cards with him all night. And the silver-shaded car was borrowed for the occasion, or stolen, or the license plates weren't right. No."

"Coffee and cake?" de Gier asked.

"Hello, Jane," he said in the canteen.

"Can I join you?" the female officer asked.

Grijpstra jumped up. De Gier fetched a chair. "You know," he said, "it wasn't wrong what I did. I got him rattled. I made waves in his soul. Didn't Newton say that action gives reaction? I made him angry. Wever has lost his cool—he's got to slip up now."

"What are you two talking about?" Jane asked. "Don't I get any coffee and cake?"

"You're a sweetheart," de Gier said. "You're actually asking. Feminists get their own coffee. You're a real woman and a beautiful woman, too. I can hardly believe your beauty. You instill tender and protective feelings in my deepest mind."

"The sergeant," Grijpstra said, "likes to work on people's feelings."

"I love it," Jane said. She pushed back her chair and crossed her legs.

"You have good legs," Grijpstra said. "It's a pity I never paint human figures. If I did, I'd ask you to model for me."

"Model," de Gier said, returning with Jane's coffee. "Cora was a model. It seems that the universe is unlimited in its manifestations, but deeper reflection might show that everything is a variation on a single theme."

"What was that?" Jane asked.

"You look like Cora," Grijpstra said.

Four hours later de Gier's apartment buzzer buzzed. The sergeant put his cat on the floor, placed his book on the table, and opened the door.

"Evening," his visitor said. "My name is Freddie."

Freddie sat down. The cat jumped from the chair.

"My cat was sitting there," de Gier said.

"Stupid cat."

"Yes?"

"Listen here," Freddie said. "I've come to bring you money. Here you are." He put an envelope on de Gier's book.

"What's in that?"

"Ten thousand. There'll be more later, but then we will require your services. This is a present. You don't even have to *not* do something because you can't do anything anyway. You have no proof."

"You're not providing me with news," de Gier said.

"You're fuzz," Freddie said, "and fuzz is for sale. Because you're good fuzz, I bring you money straightaway. The fuzz we have so far is little fuzz. They're okay for a bit of information now and then, like so that we won't be there when you're preparing a raid. But it would be nice to have some big fuzz on the payroll, too."

"Yes?"

Freddie smiled. "Yes."

De Gier lit a cigarette.

"You're not offering anything?" Freddie asked.

"No," de Gier said. "You're unwelcome company. Maybe I don't want your money either. Maybe I'll shoot you in a minute or so. I don't want to fight you. This is a small apartment and we'll break the furniture."

"Once we start fighting," Freddie said, "I'll break you, too. The boss has lost his temper. You've been rude to him. The boss likes people to be polite and helpful. So he's not giving you a choice. You've got to work for us and you've got to take our money. If you refuse, we'll be nasty."

"Like what?" de Gier asked.

The cat walked past Freddie's leg. Freddie picked up the cat and turned it over. He slid a stiletto from his pocket. The point of the stiletto scratched the cat's chin. The cat purred. "Stupid cat," Freddie said. "I can open him up, like they opened up Cora today. But I won't sew him up again. I'll leave him here, open."

"Maybe you shouldn't do that," de Gier said.

Freddie pushed the cat from his lap. "Not yet, but I might later on if you happen to be disobedient. I'll kill your cat and your old mother and anybody else you care for. If I happen to be busy, someone else will do it. The boss is rich, unbelievably rich. He can buy anybody. And whoever he buys makes more money for him."

"Yes?"

Freddie grinned, slowly and completely. "Cocaine and heroin prices are going up again, and the customers carry the money in without the slightest prodding. There's no end to it. Money is good. It buys good cars and good trips. Look at my color."

"Nice tan," de Gier acknowledged.

"Bermuda. I was there last week. I'll go again. I've been in the Seychelles too and in Indonesia. You can make nice trips, too. You can use this money."

"Not a bad idea."

"I'm glad you agree." Freddie got up.

"Good-bye," de Gier said, and closed the door behind Freddie. He waited until he heard the elevator going down and sprinted down the staircase. He was outside before Freddie got out of the elevator.

"Psst," de Gier said.

Freddie approached him with his legs astride and his fists up.

"Not here," de Gier said. "We don't want to make a spectacle of ourselves. Over there, in the park."

"You can't be serious," Freddie said.

They crossed the street together. It was late. The sky carried few clouds. The moon caused delicate shades on the lawns. Ducks in the pond woke for a moment and murmured sleepily. A swan bobbed, propelled by one foot. De Gier walked next to Freddie, his hand on his back. De Gier was tall, but he wasn't a giant. He exercised regularly, one evening a week, sometimes two. He had a black belt in judo.

Freddie was a giant. He also exercised regularly and he had a high grade in karate. He could split bricks. Freddie drank heavily, de Gier moderately. They both smoked.

"I'll take you apart," Freddie said. "But not altogether. The boss likes things to develop slowly. He warns first."

De Gier smiled. They passed a tree, and a thrush opened an eye and tried a slow trill.

"What's funny?" Freddie asked.

"That I don't give warning," de Gier said. He kicked and hit simultaneously. His foot hit Freddie's shin and his hand made contact with his belly button. Freddie almost fell. De

Gier half circled him and extended an arm, holding his waist in a friendly manner. He shuffled sideways until his foot touched Freddie's, then he swung swiftly.

"Hey," Freddie shouted as he fell.

"Here you are," de Gier said, and closed Freddie's eyes with his fist. Then he hit him on the chin.

"Yes?" the lady in charge of ambulance movements asked.

"In the Southern Park," de Gier said, "just north of the larger pond, there's a man on the gravel. He's been knocked down and he's unconscious."

"Did you phone the police?"

De Gier replaced the hook. "No," he said to the quiet telephone. "They know my voice."

He picked up the phone again.

"Yes?" Constable First-Class Simon Cardozo, temporarily attached to the Criminal Investigation Department of the Amsterdam Municipal Police, asked.

"Listen," de Gier said. "My cat has been threatened."

"Tabriz?" asked Cardozo.

"I have only one cat. Can she stay with you?"

"Long?" Cardozo asked.

"I'll bring her over now."

"I'll fetch her," Cardozo said. "You don't have a car. Give me five minutes."

A burglar cycled into the suburb Ouborg about two hours later. The burglar broke into the mansion where Cora Fischer had lived such a luxurious life. Nobody was home, and the burglar found a suitcase and filled it with clothes and jewelry. He cycled away again and was spotted by a patrol car. The car didn't stop.

"Three o'clock in the morning?" the constable next to the driver asked. "A cyclist with a suitcase?"

"His lights were in order," the driving constable said. "You don't see that very often. A cyclist with working lights is okay."

"Well, what do you know?" Wever said about nineteen hours later. "Bit of a fool, aren't you, Sergeant? Do you know that Freddie has been admitted to the hospital?"

De Gier sat on a low leather chair. He drank beer. "Nice place you've got here, but too expensive, I would think."

"Join us," Grijpstra said. "You interfere with my view of the musicians."

Wever sat down. He cracked his fingers. A girl brought drinks. She was a nice-looking girl in a miniskirt and on high heels. She wasn't wearing anything else. "To think," Grijpstra said, "that Noordwijk was a rustic little port once and that there were sailors and fishermen in the cafés, smoking stone pipes from their beards. To think," Grijpstra said dreamily, "that their wives and girlfriends wore blue calico underwear right down to the knees."

"Listen," Wever said, "Freddie tells me he forgot an envelope in the sergeant's apartment."

"One of the reasons for our visit," de Gier said, and put the envelope on the table. Wever picked it up. A combo consisting of a pianist, a drummer, and a bass player played a European version of "This Here."

"Is your paneling of rosewood?" Grijpstra asked.

De Gier observed the suspect. He saw that Wever had a soft face, not soft from sensitive but soft from weak. He has been doing too well for too long, de Gier thought. His spine is dissolving. He was a tough guy once but now his muscles are yellow fat.

"Don't get up," de Gier said.

Wever's big fingers, flashing with diamonds, clamped on the sides of his chair. His buttocks were off his cushion. "Why not? This is my place—I can do what I like."

"You're under arrest." De Gier sat. "Drop down."

Wever's body flopped back onto the cushion. "Arrest for what?"

"For serious suspicions. I suspect that you're dealing in drugs, that you make money out of prostitution, and that you allow your customers to engage in illegal gambling."

Wever's cheeks rippled. He gestured. Grijpstra watched the moist spots on the armrests of Wever's chair.

"Are you crazy?" Wever asked. "This is today. Today anything goes. What's wrong with keeping whores? I have a sex club here, not a brothel. Brothels are out. And so is the law!" He looked about him. He pointed at guests. "And why did you bring all these cops? Do you think I can't smell cops even when they dress up like real people?" He began to get up again.

"Down, boy," Grijpstra said. "Didn't the sergeant just tell you that you're under arrest?"

"I've got to go to the restroom."

"Need a sniff, do you?" Grijpstra said. "That won't help you now. Those days are gone. You've done too much. You even tried to bribe my colleague."

"Why not?" Wever asked. "Aren't you all corrupt these days? Even a commissaris can be bought. Corruption has become a way of life."

"Not quite," Grijpstra said. "The ten thou is back in your pocket. Cat-threatening is bad, too—we'll have you for that as well."

"And," de Gier said, "you had your girlfriend killed. That's really going too far."

"Proof?" Wever asked.

"Quiet," de Gier said. "That piano player is good. Let me listen for a while. I'd like another drink, too. . . . Miss?"

Wever didn't look happy, but the general atmosphere improved. The topless waitress brought drinks, and more later. Wever was allowed a visit to the restroom under Grijpstra's supervision. The adjutant frisked his suspect and confiscated one gram of cocaine and a stiletto. The combo, encouraged by applause from the plainclothesmen and the other guests, improved. The pianist played meticulously, although he increased his speed. The drummer was also a percussionist, doing well on cowbells and wooden gongs. The bass remained steady, providing a strong drive.

"Some flute maybe?" Grijpstra asked.

De Gier produced a piccolo from his inside pocket, deftly joining its parts. He got up and repeated the main theme of the song. The audience cheered. De Gier tried an arpeggio, them improvised freely. The combo adjusted easily.

Grijpstra studied Wever. He's afraid. Grijpstra thought. Things are going well. De Gier has set up the scene properly and we're getting close. But now . . . but now . . .

The moment came. The revolving door introduced a tall but slender woman, a lady in the full glory of her beauty. Her hair had been elaborately arranged. She was dressed charmingly in a linen gown hand-painted with Chinese designs. Jewels bedecked her hands and neck. She sat down in the rear of the establishment.

De Gier still played his flute, encouraged by the musicians and the audience. Grijpstra waited. Wever looked about. He finally saw the woman. The light was dim—he could see the lady's general appearance but no fine details. "Cora," he whispered.

De Gier bowed and put his flute down. Grijpstra sucked on his cigar. He waved with his free hand. A young man with unruly curly hair and dressed in a threadbare corduroy suit got up and walked toward him. "Cardozo," Grijpstra said, "it's time." He produced a document, unfolded it, and handed it to Wever. "This is our permit to search the premises. You stay here."

Wever sweated, cursed, and muttered four-letter words.

Grijpstra waved again. Two men jumped up. "Sit here," Grijpstra told them, "and make sure the suspect doesn't move."

He and de Gier left the table as the two men sat down.

"You know," de Gier said a quarter of an hour later, "if we don't find anything, we've wasted our time."

"No negativity now," Grijpstra said. "We found the roulette, didn't we? Roulette is illegal. We have a charge."

"Nah," de Gier said. "The roulette wasn't being used. Wever'll provide some excuse. He can afford the best lawyers. Even the corruption charge won't stick. I want him for heroin—and murder, of course."

They were in a large room, leaning against exotic wainscoting, their hands in their pockets, their chins on their chests. Plainclothes cops wandered about, picking up objects and putting them down again. "Adjutant?" Cardozo asked.

"Constable First Class?" Grijpstra asked.

"Look," Cardozo said, pointing at an oak shelf above the open fire. "I noticed it," Grijpstra said. "That's a small statue of a reclining Eastern goddess. We've seen the type before. They're hollow and contain heroin when they cross the border, but by the time we see them, they're always empty."

"They're always hollow," Cardozo agreed, "but that one is solid."

De Gier walked over and picked up the statuette. He showed it to the adjutant. "Cardozo is right—it's solid."

"Exactly the same type as the ones we've found before," Cardozo said, "in Chinese restaurants and junk stores and so forth. They've always been hollow, but we've found traces of heroin inside. This one is solid." He weighed it on his hand. "A little over two pounds, I would say."

"Odd," said de Gier, scratching the statue.

"Careful," said Cardozo, "I tried that, too. The stuff flakes easily."

"Gypsum doesn't flake so easily," Grijpstra said.

"It isn't gypsum," Cardozo said.

"If you're right," de Gier said, "you have a fortune in your hands. A million maybe—at street level, that is."

"I am right," Cardozo said. "And we are in a retail outlet."

Grijpstra whistled—and the room filled up with cops.

"The treasure has been found," Grijpstra said. "Have all employees arrested and have extra staff alerted at Headquarters."

"The suspect downstairs," one of the men said, "seems to be suffering a mental breakdown. He's accusing himself of murder, committed on a certain Cora Fischer, and keeps pointing at our Jane."

Sergeant de Gier, about ten hours later, admitted that the course he had taken, and subsequently helped to direct, could be defined as irregular. He made his statement in the commissaris' office. The commissaris was facing him from behind his imposing desk. Grijpstra stood near the window, admiring a geranium in bloom.

"Yes," the commissaris said, "but that fellow Freddie had been threatening your cat, which is an extenuating circumstance. The results are excellent, fortunately. I hear that Wever is not retracting his confession."

"Freddie has confessed, too," Grijpstra told the geranium. "It seems that he's been under some stress which has weakened his nerves. He also objects to being called the murder weapon by his boss."

"Your cat is not too disgruntled?" the commissaris asked.

"She's doing well, sir," de Gier said. "Cardozo took good care of her and she's home again."

THE MACHINE GUN AND THE MANNEQUIN

He sat on the porch in a cane chair dating back to the time the mansion was built, back in the days when the rich still owned plantations in the colonies. He was a little sickly-looking guy, smoking a cigar. The cigar didn't function too well either—he had to press the torn leaf on the side to suck smoke out of it.

He wasn't a plantation owner, of course, just another nut, and I was on my way out and ready to walk by him. The mansion was now a home for the elderly disturbed, and I had been visiting my aunt, who isn't right in the head. One must be thoughtful once in a while and that's why I was there, but I had been thoughtful enough and wanted to go home. My aunt hasn't a thought in her head anymore— she only clicks her dentures and doesn't know what's what.

The little old guy waved to me and pointed at another cane chair that was ready to fall apart. I sat down. He was all alone on the porch and maybe he had something to say. He looked nutty, all right, with his few long hairs waving around his shiny skull. There were buttons missing on his shirt and his slippers had just about frayed off their soles. The bridge of his spectacles bit into his bony nose and his black raisin eyes stared at me over the round glasses.

"No visitors for you, today?" I asked. He wasn't saying anything yet, so I might as well be polite.

"Never have any." It wasn't a complaint, just a statement that loosened more words. "Don't know anyone, except the woman who used to clean my place. She'll be cleaning for the next guy now, don't you think?"

I nodded. He was there for keeps.

"Yep," the little old guy said. "Willems is my name, but here they call me Gramps."

"Treating you okay?"

He said they were and that the food was fine. And he was allowed to smoke, which was fine, too.

I said it gives you cancer, but he began to cackle and said that cancer is like worms, pretty-colored worms that dig around inside you and finally carry you off.

"You don't mind being carried away?"

He said he didn't. I wanted to go then, but he offered me a cigar. He still looked lonely, so I thought I'd wait.

"I've been lucky," he said. "I'm over sixty-five. If I'd been under, they would have put me in the institution that makes you go to class. Know what I mean?"

"Not quite," I said.

He gave up on his cigar—the leaves kept coming off—and shook the tin. The tin was empty, so he looked at my cigar. I gave it to him. He thanked me. "Class is terrible," he said. "Frightening, too. I was in the institution maybe ten years ago.

It scared me, so I got normal and got the hell out." He shook his head. "Such goings-on. They give you wooden shoes and clothes that scratch, and when there's food, they ring a bell and you can't just go and eat—they expect you to play hopscotch in the corridors first." He mused for a while. "There was a big guy who scared me. In class that was. He would crush cans with his bare hands and look at me like he wanted to do the same thing to me."

"So you got out?"

He showed his brown teeth. "Yes. I told them the urge had gone. It hasn't, but what the hell. I got into the business of the mannequins. It kept me busy, I had to work for a change." He waved his hands excitedly. "I got up early, went to the fairs, sold them, delivered them myself in the van. I was all over the place."

"And the urge?" I asked—he had me curious now.

"Still there," he said, not too unhappily. "But I took care. I didn't shout 'pow-pow' anymore, and I didn't point at them. I just sort of mumbled. They couldn't hear what I said."

"Mannequins?"

A nurse came. "Visitors' hour is over, Gramps," she said.

I was ready to go, but Willems pushed me back into my chair. "You're cute," he told the nurse. "I wish I'd known you when you were still in the colonies. I would have lured you from the jungle with some beads and then, while you played with them, I would have jumped you. Ha!"

"You would?" the nurse said. She was brown and Indonesian and very pretty.

"Can't he stay?" Willems asked her softly. "I never get visitors and I haven't finished telling him my story yet."

"Right," the nurse said. "I'll go back to the jungle for a while. But don't take too long. We've got to clean up here, and you'll be needing your nap."

She left the porch and Willems and I looked at her leaving. She had long straight legs and there were strong supple lines under her tight uniform.

"Nice," Willems said. "I had a mannequin like that once. I sold her in the end. Pity. But the customer offered a good price and she was somewhat damaged here and there. She'd been in the van too long and the van was soft in the springs. If they bounce around too much, they scratch."

"So what were these mannequins?" I asked.

"For the window. My dead uncle used to own that business. He got them from the factory in Germany, slightly damaged merchandise, sold at a discount. I used to help him, and when he croaked, I took over. It was easy, really. If I paid the invoices, the Germans would send more. You should have seen them.

"I went to all the fairs where the storekeepers buy, and I would sit in my own little corner, with all the mannequins around me stark naked, and I would adjust their arms and heads so they could beg the clients to take them away. 'Release us from this wicked sorcerer' they would scream, and I would sit between them, quietlike."

"Were you gesturing, too?"

"Me? Never. I just looked pathetic. When I don't make an effort, I always look pathetic." Willems pushed up his glasses and stared at me. His eyes didn't focus. The corners of his mouth hung down—his cheeks, too. "Well? Am I right?"

I agreed.

He was grinning at me again. "The business sort of prospered. Because the mannequins were cheap. I didn't earn much, but I wasn't starving either. Not that I ever needed much money. I lived in my room with a view of Leyden Square. I had a good position—my windows were right above the sandwich shop there. All I ever wanted to do was sit at the window, look at the crowd, and polish the Maxim—oil its works sometimes, tighten a screw here and there, adjust a spring."

I thought I hadn't heard right. "The *Maxim*, Mr. Willems?"

He was distracted by a sudden gust of wind that made the glass doors of the porch rattle, but I managed to catch his attention again. I'm still a policeman, after all, even if I only run the uniform store these days, and a Maxim is a machine gun.

He was rubbing his hands. "Yes. The cops took it away. Good thing, maybe. Perhaps it was time to retire. The cops said the Maxim was too much of a risk. Fully automatic arms are illegal and possession will take you to jail—and in my case it was worse because the gun was loaded, complete with all its parts and a couple of boxes of ammo."

"You mean you had a point-fifty machine gun?"

"Sure had. But it was easy to get. I served with the RAF during the war, and later with the Dutch air force here. I was even a hero. You want to hear?"

I wanted to hear.

"I escaped to England," Willems said. "In 1943, the Jerries wanted me to work in a factory somewhere, but I wasn't game. I lived on the coast before they moved us to make room for the Atlantic Wall, their bunkers and so forth, but I still knew the way. My brother knew the way, too, and he found out where the Jerries kept their boats. He got us one, engine and all. We dressed up to look like Kraut sailors and one day we went. They saw us, but on account of our clothes they thought we were them. Easy, like eating Momma's pie—it always is when you really want something.

"Once we were out, the British saw us and picked us up. We joined the RAF, him as a pilot. But he crashed somewhere. I flew on a Lancaster, in one of them plastic bubbles. She was a big mother—four engines, guns everywhere, full of bombs. Up and down we went, to Germany and back, me with my Maxim. I was lucky, too—I got one of them Messerschmitts coming right at me. Press the button, there she went in smithereens. That's what I always wanted—know what I mean?"

I didn't, but Willems explained, rubbing his pointed chin, dribbling a little spittle every now and then. As a kid he used to have toy guns, and he pointed them at pedestrians and cars—"*Pow-pow*, you're dead." People laughed then, but they stopped laughing when Willems wasn't a kid anymore and was still shouting "*pow-pow.*"

"Why did you want them dead, Mr. Willems?"

He gave me a surprised look. "*Because.* Logic argumentation. The only way."

I pretended I agreed, but he didn't seem to believe me.

"No! You don't use logic—nobody does! Listen, Mister Visitor, this world is no good. I knew that from the start. My father used to clean windows and he was drunk most of the time. One day he missed the ladder and *whap*, there he was, out of it. Very clever of him. This life isn't even for the birds. It's a mistake, nothing else.

"Look at us—you ever see anyone smile? Or even take quiet pleasure in what he does? Life's nothing but trouble, hard labor, and misery—nothing works out. Meanwhile, it rains. With death at the end. Notice I don't even mention war. There's that, too, and disease." He shook his head. "Never get into it."

"But you did get into it, Mr. Willems," I said.

His bird's claw grasped my knee. "Could I help it? Did I have a choice? No questions asked, there I was." His small eyes glinted.

"Do you really mind that much, Mr. Willems?"

He laughed. "Maybe not so much, but that's because I found a way out. Here in Holland everybody always builds, always makes things bigger. Better. Healthier even." He raised a finger. "But that's where we are wrong. We've got to think the other way around. We don't have to build, we have to *break*. I thought the Jerries understood—they destroyed a lot when they came. Rotterdam, for instance. I happened to be there when they dropped their bombs. Did that city burn! For days I ran about, fire anywhere I went—bricks flying, beams bursting." And his finger touched my thigh. "I thought it was destroyed. But I was wrong."

"Rotterdam didn't burn?"

"Yes, but not enough. And the Germans wanted to build,

too. Destroy, yes, but then build forever—a new world, sky-high, fools that they were." He was whispering now, but a new thought cheered him up. "The British were better. You should have seen what that Lancaster did, and the other planes. All of Germany was burning down.

"Night after night I watched from my bubble on that airplane's belly. Everything below was red with flames, even the smoke. And the Maxim in front of me was always ready to fire, like when the Messerschmitt popped up. Yes, and pop she did, into a thousand bursts and bangs."

Willems was lost in his thoughts.

"And they let you take the Maxim home?"

He laughed and slapped my knee. "Now what did you think? Because I'm crazy I only talk craziness? Never. When the Führer gave in, they sent me back to Holland. I was security sergeant at an airport. When the Maxim arrived in a box, all I did was fill in a form. 'There you are, sergeant,' the soldiers said. 'Thank you, boys,' I answered."

"As easy as that?"

He shrugged. "Just after the war? With everything upside down?"

"Where did you take the gun?"

He looked sly. "Stored it safely and then had it taken to my room when they demobilized me. Then I reassembled it carefully, loaded it, and pointed it at the crowd on Leyden Square."

The thought staggered me. "For thirty-five years?"

"Most of the time."

"Loaded and ready?"

"Only during the evenings. Otherwise I locked it away."

"But you were in an institution," I said.

"Only for six months. I kept my room, and the Maxim was in the box."

"But you never fired it."

He scratched behind his ear. His spectacles came undone. "No."

"Good."

"*Bad*," Mr. Willems said loudly. "*Bad.* And weak. To think of the right solution is one thing, to go ahead is another. I've been childish, I know. I should have fired my darling, just once, on a summer night. A long burst, and then another. To prove a point." He produced his handkerchief and dabbed at his eyes. "I only fantasized instead, night after night. And now I'm here. A wasted end of a wasted life."

He was crying and rubbing at the tears impatiently. "The detectives have my Maxim. They came one evening. I still remember the older one's name. Grijpstra, he's called. They took the gun and wished me good night, and the next morning the ambulance came and took me here. It was my own fault. I'd still be home if I hadn't placed the mannequin on the roof."

The nurse was back and stared at me. "Yes," I said, and shook Mr. Willems's hand.

It was my day off, but I drove back to Amsterdam. I'm still with the police, although they won't put me on active duty since I lost the use of one leg. I went to Headquarters and found Adjutant Grijpstra in the canteen, together with his sergeant. The sergeant's name is de Gier, but he's often called "the movie star" because of his good looks. Grijpstra is my age—fifty-two. I know him well; we went to police school together. I went and sat next to him and interrupted his argument with de Gier. They were each claiming that it was the other's turn to pay.

When I paid, they calmed down somewhat.

"A Mr. Willems," I said. "The name is familiar?"

They thought for a while.

"Tell me more," de Gier said.

"A machine gun, and a mannequin."

Grijpstra eyed me morosely. "What's he to you? Not a relative, I hope?"

I described my meeting with Willems.

"Oh—right," Grijpstra acknowledged. "Thanks to de Gier's

intelligence, we nabbed him. When the chief constable heard about it, he came all the way down from the top floor to shake the sergeant's hand."

"So what's the story?"

Grijpstra pointed at de Gier.

"No," de Gier said. "Not me. I should never have interfered with that business. I've told you before, Adjutant, we should have let the suspect be."

Grijpstra is a kindly fellow. He married badly and lives an unhappy life, but if you don't raise your voice and keep pushing, he'll open up.

"Yes," he said now. "You know Café Tivoli? Big building on Leyden Square? Flat roof? Went broke a while back and has been empty ever since? Okay. There was a mannequin on the roof a few months back, the kind they use in store windows. But it had been dressed up to resemble a little old guy. He had a bald head, with a bit of fringe left on, and a small nose with spectacles stuck to it. A suit, shoes—very realistic. And beside the mannequin was a machine gun, pointed at the square.

"It was imitation, naturally. The weapon was a stovepipe with a funnel attached to one end of it, the ammo consisting of pinecones sewn into a strip of canvas. The sight was made out of twisted wire. It looked real enough, especially from the square, and frightened civilians so much the desk sergeant thought he should send somebody to check it out."

"We happened to be around," de Gier said.

"So we went up," Grijpstra explained. "I tore my trousers and got myself dirty and the sergeant almost slipped off the roof—there's a lot of bird dung up there and it was raining, of course—but we did make it in the end. De Gier insisted on a thorough investigation—he even went back to get a camera."

De Gier nodded. "Of course."

"Of course," Grijpstra repeated. "The sergeant is an artist, you see, and a psychologist as well, and interested in furthering his career. We removed the mannequin. It fell apart on the way down, but we still had the photographs, so the sergeant put them up in our room at Headquarters and spent a day or two studying them."

I looked at de Gier. He looked away.

"And finally," Grijpstra said, "our supersleuth came up with this. 'Whoever created this apparition,' he said, 'is crazy, and evil, too. We will make an arrest.' "

"Which was wrong," the sergeant said.

"Which was right," said Grijpstra.

"Yes," I said. "And then?"

Adjutant Grijpstra rubbed the tabletop with his hand. "We found him. It wasn't hard. We knew what he looked like and that he had to be around the square. We ran into him the next evening when I took the sergeant to the sandwich shop to spend some money on him."

"Ha," de Gier said. "The smoked eel was on me. But the adjutant is right. We walked into him easily enough and followed him to his room. The machine gun was there, oiled and greased and fully loaded."

"So you had him removed to the nuthouse," I said.

"Where else?" Grijpstra asked. "How is he now?"

"Fine," I said. "Having his meals on time and being looked after by an Indonesian beauty. Very good of you, Adjutant. A true danger to society if I ever came across one. Not a nasty sort of chap, really, but had he ever pressed that trigger, there would have been a lot of blood on the cobblestones."

"It is the task of the police to protect the civilians against themselves," Grijpstra said.

De Gier got up. "We should have left the suspect be. What he explained that evening is absolutely dead right. An original thinker reasoning from a correct point of view. If we learn to destroy the environment and keep at it until there's nothing left, we have done with all misery once and forever. Life is suffering, so it follows that no life equals no suffering. Getting rid of the whole thing is the only way out."

De Gier walked to the canteen's counter and engaged the girl behind it in flirtation. She is a lovely creature, of the same order as Willems' nurse.

"One wonders," I said to Grijpstra, "if your sergeant should really be allowed to be a policeman."

Grijpstra got to his feet. "I have to go on patrol. The Lord only knows what the civilians are up to now."

I repeated my query.

"De Gier is an excellent policeman," Grijpstra said softly. "Bright and diligent. He has been studying Buddhism lately and contemplating the meaning of suffering. But I don't think he has obtained the right insight yet. Nice to see you again." He started to leave. "Do you think Willems is happy in that home?"

I thought about it. I said he probably was.

ᏁOUSEFUL OF ᏁUSSELS

"One dead professor," the girl operator at Amsterdam Municipal Police Headquarters said into the telephone. "Nice job for you, Adjutant. Close by, too. Five-minute walk."

Grijpstra was still trying to claw through the fog of deep sleep. "Whuh?"

"Where? Okay. He lives—eh, lived, isn't this sad? Poor chap—at 143 Leyden Quay. Isn't that close?"

"Yuh."

"Are you asleep, Adjutant? It isn't eleven yet."

"Up and about all day," Grijpstra said. "Off duty now. Tired. Phone Sergeant de Gier. *He's* on duty."

"He's there now, Adjutant. The commissaris says you'll have to go, too, because of the corpse being a professor. Makes it more involved, don't you agree?"

"Nuh." Grijpstra replaced the phone. He looked, unhappily, first at his three-piece dark blue suit, then at his pistol belt, before putting it all on. He pushed an almost toothless comb through short white bristly hairs that kept standing up as he stared at them in the mirror. "What's up?" he asked his heavy image. "Suicide? That'd be better."

He repeated the thought as he strolled under elm trees that answered by rustling their leaves in the soft warm breeze. Ducks, hoping to be fed and talked to, followed alongside, paddling furiously in the canal. Professors overthink, Grijpstra thought. They know the world is about to fade or fold. They're too intelligent; they can figure out the future. They anticipate this environment's total destruction. Can't carry their insight— I'll confirm that in my report, which de Gier can then type out and sign on my behalf. Meanwhile, I will be in bed again, enjoying an oblivion due to me because of higher status and rank.

He stumbled and almost fell, tripping over a mostly-dachshund, squatting unobtrusively in weeds. "Oops." The dog yapped kindly. They walked on together to the dead man's house, labeled as such from afar by the sweeping blue lights of two patrol cars. A crowd had gathered, lusting for blood. "Away," Grijpstra said, pushing through slowly. Constables guarding a mighty oak door saluted smartly.

"Suicide?" Grijpstra asked cheerfully.

"Murder."

"How so?" Grijpstra frowned.

"We found no weapon. Subject was shot in the forehead. Neighbor lady heard the shot and telephoned at once. Ten-thirty P.M. this happened. We arrived at ten-thirty-five."

"You were expecting the mishap?" Grijpstra kept frowning.

"Patrol cars are supposed to be slow. Did anyone see anyone leave?"

"No."

"How did you get in?"

"Neighbor lady had a duplicate key, Adjutant."

"No crying wife or live-in love?"

"Just a million mussels, Adjutant," the constable said. "In aquariums. All over. Even in the bathrooms. And this ghastly green light, and little bubbly tubes, and pumps that thump and suck, and the mussels opening and closing, yawning and gaping. Scary. *Yagh.*"

"Mussels," Grijpstra said. "Right. Just what I expected. My sergeant is in here?"

"Yes, Adjutant."

"And the technical gents?"

"On the way, I'm sure."

Grijpstra read a name, hand-lettered nicely on the door's gleaming green surface: HANS STROOM.

"A mussel professor," the policeman who talked said. The policeman who didn't nodded.

"Mussels have been getting pricey lately," Grijpstra said.

"Logically," the policeman who didn't talk said. "Once the high gents get into something, the price goes up, right? Musselologists must be earning a fortune."

The door wasn't closed. De Gier was waiting in the hall. Sergeant Rinus de Gier is a tall man, wide-shouldered, narrow-hipped. He wears tailor-made jeans and jackets that he cheers up with multicolored silk scarves. His curly hair shines softly and his huge handlebar mustache is carefully brushed. High cheekbones push his kind brown eyes upward. His age is unclear, although he knows it to be close to forty. Grijpstra is close to fifty, also from the final side. De Gier doesn't have a female friend right now; Grijpstra is separated. De Gier is reputedly still searching for happiness. Grijpstra reputedly no longer cares.

"So?" Grijpstra asked.

"So," de Gier said, "our man is dead. The doctor will confirm his total absence." He pointed.

Grijpstra walked through the indicated door and bowed down. "Oh, dear." He put his hands in his pockets. "Nicely laid out. On his back. Mouth closed. Eyes open." He raised his voice to make himself heard, for the water pumps bubbled loudly. He also raised his hands, as if to protect himself from the green light illuminating the aquariums' wavy water.

"Makes the little fellows grow," de Gier said. "Stimulates plant life—maybe the mussels eat the algae? Our professor is an oceanographer. This is a mussel farm, government funded. He lived here, sharing his life with the black and blue chappies."

"TV?" Grijpstra asked, indicating a screen.

"A computer monitor. Must have been working with it. Those figures seem to be some mussel-food formula."

Grijpstra sat down on a yellow plastic case. "Tell me more."

"The neighbor lady was here when I arrived. She phoned the police when she heard the shot, then came to visit. An older lady—the professor's present state upset her, so she went home to take half an overdose of valium."

"A suspect?"

"Unlikely."

"But she had a key."

"So that she can take care of the place when the professor has to leave. She feeds the mussels, checks temperatures, oxygen, whatever. She gets paid for her troubles."

"Nice-looking laddie," Grijpstra said, bending down toward the corpse. "Good beard. Great tan. Athletic."

"Scuba diver," de Gier said, opening up a cupboard. "See the equipment? I checked his passport—it's on the desk over there. Reached the age of thirty-nine. Unmarried. Lives alone, according to the neighbor, but he does have girlfriends, two, both his assistants, one junior colleague and a much-better-looking student.

"Who exactly?"

De Gier checked his notes. "Bakini Khan, late twenties, and Truus Vermuul, a lady of uncertain age. Got addresses." He tapped the notebook. "Got phone numbers, too. Both of them live in the area."

"Listen here," Grijpstra said. "This will be simple." He scratched his chin. "Just before the shot there was an argument. Someone heard that."

"Nobody heard an argument," de Gier said. "Neighbors on the other side are on holiday, and my witness is somewhat deaf. She did hear the shot. She also heard the front door slam. I agree with you, though. This student Bakini would be exotically attractive." He pointed at the corpse. "This professor used his chance. They lusted together. Bakini wants to transform the emotion into love. The professor seems to love mussels better. Bakini now hates the forever-opening-and-closing little beasts. She makes her friend a proposition he couldn't possibly refuse, yet he did. So he died."

Grijpstra squatted. "Classical, don't you think? A true murderous wound, Sergeant—haven't seen one in a long while. It's all automatic these days. Remember the Chinese last week, with the sixteen wounds? Half an Uzi's clip, fired at random. This is professional. I like this better."

De Gier squatted, too. "Bull's-eye, all right. First prize. I say, do you think he looks like a professor?"

"More like a pirate," Grijpstra agreed. "Including the golden earring. Dashing, very. Women like pimps and pirates better. They help themselves and run off smiling. Women like that, you know, but they get them later."

"Love-related," de Gier said. "So you think so, too. This corpse abused a vengeful woman."

"Are the sleuths done sleuthing?" a gentleman asked, leaning through the open door. "Can my colleagues and I now apply science?"

"We left some fingerprints," de Gier said, "but we haven't found the cartridge yet."

The gentleman found the cartridge. "Thirty-eight caliber."

"A ladylike weapon." De Gier rubbed his hands. "Hides in a handbag. Coming, Adjutant? We can phone from the pub."

"Just a minute," Grijpstra said. "You, sir. That's a Polaroid, right? One gruesome photograph, please, of this gruesome corpse. Don't be easy on the blood."

A flashbulb popped. The snapshot became more detailed as they watched. "Nice," Grijpstra said. "Blood coming out of nostrils and mouth. Just what I wanted."

Grijpstra used the café's telephone while de Gier sipped coffee and drew diagonal lines on a napkin. Line 1: a dead professor. Line 2: a million mussels. Line 3: two unknown female suspects. The gun didn't deserve a line of its own—it was merely the extension of a killing arm. What else?

"Miss Khan," Grijpstra asked the mouthpiece in his hand. "I'm sorry I'm bothering you this late. This is the police, Adjutant Grijpstra, Murder Brigade. Something quite unpleasant happened and my sergeant and I would like to call on you, yes? . . . Right now? That's nice."

"That's nice," Grijpstra said half a minute later. "No coffee for me? Then I'll have yours. Thank you—very nice coffee. The nice lady's nice street address is just around the nice corner. We can walk. Nice weather outside. Ha-ha."

"Like your job, do you?" de Gier asked grimly.

"No," Grijpstra said.

"I was thinking again," de Gier said. "Did you notice the hard yellow plastic boxes at the professor's?"

"I sat on one, didn't I?" Grijpstra asked. "So what? So nothing."

"Those boxes didn't look right," de Gier said. "I thought. A hard commercial color in between all those soft greens and blues."

Grijpstra pushed the empty coffee cup away. "You see colors? *I* am the artist."

"You are?" de Gier asked. "Maybe you should paint those mussels. The pure white sands, those swaying dark shapes. And then there were those ugly yellow boxes, with Chinese characters stamped on their sides. And the neighbor lady says the professor had just returned from Taiwan."

"The boxes are connected?"

"The boxes are contrasted," de Gier explained. "Crime associates with contrasts. Remember the junkie driving the Rolls-Royce? Remember the classy lady running barefoot around the queen's palace? Our best cases of that year."

"Boxes?" Grijpstra asked.

"Never mind." De Gier paid for the coffee.

Grijpstra mumbled as they walked. "Hi," de Gier said to the mostly-dachshund. The doggie wagged. "Friend of ours?" De Gier asked.

Grijpstra nodded. "You know what we are? I wonder about that at times, now that I'm older and more aware. We're ghouls. And we like that. Just now, when I spoke to the nice lady on the phone? I was *scaring* the nice lady."

"I heard you," de Gier said, stooping down to pet the dog. "The *Murder Brigade*; something *very unpleasant* that happened."

"We're werewolves," Grijpstra said sadly, "creeping around being weird, to freak out the nice ladies."

"So she is innocent?" de Gier asked.

"Of course," Grijpstra said. "Why would a lovely young lady shoot her very own lover/teacher? Because of his horrible spell that he cast on her? She wasn't getting straight A's anymore because she refused to humble her tender spirit, because she wouldn't give in to his lustful whipping and sexy kicking?"

"Right," de Gier said. "My idea entirely. Perhaps she did do away with him, but she can be excused. Didn't like the chap myself. Sinister, rather. If anyone is to blame, it's *us*. Corruption and liberal laws have weakened the police so that the citizens increasingly rely on their own defenses. She knew that her situation could only worsen if she called us. So she shot him herself."

Grijpstra tripped. "Damn dog." He wagged his finger. "What's with you? Your bladder too small? Stop squatting in front of my foot. Get lost." The mostly-dachshund limped. Grijpstra picked it up, felt the sore paw, scratched the dog's neck, and put it down again.

"Putter onner," de Gier said gruffly. The little dog grinned.

"Ugly yellow boxes," de Gier said. "Subdivided inside, with spirals everywhere. What for?"

Grijpstra rang a bell. The door clicked open. Dainty naked brown feet appeared on a steep staircase, lengthening into slim ankles and long legs. A young woman presented herself. She would be in her early twenties. She had doe eyes and long black hair, cascading down her slender shoulders. A sarong of batik cloth was draped around her body.

The detectives showed their ID, which she carefully studied.

I do sometimes like my work, de Gier thought as he followed Bakini up the stairs. Crime is usually unattractive. Suspects mess up society and we hold our noses and are forever trying to rearrange, making things worse. We deal with monstrosities spawned by perversity, but there's always the exception. Now look at this. A graceful suspect, descending from an Oriental heaven. Aren't our private surroundings our own projections? Well? What about these tasteful rooms?

"Tea?" Bakini asked sweetly. She poured, from a red copper kettle, into earless little cups. "No sugar or milk, I'm afraid, but they would only spoil the jasmine fragrance. Would you mind taking a cushion and sitting on the floor? I don't have chairs."

Doesn't even want to know what's up, de Gier thought. A truly polite spirit. The quiet acceptance emanating from Far Eastern philosophical solutions. Here we come clodhopping in, intending to misuse her for our egotistic goals. Wouldn't we like to clap her in irons, drag her to our lair? She knows, but she keeps nicely quiet. Good strategy—true kindness is a most fearsome weapon. He sniffed at the incense smoke that reached him from an altar on a low table, next to an aquarium where mussels quietly opened and closed. Bakini had sat down, tucking her legs into each other, hiding them under a fold of her sarong.

"Good tea," Grijpstra said.

"I love your rooms," de Gier said, trying to copy the all-encompassing smile of the little Buddha statue on the table.

Bakini smiled.

"Professor Hans Stroom?" Grijpstra asked.

"Is he dead?"

"He is," de Gier said. "Shot through the head."

Bakini looked at him calmly.

There we go again, de Gier thought. Easterners have a better way of reacting. I cringe when bad news hits me, but she sits up straight. I flap my hands; she folds them. My eyes go wide; she almost closes hers. It all goes with the smell of the incense, the bubbling of the water pump.

Grijpstra made an effort to keep looking stern. Now what? the adjutant thought. We can't lose tension. "Were you born here?" he asked.

"I was born in your former South American colony, Surinam," Bakini said softly. "My forefathers were indentured laborers from Pakistan. I knew the professor well. I worked at his mussel station on the coast and assisted with the experiments here at his home. We traveled together—earlier this year we were in Karachi."

"Not in Taiwan?"

"No, Truus went to Taiwan. We do a lot of traveling in our department."

Grijpstra cleared his throat. "You're very calm. Don't you want to know how your teacher was murdered?"

"Yes." Bakini's voice vibrated slightly. De Gier apologized to himself for the pleasurable shiver down his spine.

Bakini bowed her head. "Death is part of life. Especially scientists should accept that. Life and death flow from each other. It would be unthinkable to hold on to either."

"Why did the professor travel?" de Gier asked, trying to keep his voice flat and cold.

"We visited mussel farms mostly."

"You were here all night?"

"Yes."

"You spoke to him?"

"By telephone." She nodded. "He wanted me to come over, but I said it was no use."

"An affair?" de Gier asked.

"Yes."

"When did it stop?"

"Yesterday," Bakini said quietly. She got up in one supple movement, without touching the floor with her hands. "More tea?" She poured into the little cups, respectfully held up by the detectives. "I broke up with Hans because I thought he had become too greedy. Scientists should serve society. Our world is three-fourths water. The oceans could feed all of human life if they were managed properly, but we selfishly rob and rob, pollute, don't replace what we take out. Less food is available each day. Scientists may reverse the process."

"The professor didn't share your ideals?" de Gier asked.

"No." Bakini replaced the teapot daintily. "'Hans was paid quite well as a university professor, about the maximum income that this rich country can provide, but he still had to be a businessman, too, buying cheap mussel seed from Karachi and selling it here through his own company at a large profit. When he and Truus came back from Taiwan, he brought plastic starting boxes developed by Chinese mussel breeders. He had taken out a sublicense for Western Europe and was about to have them manufactured here."

"For private profit?" de Gier asked. "That tainted the relationship. You wouldn't be his student either?"

"Oh, yes," Bakini said. "I do want my degree. He will continue to teach me."

"He's dead," Grijpstra said.

"I rather doubt," Bakini said, "the linear essence of time. Much that he showed me will continue to work."

De Gier looked up. "I keep forgetting to ask you. Are you a good shot?"

She smiled. "Yes, I think so."

"With a pistol?"

"A spear gun." Her hand swept up and indicated an array of long metal arrows decoratively arranged on the wall. The gun itself was on the floor, looking deadly and in good order.

"What time did Hans phone you?" Grijpstra asked.

"Ten o'clock." She arranged a strand of hair on her temple. "I remember because I was going to watch a nature program on TV. I didn't after all. I sat here instead."

"You had a feeling?" de Gier asked.

"I almost knew something was very wrong," Bakini said, "but I had no idea what."

Grijpstra dramatically produced the Polaroid picture. She took it from him and reverently pressed it to her forehead, saying something in a sing-song voice.

"Beg pardon?" de Gier asked.

"I wished him a good journey."

De Gier released a cramping leg. "You know," he said slowly. "In some countries crimes against the people are punishable by death. What sort of fish do you shoot when you're out hunting?"

"Sharks," Bakini said. "I shouldn't, perhaps, but I like the challenge."

"Wasn't Hans a shark?"

"The tribal laws of the Netherlands," Bakini said, "disapprove of doing away with our own species. My own law is to wait, once I've legally done all I can."

"She didn't have to wait long," Grijpstra said when they were back in the street. "Nice lady, but I'm glad I'm no shark."

"Hmm?"

"Hello?" Grijpstra asked, thumping de Gier's arm. "Hello? Tackle the other one now? Call first? The cafés around here should be closed by now."

De Gier checked his notepad. "Let's ambush the lady."

Dr. Truus Vermuul's apartment was the top floor of a restored little gabled house in a fashionable mews.

"Both suspects live within a ten-minute walk from the dead man's house," Grijpstra remarked. "A coincidence, perhaps?"

"For sure." De Gier rang the bell. "Has she done it?"

"You were right about the boxes," Grijpstra said. "Has she?"

De Gier shrugged. "Don't know. I hope so. I'm not going

to arrest Bakini. What's the penalty again for assisting a criminal to escape?"

"Go away," the woman yelled at the top of the stairs. "I don't want to believe in Krishna. Piss off or I'll pour this boiling oil on your heads."

"Police, ma'am," Grijpstra shouted, waving his card.

"The other chap, too? He looks like a Krishna."

"Are you?" Grijpstra asked de Gier. "You save the lovely lady?"

"I wouldn't save you," de Gier yelled, "if you begged me on your knees."

Grijpstra was halfway up the stairs. De Gier bounded past him, heading for the pot she was holding. "It's all right," Truus said grumpily, "I'm boiling up a mess of mussels, a new recipe. What's wrong?"

"Professor Hans Stroom got himself shot dead tonight," Grijpstra panted. "We're making enquiries. Can I sit down?"

"Have a warrant?" Truss asked. She was a big woman in her forties, amply proportioned. Her large, bulging blue eyes weren't focusing too well.

"I can get a warrant," de Gier said. "Back in a jiffy."

She waved him to a straight-backed chair at the bare table under a high white ceiling. The fairly large room was lit by fluorescent tubes.

"Shot?" Truus asked. "You're kidding. I saw Hans today at the university. Who would shoot that fool?"

De Gier asked if he could use the phone. "You guys know anything more about the cartridge?"

"Can't be sure," the ballistics voice said. "Probably a Walther PPK. We have the slug, too—dug it out of the skull. All the nasty little gunmen have PPKs now. The weapon is in vogue. You can buy Walthers through the coffee shops where pot is supplied. Someone must have brought in a truckload of the suckers."

"A Walther PPK," de Gier said to Grijpstra. "Fits in a lady's handbag."

Truus had sat down, too. "Are you planning to blame this

on *me*?" she asked. "Are you mad? We're friends. We've just been to Taiwan together."

"You don't look sad," Grijpstra said.

"Should I?" She hit the table with the flat of her hand. "We'll have a new professor-man tomorrow. There are plenty of professor-men around. Shooting them doesn't help."

"Friends?" de Gier said. "You were friends, you said."

She pulled up a shoulder. "Friends . . . okay . . . but I wouldn't shoot him. I wouldn't be able to get his job anyway. The university uses women for menial work only."

It became quiet in the cool room. Truus fetched plates and forks from a cupboard. "Some mussels, boys? May as well make yourselves useful. I'm into new recipes, to advertise our clammy friends. I have white Beaujolais, too—not too clever a wine, but it's got a good wallop afterward."

"Just mussels," Grijpstra said.

She filled her own glass. De Gier waved his refusal of the wine. He dug into the mussels. "Terrific."

Truus tasted the Beaujolais. "So is this. You sure now? You don't know what you're missing."

"You live here alone?" Grijpstra asked.

"Hurrah." She held up her glass. "To old Hans. Sure I live alone. Don't need you get-in-the-ways here. Polluters of the good planet. Multipliers of the bad seeds. Away with all men. We'll be cloning ourselves soon. Won't that be fun?"

"Can I hide somewhere and watch?" de Gier asked.

She reached for the bottle. "No pornography, please. Cloning is clean fun. Every time the body gets old, the clone will replace it. Throw the old body out."

"Where was your body at ten-thirty tonight?" Grijpstra asked.

"Right here." She peered owlishly at her glass while the fluid's level came up. "Cooking the old mussels." The bottle ran out. " 'Xcuse me." She fetched another. The corkscrew didn't work too well. She impatiently slammed the cork into the bottle.

"You eat all your mussels yourself?" de Gier asked.

"I sell them to a deli further down the alley," Truus said.

"Making a bit on the side. Learned that from Hans, I did. But he did it bigger. Yah-hoo, boys." She drank.

Grijpstra pushed the Polaroid photo of the corpse across the table. She looked at it. "Well, well." She pointed at stacked yellow mussel boxes in a corner of the room. "What's to become of those now, eh? His nice new line of merchandise?"

"Now, my dear," Grijpstra said, "who might have wanted to shoot your superior? Why don't you tell us?"

"Might?" Truus asked. "And have? And wanted? And shoot? Lot of verbs you have there. The Chinese maybe?"

"Please," Grijpstra said. "Do we have to go that far? And there are so many of them. Why the Chinese, dear?"

"Don't *dear* me," Truus bellowed, hitting the table with both fists, making the dishes and her glass hop around. "Those mussel boxes are good business. They'll sell themselves. By the hundred thousand. The Chinese were crazy to sign their rights away for all of Western Europe. They must have realized it by now, so they came over, and *plop*?" She winked. "Eh?"

"That's heroin," de Gier said. "Not mussel boxes. You got yourself mixed up."

"Yes?" The wink became heavier. "More mussels, my boy? Mind if I drink by myself? There we go." She stared ahead glassily, drops gleaming on her chin.

Grijpstra leaned over to de Gier. "I think our hostess is nervous," he said loudly. "Why? No alibi perhaps?"

"Don't need an alibi," Truus burst out happily. "It's nice to have one, but there's no need, really. Not if I didn't do it. I live here. This is where I can be as much as I like."

De Gier nodded solemnly. "You could be right, Adjutant. She knew the professor intimately, traveled with him all of the time, hotel rooms, you know what it's like."

"You do?" Truus asked. She put out her tongue. "Yuck." She tried to stare de Gier down, but her eyes kept slipping away. "I always had my own room and Hans was always knocking on my door and I never opened. Ha."

Grijpstra pursed his lips. "Yeh."

"Yeh what?" Truus shouted. "More mussels?"

"Jealousy?" Grijpstra said. "The great motivation of most human mistakes. Keep running into jealousy, eh, Sergeant?" He held up the photograph. "Hans doesn't look too good here, but we can still see that he was handsome. And intelligent— must have been intelligent, a professor. . . . And this older woman wanting him, and that young thing in the way, that exotic young thing. What a beauty—Bakini, right?"

"What?" Truus shouted. "Me? In love? With a *man?*"

"A woman scorned," de Gier said sadly.

"More mussels?" Truus yelled.

"No thank you, ma'am," Grijpstra said. "Really. They're delicious, but I'm quite full. What about you, Sergeant?"

"Not right now," de Gier said.

"Jealousy," Truus said. "What nonsense. Moral outrage, you mean. It's hard to tolerate a swindler like Hans, but we're still underneath—it doesn't do us any good to rebel." She brightened up. "Come on. A little glass? Such a nice evening. So good of you to come. Shall we . . ."

She thought.

"Tell you what," Grijpstra told de Gier. "This probably isn't even murder. She went to see her beloved. She was, once again, refused. She doesn't know the terrific strength of her own sexual longing. She had a gun. It went off."

"Yes?" de Gier asked. "Got him right between the eyes? Wow. Some urge."

" . . . celebrate," Truus said. "Couldn't think of the word. Want to celebrate, boys? Okay, now you have some motivation. I've been reading this book on detection. What comes next again? The weapon?"

"Fingerprints," Grijpstra said. "You must have left some."

Truus laughed. "Of course. I often work there."

"Maybe we should go home," de Gier said. "Got to play this fair. A drunk suspect?"

"I'm fine," Truus said. "Don't pity me." She grinned. "You really think I'd get drunk if I was guilty?"

"Good." De Gier folded his hands. "The weapon comes next. You're right. Where is it? Where is the horrible tool used in *la crime passionnelle?*"

"*Crime* is masculine," Truus said. "*Le crime.*"

"The gun?" Grijpstra said. "It's here. She could have thrown it away, but there's only one short stretch of canal between the professor's house and here. Our divers could find it. No, it's here, don't you think?"

"A Walther PPK is expensive," de Gier said. "She would also want it for self-defense. Better watch her, Adjutant. Drunk. Violent. A loaded semiautomatic high-quality murder machine can pop up any moment."

Grijpstra looked around. "Oh, dear."

"Mussels?" Truus asked, looking into the pot. "There's plenty left. Don't you like my herbs? Don't they bring out the flavor?"

"Remember how you lost the tip of your toe?" de Gier asked. "Let's see now. Suspect hides his gun in your coat. We look everywhere. We don't look in your coat. Then suspect helps you into your coat and takes the gun out. I saw that. I hit his wrist. The gun dropped on the floor and went off."

"I'm not wearing an overcoat today," Grijpstra said. "Neither are you."

"I don't understand you two," Truus said. "You know what the street stalls are asking for fried mussels these days? Four-fifty a scoop. Mine are free." She leaned her head on her hand. Her elbow slipped. Her head dropped, then jerked up again.

"Watch it," de Gier said. "I'm sorry. You kept telling us and I wouldn't hear you." He took the spoon from her hand and dug about in the pot. There was a clank of metal.

"Go easy," Grijpstra said. "Don't want the shells to explode in that hot brew. Easy now."

De Gier turned the pot over. Grijpstra wiped the pistol clean with a dish cloth. He shook his head. "Really, a scientist who doesn't respect a tool. Look at this. Fully loaded, cartridge in the chamber, safety off. There. That's better." He had removed the clip and made the chambered cartridge jump free. "She must have dropped it in when she heard me ring the bell."

"I won't come with you," Truus said. "You'll have to drag me."

De Gier telephoned.

Two policewomen climbed the stairs. "Where's the patient?"

"Inside," de Gier said.

"Couldn't bring her in yourself?" the older constable asked. "Shame on you."

"Didn't dare," de Gier said.

"Charge?"

"Manslaughter. She shot her boyfriend. Murder maybe."

"She's drunk," Grijpstra said as the constables marched in. Truus looked at them sleepily, then pushed over the table. She ran into the kitchen and came back with a long knife. The constables pulled their guns.

"No, no," de Gier said. "Truus?"

She swung the knife at him in a wide arc, and he blocked it, turned to the side, wrapped his arm around suspect's arm, clamped his hand on her wrist. A sharp twist and she yelled. The knife clattered on the floor. De Gier stepped behind suspect and handcuffed her smartly. "There you go."

The mostly-dachshund had been waiting outside. Grijpstra stumbled. De Gier caught him. "Dumb doggie," Grijpstra said, "are you teaching me awareness?"

De Gier picked up the little dog, turned it around, checked, put it down on its legs. "The female mind," de Gier said, "is both devious and relentless. She's offering herself and I would advise you to accept."

"Yes?" Grijpstra asked the mostly-dachshund. The dog held her head to the side, waved her long tail once, barked inside her long snout.

"Poor Truus," de Gier said.

"Poor Bakini," Grijpstra said.

"Why Bakini?"

"Won't you be after her?" Grijpstra asked. "Comforting?"

"She might comfort *me*," de Gier said. "She has access to heaven."

"She might," Grijpstra said. He began to sigh and grumble.

"Don't be jealous," de Gier said. "See who'll be comforting you." He pointed down. The mostly-dachshund was sitting up, offering both paws. Grijpstra squatted and shook them. The dog wore no tag and looked like she had been living an irregular and needy existence.

"A stray?" Grijpstra asked.

"Yours for the taking," de Gier said. "Sleep well, you two." He turned and strode off.

The dog woofed invitingly and made a believable attempt to frolic.

"You sure?" Grijpstra asked. "I'm not an easy man."

The little dog's ears waved, her tail wagged.

"You're not into mussels? You won't get fat? You won't watch TV?"

They both waited.

"Be my guest," Grijpstra asked. They walked off.

LETTER PRESENT

I just had a look at the visiting card again, after I found it in my file. It was neatly glued to a sheet of clean paper and put away under the letter *G*. Evidently, I knew I would need it sometime. The tiny document is filed under *G* because the person it refers to is called Grijpstra, Hank Grijpstra, adjutant of the Municipal Police, Murder Brigade.

The adjutant, a paternal type with short gray hair that sticks up like the bristles of a well-worn brush, came to see me to inquire, as he put it, "about your father's untimely demise." That's the way the old bird of prey likes to express himself.

I would choose my words differently, but then I'm a bit of a scholar in my time off and a publisher of literature by trade.

"Sorry to disturb," Adjutant Grijpstra said kindly after he lowered his bulk into our easy chair reserved for visitors. For a moment I felt relieved, as a respected citizen in our free country. That the police were visiting me, the adjutant explained, was due to a regrettable fact, the possibly unnatural death of Dad. The authorities protect the citizen in a true democracy. The adjutant pointed out that I, as the bereaved party (isn't it terrible when a son loses his beloved father?) could be sure of receiving help. Isn't the state a father, too? I could rest assured. I felt immediately threatened again, however, not so much by the polite and well-mannered adjutant but by his companion, a quiet detective sergeant, who had also given me his card. The sergeant's card found a place in the wastepaper basket after they left. One hint of conscience was sufficient in my case. The sergeant's name was Rinus de Gier.

Gier means "vulture" and both officers reminded me of deadly powerful birds. There I was, stretched out on the glowing white sand of a helpless desert; there they perched, flapping their transparent batlike wings on the branch of a dead tree; just another few seconds *and the vorpal blades go snicker-snack.* I read too much and always remember the wrong passages, which frighten me, and which grow in horror in my sick but fertile imagination. The sergeant himself didn't really resemble a bird at all; he is a much too handsome hero in his early forties, with the mustache of a romantic cavalry officer of days gone by and the profile one finds in the expensive advertisements of fashion magazines. A movie projection, an exaggerated female dream; did I have to become all nervous because of his glossy image? Couldn't I just shrug my shoulders while I observed the sergeant's with-it casual gear, the well-fitting suit cut out of denim, the gay (I didn't think *he* was) baby-blue silk scarf knotted loosely under his strong but not uncharming chin? Couldn't I define his presence as merely irritating and meanwhile keep listening to what the adjutant was saying? The adjutant spoke with just a touch of the musical

Amsterdam accent and looked at me sympathetically from pale blue deep-set eyes. He had a second chin and voluminous cheeks. Adjutant Grijpstra was regretting my father's sudden heart attack and mentioned that he thought it "embarrassing" that untimely Death had grabbed Dad from the arms of a woman he wasn't married to. He thought I might know my father's girlfriend—the lady who left Dad in the grip of Fate, who ran away without even calling a doctor?

I tried to control my trembling lower lip. Surely, I might be a little nervy. Wasn't I Dad's only child, and couldn't I be expected to feel lost and alone? But if I lost my cool altogether, these sleuths, whose eyes were now drilling into my face, might be led to believe in all sorts of dangerous conclusions. The interview, as the adjutant had said, was a formality, no more. They expected me to provide them with short and exact answers; if I could satisfy their curiosity briefly, this painful interlude would come to an end.

"Yes," I croaked. "She's an acquaintance. Her name is Monica and she's really my friend Hubert's, well, eh, sort of mistress. I've known for a while that she rather liked Dad. He liked her, too. Dad was discreet, of course, but my mother died many years ago" (I didn't tell them how Mom met her end, for information should never be too complete) "and Monica is rather attractive and does prefer older men" (I tried to smile in a know-it-all way, for this is Amsterdam and we're all supposed to know what's what in our wicked city).

The adjutant was decent enough to accept my words in silence, but the sergeant opened up. He saw a contrast between reality and my glib talk. Monica and Dad? An intimate relationship? And Monica was my friend Hubert's girl?

"Quite," I said firmly. Maybe it was my turn to throw out a question. "Isn't reality rather complicated at times? Look here, Monica is extraordinarily attractive. Hubert likes beauty—to admire, so to speak. He collects works of art and some of them are allowed to be alive. But she should never touch him, if you know what I mean. He allows Monica to be his companion; if there's anything more intimate she can offer, he doesn't want to know." That Hubert is fond of boys I didn't mention. Like Dad, I can be discreet. That conclusion could be theirs.

The detectives kept looking at me while they digested my information. What were they seeing? That I'm most intelligent? My IQ is high and I'm a sensitive person. If there are other assets to my character, I haven't noticed. I'm short, bald (only thirty-two years old), somewhat bent over, shy to a fault, and seem rather slavish, but I only project that modesty. Under my servility hides a dictator and I can, in a roundabout way, be ferociously aggressive. Know thyself, Socrates said. He also said that self-knowledge is almost impossible to achieve; but others, unfortunately, can see my self most easily.

I attempted to fathom what the gentlefolks of the Murder Brigade were thinking, while they tipped their small cigars and stirred their coffee. They theorized that Hubert, if Monica loved my father with Hubert's permission, was giving instead of taking, even if Dad's passion did finally kill him. In my case there could be motivation. Wasn't I Dad's sole heir? All his possessions passed to me, to wit one profitable publishing company, one regal mansion just outside of the city, and one sixteenth-century restored gable house on the Emperor's Canal, complete with a luxurious apartment on the upper story, where Dad took his naps and occasionally spent the nights. There was also cash, bonds, and shares. Hubert wasn't getting any of the loot. Now why should Hubert, this collector of beautiful objects, so far unknown to the detectives, instruct Monica in such a manner that she, by showing off her luscious lines of living flesh, might increase Dad's blood pressure to the point where a vein would burst and stop his works?

It's pleasurable to try and analyze the others' hidden thoughts, but only if the observer is a disinterested party, for if he's part of what's going on, he may be taken out by the equation, and knowing that, fear makes him sweat.

Were Adjutant Grijpstra and Sergeant de Gier trying to prove any intent on my part? Princes are forever trying to usurp the king. I had read the murdering genre of literature and knew that heirs are the first to be suspected. But really, was I a British prince in a Shakespearean tale or some ungodly shadow figure in an early Greek play? Nothing exotic, if you please—weren't we in the flat Netherlands, where nothing out of the way is ever imagined behind our all-protecting dikes? Were these solid policemen really prepared to soil their placid minds with foreign poetry?

How much attention could they muster for that one single suspect circumstance? Monica wasn't present when the detectives answered the emergency call and entered the apartment furnished with antiques; but she did leave a trail. Her bag was found next to the bed. *She* was found that same night, in the bar at the Brewers' Canal, where she had stupefied herself with alcohol and the forgetful weed. Noteworthy: why hadn't Monica called a doctor? Why did she run when Dad had trouble breathing, held on to his neck, groaned in agony? Yes, she said, she had been unnerved and had escaped to the trusted support of her favorite tavern.

"But, miss! Mr. Habbema was obviously ill. Didn't you think you'd better be of help?"

"I thought he was angry with me."

Right. How clever to pretend to be drunk, stoned, and silly. Could be genuine. Dad wasn't altogether comatose, for he did manage to telephone his friend, the M.D. in his suburb. The doctor did show up, even if he had to leave a jolly party with friends.

Can a heart attack indicate murder? Isn't the connection a little far-fetched? Not to me, for I read literature. Tanizaki, in his subtle novel *The Key*, makes a young wife excite her husband to the point of death. Was it accidental that the sergeant was playing with his key ring while he kept watching me, stealthily, through his long lashes? Hubert would have been excited if he had been the victim of such quiet, veiled interrogation, but I'm sexually normal and felt severely harassed by the implications the sergeant's mime provoked.

So how about this Hubert, the sergeant wanted to know.

The police like straight lines. What do we have here now? Girlfriend of third party, in bed with the victim. How does the accusing pencil connect the given points? How well did I know this Hubert?

I replied in detail, for the line was missing the important point. Certainly, I had known Hubert for many years indeed; we started school together and were joined right through university. Together we started our careers in publishing, but Hubert joined another firm, which didn't compete with Habbema & Son Incorporated.

Hubert's manipulators publish scientific work, and we're more in the popular sector, in herbs and health food and the mystical meadow. While I write this essay, our latest project is on the table, an inane survey of telepathy in animals: *Do You Know that Puss Can Read Your Thoughts?* That's pure nonsense, because cats can't read. They can't even think; at the most, they can feel a little. Whoever owns an animal knows that human moods can be sensed by animals and that they will react to the impulses we emit. This speechless contact is the subject of our book. The author, who, commissioned by my firm, fills two hundred pages on the simple subject, can't do much more than repeat himself in vague terms and quote some examples that are "clarified" by unprovable imagination. That's exactly what he did, and we took care of a striking jacket, illuminating illustrations, and some artful photography. The reader will see what he should have known for some time, confirmed in clear print; and supplier and client can continue in peace. The book is meant to be a suitable Christmas present and can't do much harm, but for me it's depressing. Dad's trusted pussycat is still alive and set on revenge. The pliable, animated plaything of the past is turning into a hellish tiger, and hisses and snarls even when I bring him his food.

Hubert's firm prints science for the universities and we entertain, but the positions that Hubert and I filled, before Dad's death, were about equal. We both served the capitalists above. Routine tasks humiliated our brilliant minds. Two Ph.D.'s sorting spelling mistakes. We demurred volubly during the many drunken hours that we wasted in the bar at the

Brewers' Canal, and Monica pretended to listen to our variations on the theme of self-pity. Her only gift was her beauty, and we allowed her to tack on to us so that we could have something to pride ourselves on. Her seductive presence confirmed our faith in ourselves and the possibility of eventually improving our positions. How? By increasing our status. And what would we eventually do? Publish books ourselves. Which firm would give us our chance? Habbema & Son. What was in the way? Dad's everlasting presence.

Hubert and I generated the same idea simultaneously, after discussing a little Tanizaki. The sexual urge can destroy a man and make him a willing victim along the final way. Would my father be willing? Tanizaki evolved no new thought; the urge has been around since the creation. There is no novelty in the basic themes, but variations and combinations are, fortunately, endless. The genetic codes are given and can, once they're understood, be used. Our joke would be another way of manipulating what circumstances offered so freely. Dad's high blood pressure, Monica's beauty. $1 + 1 = 0$. We ordered fresh drinks and winked at each other, Hubert and I. The zero of Dad's death amused us no end. While we were at it, we worked out the future.

Hubert, who likes to reach out and knows how to ensnare potential clients, would be our commercial director, earning top wages and entitled to spend his savings on part of the stock; I, with the majority of the shares, would fill in the background, control the final choice of work to be published, and be responsible for artwork and the appearance of the product. Hubert would sell my creations. A deal? Hubert was delighted. "And I?" Monica asked.

"You want to work?" Hubert asked.

"Well, work—"

"You'll be on the payroll," I said at once, because we would need her and she had to stay around. "You'll be our hostess," Hubert said, "or something like it." He underlined his statement with a lopsided grin. We raised our glasses. She'd be worth every penny we would push her way, with her long slender legs, tipped-up bosom, tight waist, ever slightly opened moist lips, and the eyes of an angel.

That's what Hubert was thinking; he's the expert of good taste. I'm a little more. My line of thinking always ends in a climax.

Dad's climax this time. Dad was overweight, his hands trembled, and he walked with some trouble. He should not excite himself; his doctor friend kept repeating the warning. I was forgetting at that time that Dad was also a kind old man, not just a fat fence that had to be kicked down to open our way.

"But," I said, "would a man of his age and condition still be capable of fullfilling his desire?"

Hubert, slurring his words, held forth on the power of positive thinking. Monica admired her delicate hands; so did I. I knew her hands quite well; they had been all over me often enough, with Hubert's approval. Hubert, my good friend, always willing to share. He only wanted Monica as a decoration, I needed her to play my sneaky little games. Waiter! More to drink. We did enjoy ourselves in our ghoulish way. I can see that now, a little late.

Demons from the nether spheres: me, in a dirty sweater and frayed jeans with a zipper broken by belly pressure. Hubert, in his leather outfit set off with thin bright chains. Monica, the living mannequin, a painted pawn pushed around by our smudgy hands. How clever we thought we were.

I'm writing all this down to analyze the goings-on and to formulate a clear confession; read on, Adjutant Grijpstra and Sergeant de Gier. As you see, I'm behaving properly in the end, for he who says good-bye should do everything in his remaining power to cause the least trouble to those who remain on the human battlefield. I know the rules because I once heard two cops talking to each other, with me on the backseat of their patrol car, arrested for drunken driving. The officer at the wheel recalled that the previous night he had visited a home where a suicide had taken place. "Letter present?" the other cop asked. "Yes, he knew how to behave, the sucker." A decent chap who hadn't broken the last rule. Their man hung himself but pinned a note to his chest first: "Good-bye. Couldn't take any more of this." Signed and all. No blame on another. That's why I'm typing away tonight; I'm expressing my error. I've failed sufficiently; when this envelope with contents reaches you, you can close your file.

Who is to blame? Monica had a bad youth. Abandoned as a child, she was raised in state homes, abused to a level where she could only withdraw into the remnants of her self; and even to us, her companions of a latter day, she could open up only a little. She selected Hubert, whose perversion created distance, and me, whose ugly exterior matched the sadness of her soul.

I'm trembling now because I'm seeing more than I can stand and because the end is slipping into sight. The end of the torture, of my pain, but first I have to take proper care of the final formality. I'll have to call you and press the trigger afterward. I first intended the tiny projectile to enter my brain between the eyes, but I read somewhere that a .22 bullet—the instrument that's waiting so patiently next to my telephone isn't much more than an improved toy—may be too light and could get struck in the bone of the forehead. It would be better to direct the shot through the mouth, with the barrel pointed slightly upward; then the mind can be reached easily from within. Oral and ultimate satisfaction. Not too tasty. I sucked the barrel just now—pistol grease is sickly sweet.

Read on, upholders of the law. A son who murders his father is no good, I quite agree. We should be more careful, chipping away at our taboos, but people in your profession aren't too easily shocked. You'll take care of this, won't you? You'll write me off as a sinner who'll have to put up with his just reward?

Dad was a good guy who looked after me well, and after Mom, too, but Mom paid no attention to traffic that afternoon in the past; no, please, I had nothing to do with that, I was in summer camp, at a safe distance. Dad's only weakness was his overeating. I inherited the trait and even the pets picked up the habit. Dad's weakness mattered to us conspirators, it came up during that fateful conversation in the bar that I haven't visited since then. "Where can your father be hit?" Hubert asked. "We've got to know, if we want to pull this off."

Dad fancied his snacks but he could manage the problem—during the day, that is—when he followed Doctor's instructions. At night he slipped into the kitchen—the dog would wake him. Together they sneaked about and emptied the refrigerator. Cheese, fat slices of ham, olives, pickles, buttered toast covered with sardines, creamy soups—the parties lasted for hours. To counter the results, Dad exercised a little and the dog climbed a stepladder. In the old days he could get off, but through the last year Dad would have to pick him up and put him carefully on the floor. Then they returned to bed, after a visit to the bathroom and some intake of medications. The dog got some, too.

Hubert had seen the movie *La Grande Bouffe*, a melodrama in which elderly gents, suffering from incurable disease, exploded themselves with previous intent. "Something like that," Hubert said. "We arrange the final feast and he'll pop."

"Too difficult," I answered. "You underestimate Dad's defenses. We have religious genes, so guilt slows us down. If we're too coarse, he'll smell the devil. Don't forget that Albert Habbema, my grandfather, could start the publishing firm thanks to the sale of a collection of valuable antique Bibles that he inherited from *his* dad. A little subtlety, old pal."

"Sex is subtle," Monica said, posturing gently.

Hubert moved an inch away from her. "Your father fancies women?"

"Surely," I said brightly, paying no attention to his expression of disgust.

Dad didn't practice sex, of course. A proper widower, well in control of lower lust. "However . . ."

"Yes?" Hubert asked eagerly, trying to dry his hands on the smooth leather of his jacket. "Let's have it, comrade."

He knew that this approach always caught me off guard. To

call me "comrade" meant a direct appeal to the core of our friendship. We had been comrades at kindergarten when we defended ourselves against the gang of bullies. We were both minorities; all the others were healthy and sane. Together we managed through the early and later formative years. Friendship? I'm not so sure anymore. Fear kept us together, and we became each other's shadow, which darkened through the years, a composition of black shades to which Monica joined hers later.

I told Hubert what I knew about Dad's sex secrets. There was a family gathering and Dad, drunk, beckoned me over and made me sit at his feet. We mellowly discussed erotic pleasures. The next day he avoided me, but by then I knew more. He always liked to squeeze tea bags, looking naughty. That evening he explained why. They reminded him of breasts, of course, which, when properly handled, emit the feeding fluid. "Nothing in this world," Dad said dreamily, "excites me more than the female bosom." He told me about his very early youth, when, as a boxed-in baby, he rattled his fence when his nurse stripped slowly to titillate her captive audience. Toddler Dad would get so frantic that he was attacked by hiccups and had to be lifted out and fondled, and he would fondle in turn. "Amazing," Dad said, "such a strong memory, and the very first; I wasn't two years old."

I thought that was it and wanted to rejoin the party, but Dad's heavy hand restrained me. The nurse stayed with the family and later, when Dad was in puberty, lured him to her attic, for the game wasn't over. The fondling continued but was never fullfilled, for she was religious, too, and believed that complete enjoyment had to be reserved for the heavenly spheres. A little of the way was perhaps all right, so here we see the ripe woman and the forming youth together between the sheets, feeling away but not quite . . . well, yes.

Until the couple were caught, by furious Granddad, and Nurse was thrown out, sobbing, dragging her bursting cardboard suitcase.

"I had to let her go," Dad said, "but the desire clung."

And now the clash of cymbals, clanging into my ears, after Dad had tipped back his umpteenth glass of jenever. "Nurse, Son, looked just like Monica."

"*Right*," Hubert shouted. "Where's there's a will, there's a way. Good luck is with the relentless pursuer. Right away the solution jumps us. Our adventure is blessed."

Dad knew Monica well; I often took her home, with Hubert, and the four of us would dine together. Dad was always most polite when addressing our companion. How could I ever have guessed that she resembled the lurid influence of his early days? If he hadn't told me, he might still be alive. But did we have a choice? I often wonder.

Hubert instructed Monica in the fine art of seduction. I assisted his efforts. I suggested to Dad that our garden needed a new design and that my friends would like nothing better than to join the project. While we dug—Hubert and I, for this was manly work, and Dad was too old and Monica too tender— and carried rocks, raked gravel, constructed a bamboo gate, Monica was left with Dad. On the back porch, well out of our sight, Monica displayed her curves, accentuated and not in any way hidden by the smallest of bikinis. She kept up the show, even when she dressed, and Dad wasn't given a moment of respite. She did a good job, even if she couldn't play with the pets, for neither dog nor cat wanted to join her when she enticed them to frolic with her on the Persian rugs, so that she could continue her act.

"This is like Nazi Germany," Hubert said, lugging bags filled with soil, or sinking more lilies in the pond. "Much beauty was created there before the Power showed its true face."

Imbeciles we were, knowing full well what was dragging us along and never pausing to see what that could be.

Hubert developed some muscle and I lost a large number of pounds. We heard Dad laugh and Monica titter from the seclusion of the back porch. Except for the howling and hissing of the pets, working conditions were most pleasant. Hubert wanted to hurry, while I preferred to slow down; the status quo seemed to suit me fine.

Dad didn't want to give in, but he was sorely tempted. The seduction took a month. Meanwhile, the garden developed nicely. Hubert egged Monica on. Autumn was on its way, and we were chopping wood for the open fire by then. Monica finally managed to convince Dad of her sincere longing for his elderly caresses. The merriment on the porch gave way to deep sighs. Then they became absent, for Dad preferred the privacy of his city apartment. Sin shies away from an audience. Dad died in secret, and Monica's panic made her run away, leaving her telltale bag that invited the Murder Brigade into my office.

"So your father had an affair with the young lady," Adjutant Grijpstra was saying. "I can't stay the situation is too clear to me, but I think we have bothered you enough for today." He left, followed by the impeccably attired sergeant, who turned in the doorway to scan me with his steady gaze. *Today*. The word they left hung heavily between my walls. There was always tomorrow, as they intended me to understand. The suspicion, the charge in the sergeant's gaze was clear enough. I understood that he almost understood my motivation. For look here, something was wrong, although the facts still underlined my innocence. Monica was Hubert's girlfriend. Hubert was gay. Monica was most attractive and I was not. Dad's death moved all his property to me. The case smelled foully on all sides, but the catchers of ghouls were short of proof, as long as my resistance lasted. Cops catch the wicked, but their power is restricted, and it doesn't often happen that they meet the perpetrators while they're actually doing wrong. Their main task is preventive; they are around and they stay around, making sure you won't ever forget their presence. And while they're around, the sinner may weaken.

Grijpstra and de Gier visited me twice again; afterward they stayed away. Insufficiency of proof—and what did they care anyway? Detectives of the Murder Brigade are always ankle-deep in a quagmire of sticky evil; they could put up with the little I was adding. Whenever they visited, they allowed me to talk and observed me meanwhile, informing me wordlessly that they thought I was a slimy example of everything they abhorred. As if I needed their quiet attack. Of criticism I had a sufficiency and it was all my own. Their pointing fingers were visible, especially the adjutant's stubby index, and it hurt me that this paternal figure refused to show the slightest understanding.

Fine. Dad's dead, the company is mine. Hubert showed up the very next day to remind me of my promise, and I made him a director. Monica appeared and lay down on the visitor's couch. I tried to convince them that some patience might be better, but Hubert called me "comrade" and Monica became erotic.

I knew then I would have to be rid of them; the friendship, if our connection was ever friendly, reminded me of what we had done wrong together. How does one remove nasty people? For once and for all? A good beginning is half the work?

To separate myself from Hubert was easy enough. Hubert always underestimated me, a mistake that has terminated many a criminal mind. When you grow up together, there's enough opportunity to weigh the other. He should have remembered that my Ph.D. was cum laude, that I never lose a game of chess, and that in confrontations I always slide out unscratched in the end.

What was Hubert's weakness? Which circumstances needed to be combined? I had money, Hubert hadn't. Hubert has expensive tastes, and his worst is his longing for rough male company. He likes to be around motorcyclists with bulging biceps. Bullies can be bought, especially when they're on expensive drugs, and I found just the type in a junkies' café, who, in spite of his lack of brain, further reduced by addiction, did grasp fairly quickly what I wanted of him. I didn't tell him that Hubert's skull is thin and that, as a kid, he almost died because he fell off his bike and cracked his head. I did mention that Hubert likes to be hurt, especially on the head, if possible with a chain.

Hubert does get rather drunk at times. I took him along to the miserable quarters where the leather boys hang out and introduced him to my burly acquaintance. I gave money to the tough. "Have a good time, boys; you'll get along well." Amazing how easy it all is. Hubert was found in the morning, dying of a bleeding skull; he had been nicely arranged between two piles of garbage. He mumbled as he died. A prayer? The alley is called Prayer Without End, for it's circular and bites its own tail.

Monica was a little more tricky, but as Hubert used to say, where there's a will, there's a way. I knew her inside out and *her* weak spot was obvious. Monica is allergic to monosodium glutamate, the taste-improver professional cooks use so that they can serve appetizing leftovers. The chemical also tenderizes meat. MSG never fails to upset Monica's stomach. It also makes her dizzy, and when she consumes a lot, she's apt to faint.

I bought a little bright red can filled with MSG.

With Hubert gone, his share in Monica became mine, too. Our more intimate relationship brought along more duties. She asked for presents, and I bought her an Italian sports car with a long dainty nose. Monica likes to race in traffic. As she's a good driver, my hope wasn't fullfilled too soon. I was in a hurry; hence the can of the weakener of Monica's defenses.

Monica is vain.

All factors were available, and the day came that they would fit. We were on holiday in Paris, and I took her to a three-star restaurant, close to the circular road that spans the inner city. Monica just loved to race that highway, all day if need be, and she would change lanes, with inches to spare from the others' fenders.

During the day I was friendly enough and for dinner ordered her favorite delicacy, a filet mignon topped with rare mushrooms. "What's wrong with your hair, dear?" I asked, just when she was ready to dig in.

"Doesn't it look right?"

"No, it's all blown up. You look ridiculous, you know."

She repaired to the restroom to see if I was right, and I sprinkled the glutamate on her little steak, pressing it in with my fork so that the white flakes wouldn't show. Monica returned, ate the mignon, and got irritated by my sarcastic remarks. Monica hardly ever loses her temper but she's sensitive to criticism if it refers to her grammar. Never having been to school much, she expresses herself poorly. I said that it's very nice if a woman is attractive, but that beauty is only skin-deep and that a man does appreciate intelligence after a while. She became furious and left. I had placed the car keys on the table so that she could grab them as she stalked out. We stayed in a hotel around the corner; she knew where she could locate me once the anger passed. I got up, shouted another insult, sat down, and ordered cognac. She must have been squashed while I was on my second refreshment. The gendarmes showed me later how the accident must have taken place. "Madame was speeding." Well over a hundred, they thought; apparently, experts can determine speed from measuring tire tracks. They were short and cut through the railing that supposedly protects the highway. Monica's car made short work of it and then flew down, landing eventually on a crossing and a Parisian in a Renault, father of four kids, on his way home after working late in his office.

That nice, dead, harmless *monsieur* got to be too much for me; he appears in all my dreams and keeps asking whether I couldn't have arranged my personal problem a little better. "Four little children, Monsieur!" I might have taken them into consideration. Who would look after them, *hein*? My dream demon isn't angry; he just inquires politely.

Dad's pets pursue me, too. The dog is off his food and suffers from neurotic itch, and the cat waits for me, in hidden corners, to leap out and hiss and claw. That cat used to be my pal once; she would bring me crumpled papers and expect me to throw them and then would bring them back. Siamese cats do that, if they truly like you. I need medication to fall asleep, and instead of resting, I then keep murdering my father and my friends. Each night they die again, out of breath, clutching their broken heads, flattened in a wrecked sports car, and the

French office worker keeps returning to tell me about his starving kids.

Adjutant Grijpstra left his visiting card, with the request to call him if something cropped up. Very well, something has. I won't disturb you personally, Adjutant, although your private number is printed on your card, but it's evening now and I imagine your wife has just brought you your coffee and you're about to watch a nature film on TV. I'll call your radio room. The officers who will take care of my conclusion will deliver this note.

REPORT OF THE RADIO ROOM, POLICE HEADQUARTERS, AMSTERDAM

-- January, 198-. Time: 1937 hours.

Dialogue as taped:

"Hello, the police?"
(Yes)
"Listen. My name is Peter Habbema and I'm phoning from my office, Habbema and Son Inc., Emperor's Canal 610. I'm going to . . . eh . . . shoot myself."
(Don't do that, sir.)
"What was that?"
(*repeat*)
"Don't do that? Come on, Officer. This is a neat city. Garbage has to be cleared away."
(Mr. Habbema . . .)
"No, just a minute, please. There's a letter all ready for you, addressed to your detectives. I've left nothing out. Motivation. Why it's gotten as far as this. Complete. Crime and punishment. All I have to do now is pull this little trigger."
(*clicking sound*)
"What's this now? Just a click? Aha, I see it. Safety is still on,

I'm never handy with technical stuff. This way now, up she goes, and ready to fire. See this? The red dot is visible. There we go."

(*sound of a shot*)

REPORT OF A PATROL CAR. Number 6-7. Time: 1954 hours. . . . and we found the lifeless body of a male. Letter present. . . .

A TASTY TIDBIT

As a journalist, stationed in my home country, the Netherlands, where I work for a magazine, I often have to travel to the States. My last assignment, some months ago now, was the usual assortment of very different fish—a religious society in the deep South supposedly making use of deadly snakes (whoever enjoys true enlightenment doesn't get bitten), a corrupt senator willing to grant an interview, a Dutch professor who explained biological computers in his New York laboratory, and a Dutch writer who lived high up on the East Coast.

One shouldn't expect too much from shallow

articles illustrated with glossy photographs—at the very best they may distract patients in dentists' waiting rooms—so if I say the results were disappointing, I only mean the final results. What I really experience is worth the trouble. But I can never express my true feelings, which leads to continuous frustration.

Those idiots with their copperheads and rattlesnakes, for instance. What a marvelous show they put on, complete with a true black necromancer, jungle drums, nude young female meditators—how beautiful. And the slimy senator, that sympathetic parasite. And the delicious old know-it-all in New York who really thinks he is *growing* computers—the multicolored interconnected worms he showed me through his electronic microscope are still in my dreams. Each interview would supply more than enough material for a novel, but I'm only a piecemeal writer, not a true author—like the fourth contact I made on that American trip, the Netherlands-born "thriller" writer, Victor Verburg.

I found him available, via a telephone call to his estate on the Maine coast, and he was kind enough to pick me up at the airport. A lean, tall man with only a touch of bulge above the belt, a scholarly rustic with kind brown eyes and a scraggly mustache, affecting a modest attitude, although he is well known—or, rather, he was. The reading public forgets quickly. Which was the reason for looking him up—he hasn't been published for a while now.

"Why, don't you write anymore, Victor?" I asked in the car. (He put us on a first-name basis right away.)

"Well"—he had a pleasant, hoarse voice—"I have other interests these days."

He explained his recent activities, while the car—a long, low convertible that gave me the feeling of riding on whipped cream—slid through a freshly green landscape. He said he had asked himself, once he was well established on the international market, whether he should go on. The motivation of money is limited; after a certain amount one has all that is needed. He was spending his time now on boating and study, and in his home I found a respectable library on subjects ranging from the technical origin of life through pure abstract philosophy.

His home, a large wooden structure on a low hill with a view of the sea, was surrounded by balconies and verandas, all at the center of gardens flowing toward the sea—wavy fields carrying a crop of silver-colored plants. His wife, Victor told me, was an authority on herbs. She wasn't around—it seemed she traveled a lot, searching for rare flora.

I stayed a few days. American distances are too enormous to allow for arriving and leaving on the same day, and Verburg was a perfect host. He was a gourmet cook himself but also knew all the good eating places in the neighborhood. He poured tasty but strong drinks and would talk at length, but also knew how to be quiet. We went for walks, and the second day he took me out in his motorboat.

The coast there consists of bays and peninsulas. My own hobby is scuba-diving and Victor owned a number of complete sets of equipment. Together we dived near some large rocks where a herd of seals were sunning themselves. Victor seemed to know some of them well, and several young males welcomed us and accompanied us on our journey.

It took a while to get used to the rather muddy water, but I soon began to see mysteriously waving reeds, flashing bodies of cod and mackerel, brilliant jellyfish pumping themselves forward in their bizarre manner, and the subtle sepia colors of the bay's irregular bottom. We swam farther and farther, exploring large caves.

Then suddenly the mood changed. I didn't understand my sudden fear. The veiled light hadn't changed. Plants and fish continued their ballet. Lobsters waved their antennae and claws. But I felt threatened and seemed to be listening to the somber music of demons playing the double bass and hitting kettledrums with wrapped sticks. I couldn't see Victor, but two of the seals were with me, flapping their short forepaws nervously. We had just reached another cave, larger and deeper than the others. Rocks covered with algae were set around the entrance, and I thought I saw the white glistening of an enormous smooth body inside. I started inside, but the seals got in my way and pushed me back.

The oxygen in my cylinders was gettng low and so I floated up. Victor was waiting for me. He smiled at me from the boat and helped me aboard.

I told him about the cave and the seals' strange behavior. He nodded. "Yes, I didn't know we had strayed this far. A shark lives in there."

"I didn't think sharks would bother us in such cold waters."

"You're right," Victor said. "Sharks are okay up here, but they could still lust after flesh, and the great white shark is the most dangerous of the lot. He shouldn't hurt you here, but he may forget himself. And this particular fellow is an especially large example of the species."

"The two of you have met?" I asked.

He started his almost soundless engine, and the small boat lifted its slender bow and began to chop at the little waves, picking up speed until we planed effortlessly on the smooth surface of the bay, hardly disturbed by a soft breeze. The freshly foaming wake stretched far behind us.

"The shark and I are well acquainted," Victor told me. "He's a true giant, some thirty feet long, with wicked teeth in his evil head. But he isn't a bad chap once you get to know him. He must be quite old. I think he has retired in that cave. I never see him near the other shore of the bay, so he must be living on whatever happens to stray within his reach here."

I forgot the shark, and that evening on Victor's veranda we awaited the arrival of a full moon while sipping cognac and smoking cigars. The temperature had dropped and Victor lit the pile of debris we had gathered that morning. The largest part of his estate is covered by a forest of pines and firs, and he collects the dead wood and branches so that the carpet of reddish needles may remain undisturbed.

We watched the flames that made the cognac in our glasses sparkle and I remembered that I should be asking questions. "Don't you mind losing your following?" I said.

Verburg's was an unusual career. He lived on all the continents during the early part of his life, buying and selling irregular goods. Later on, he owned his own firm in Amsterdam but migrated to America when his books began to sell. He wrote for only some seven years, but his work was well accepted and his fame spread quickly. Some years ago he was interviewed regularly, spoke on talk shows on both sides of the Atlantic, had his own column in several newspapers, and published short stories in the better magazines. Then it all came to an end.

Victor raised his glass and laughed. The light from the bonfire made his silhouette glow. "Fame? What will that do for me? Writing was a pleasurable pastime and the profit still supports me, but I've reached the last part of my life. Isn't it time to spend my mature years on something more worthwhile? I'm studying at the local university, I observe whatever interests me. Lately I've been having a good time attempting to comprehend Einstein's ideas on relativity. The universe is fascinating, even in the dark corner that is reserved for us. Having a following distracts me from my curiosity. I don't want to waste any more time courting applause."

"Do you know a lot of people here?" I asked.

He shook his head. "And I don't want to. It's not hard to make friends here, but once you do, they gobble you up. I prefer to be a hermit."

"Am I the exception?"

He drained his glass and the silence crept back between us. His large brown eyes avoided mine. "All rules need to be broken at times, and the prospect of a visitor from my own country—I am homesick, maybe." He smiled as if he wanted to excuse a weakness.

I relaxed and Verburg seemed to, too. The glasses filled themselves again, the pile burned brightly, and the moon floated majestically above bay and woods.

"Fame," Victor said, pulling his chair closer to mine, "is a nuisance, especially when it attacks you through female seduction. When a man gets older, he likes to feel he's still in it." He took a long swallow from his drink. "Some years ago there was a girl here . . ."

The information reaching me was unsuitable for the chatty level of my magazine's articles, but I kept quiet and listened.

"My wife was ajourneying again," Victor said. "She does have to go after her plants, and . . ."

I had looked through the photo album in his study and seen pictures of his wife. A most beautiful woman—slender, calm, exotic. Victor said he had met Eleia in South America. She was still on this side of middle age, a handsome woman, looking a little like Raquel Welch but somewhat darker, and with luminous eyes.

"Eleia was on a trip," Victor said, "and a girl telephoned me, a girl from the Netherlands with a dear voice. She said she had read everything that I ever wrote, was completely captivated by the content and style of my work, and—well, you know that sort of approach. The most welcome type of fan mail, but alive and attainable. She was staying close by, on one of the islands here." He pointed. "I can reach it within an hour by boat. You can see the island if you stand on the roof. The girl was by herself, had to caretake somebody's house, didn't know what to do with herself, found my name in the telephone book, decided to call me, and hoped she wasn't disturbing me."

"An open invitation?" I asked.

"I didn't respond," Victor said. "I'm not that crazy. Eleia is rather jealous. To invite a young female here when she was away—wouldn't that be asking for trouble?"

"You went to fetch her."

Victor sighed, "How weak is man—how strong his desire. Not that I intended to, of course. I was just going for a little trip, as I so often do, and happened to get close to the island. And then felt like going even closer, to see if the kelp was doing well near the shore—"

"And there she was, displaying her lovely form on a rock."

"How do you know?" Victor asked.

I smiled.

"Indeed, on a rock. Such a lovely girl. Some twenty-three years old, exactly the right age. I allowed the boat to nose close to her and she never hesitated, she jumped aboard."

"She recognized you? Ah, your photograph is on your books."

"Yes, but she seemed surprised all the same. She kept saying I looked so young."

"And so you do," I said. "The life here must agree with you."

"The girl was flattering me, kept babbling about my virile good looks, saying she would never have thought of telephoning me if she'd known how much I would attract her."

I grinned.

"Yes, you can laugh. Little mistakes go a long way. My last published story appeared in an anthology gathered by a disorganized genius. Each story showed the birth year of the author, and in my case he was ten years off, so the girl thought I was in my sixties."

"Poor little thing."

"Smart little thing," Victor said, "with an excellent act. I ate the apple and headed for home."

"Some sexual activity?"

"After the walk across the estate, we were at each other and never stopped. She was like an unmeasurable pit and I kept falling into her without ever reaching bottom. Whatever she gave me seemed only a beginning."

"A tasty tidbit." I grinned and held up my glass. The bottle was empty and Victor staggered into the house. We had a good go at the second bottle while he told all.

The affair was idyllic. Holding hands, artist and muse trotted through the woods. They went sailing together and raced the motorboat. She learned scuba-diving and the two explored the inlet's romantic depths. He read his unpublished poetry to her and she was moved to tears. ("My rhymes make my wife sick to her stomach," Victor said, "and rightly so.") The girl got on well with the seals and helped him weed the herb gardens. She taught him new recipes. She was always cheerful. Her youthful energy kindled his own. ("My wife doesn't believe in overspending ourselves," Victor said.)

"Real love, eh?"

"I thought so for a little while."

"You wanted to marry her?"

"The frenzy got worse and worse. After a few days, I told her I couldn't live without her. I proposed lengthy journeys. I've always wanted to go to New Guinea, to study primitive masks, and what do you know, that was exactly what she wanted to do. We seemed to be made for each other."

"Are you very rich?" I asked.

"She must have been interested in my wealth. But she never asked about money. She said she was a nurse and earning a fair salary."

"Did you promise her any presents?"

Victor nodded sadly. "She said she liked small sports cars and I immediately offered to buy her one. She also wanted to learn how to fly. I said that she could become a member of the local flying club and I would give her an airplane as soon as she had her papers."

"You never saw through the magnificent soap bubble?"

The liquor had lamed the muscles of his lips and he suddenly looked like an old clown. "My wife was due to return and the girl was still around. One morning I was brushing my teeth on the balcony and realized the stupidity of the whole thing. I knew I had struck nonsense again. She had to go, as soon as possible."

"And didn't go."

"No."

"And you were too much the gentleman to push her out."

"No. Men are rather weak, don't you think? Are you any good at breaking relationships?"

"Not at all," I said helpfully.

"Good. Neither am I. Eleia came back and I introduced the

two. She saw through the situation in half a second, took me aside, and asked me what I wanted. I told her, to be rid of her."

"Of who? Your wife?"

He gave me a surprised look. "Are you all right in the head? The girl, of course. I love Eleia. To grow old together, can there be anything more beautiful than that?"

"So then what?"

"Eleia knows how to take care of situations," said Victor, wiping at a cognac stain on his shirt. He wanted to break off his story but I held on.

"No, finish the tale. What happened to the girl?"

Victor gazed at the bay below. "She's still there."

"What?"

"Her body cells must have been absorbed by those of the shark."

I was on my feet. "Did you feed her to the shark?"

"Not me," Victor said.

"Who?"

He kept quiet.

"Did she visit the old shark by herself?"

Victor turned his attention to the dying fire. "Not with me, didn't I say so just now? I once gave the shark a dead seal. I found the carcass on the rocks and thought the shark would appreciate the gift. I was right. Chop, chop, chop. The crazy animal really has a nasty mouth. Sharks devour carrion and they go after blood. Once you're wounded, you have to be careful. But when you're in one piece, you can safely visit him—I've often done it. He'll come to greet me and push his flank against my leg. Why don't you join me tomorrow and see?"

"Not on your life," I said, and waited.

In time Victor continued. "The girl stayed, and so did Eleia and I, of course. A ménage à trois in a way, although the girl and I didn't sleep together anymore. Her presence became irritating."

"Your wife must be very good at scuba-diving, too," I said. "Am I right?"

"The county's champion," Victor said proudly. "Eleia's won first prize for five years in a row. She used to be a dancer and knows how to control her body."

"So your wife took the guest along on a swim," I said, "and happened to wound her once they were submerged—with her knife, I imagine. You gave me a knife when we were diving. I strapped it to my leg. Eleia must have scratched the girl and then taken her to the shark's cave. Chop, chop, chop."

"It may have happened that way," Victor said.

"You're not sure?"

He made an effort to smile. "Eleia came back alone and we've never discussed the matter."

I woke up the next morning with a terrible hangover, treated by Victor with strong coffee, some aspirin, and orange juice. He dropped me off at the airport. I didn't remind him of the previous evening's conversation. Authors live in a world of fantasy. I understood that he had come up with a horror story to amuse me.

A few days ago an acquaintance I met in a café mentioned holidaying in the United States. I said that the world is becoming less safe by the day—only North America can be trusted. When you leave, you know you will return on the appointed day. My acquaintance disagreed. A girl he knew had left but never come back. I asked for details.

The girl was a nurse who had been baby-sitting someone's house on an island off the coast of Maine. When the owner of the house eventually returned, the girl was nowhere to be found.

"What happened?" I asked. "Was she out swimming and caught by the currents?"

"Her baggage was still in the house," my friend said. "She may have slipped off the rocks or gone under while swimming, but according to the U.S. Coast Guard, drowned persons are invariably found. Nobody found *her*."

What can I do—press charges? Without any proof, I'll make

a fool of myself. I still see Victor Verburg, telling the tale during that drunken evening, with a woodpile burning brightly and a soft white moon sailing slowly above land- and seascape. I understand now why he stopped writing. All his work is motivated by and based on fear, the fear of fantasy. That time he must have come too close to reality.

I wonder if he still visits the shark, in that greenish-black cavity fifteen feet below the cheerful little white waves of his peaceful bay.

A GREAT SIGHT

No, it wasn't easy. It took a great deal of effortful dreaming to get where I am now. Where I am now is Moose Bay, on the Maine shore, which is on the East Coast of the United States of America, in case you haven't been looking at maps lately. Moose Bay is long and narrow, bordered by two peninsulas and holding some twenty square miles of water. I've lived on the south shore for almost thirty years now, always alone—if you don't count a couple of old cats—and badly crippled. Lost the use of my legs, I did, thirty years ago, and that was my release and my ticket to Moose Bay. I've often wondered whether the mishap was really an accident. Sure enough, the fall was due to faulty equipment (a new strap that broke) and quite beyond my will. The telephone company that employed me acknowledged their responsibility easily enough, paying me handsomely so that I could be comfortably out of work for the rest of my life. But didn't I, perhaps, dream myself into that fall? You see, I wasn't exactly happy being a telephone repairman. Up one post and down another, climbing or slithering up and down forever, day after day, and not in the best of climates. For years I did that, and there was no way I could see in which the ordeal would ever end. So I began to dream of a way out, and of where I would go. To be able to dream is a gift. My father didn't have the talent. No imagination had the old man, in Holland he lived, where I was born, and he had a similar job to what I would have later. He was a window cleaner, and I guess he could only visualize death, for when *he* fell, it was the last thing he ever did. I survived, with mashed legs. I never dreamed of death; I dreamed of the great sights I would still see, whisking myself to a life on a rocky coast, where I would be alone, maybe with a few old cats, in a cedar log cabin with a view of the water, the sky, and a line of trees on the other shore. I would see, I dreamed, rippling waves or the mirrorlike surface of a great expanse of liquid beauty on a windless day. I never gave that up, the possibility of seeing great sights, and I dreamed myself up here, where everything is as I thought it might be, only better.

Now don't get me wrong; I'm not your dreamy type. No long hair and beads for me, no debts unpaid or useless things just lying about in the house. Everything is spic-and-span with me. The kitchen works: there's an ample supply of staples, each in its own jar; I have good vegetables from the garden, an occasional bird I get with the shotgun, and fish caught off my dock. I can't walk so well, but I get about on my crutches and the pickup has been changed so that I can drive it with my hands. No fleas on the cats, either, and no smell from the outhouse. I have all I need and all within easy reach. There must be richer people in the world (don't I see them sometimes, sailing along in their hundred-foot skyscrapers?), but I don't have to envy them. May they live happily for as long as it takes; I'll just sit here and watch the sights from my porch.

Or I watch them from the water. I have an eight-foot dory and it rows quite well in the bay if the waves aren't too high, for it *will* ship water when the weather gets rough. There's much to see when I go rowing. A herd of harbor seals live just out of my cove, and they know me well, coming to play around my boat as soon as I sing out to them. I bring them a rubber ball that they push about for a bit, and throw even, until they want to go about their own business again and bring it back. I've named them all and can identify the individuals when they frolic in the spring, or raise their tails and heads, lolling in the summer sun.

I go out most good days, for I've taken it upon myself to keep this coast clean. Garbage drifts in, thrown in by the careless, off ships I suppose, and by the city people, the unfortunates who never look at the sights. I get beer cans to pick up in my net, and every variety of plastic container, boards with rusty nails in them, and occasionally a complete vessel, made out of crumbly foam. I drag it all to the same spot and burn the rubbish. Rodney, the fellow I share Moose Bay with—he lives a mile down from me in a tar-papered shack—makes fun of me when I perform my duty. He'll come by in his smart powerboat, flat on the water and sharply pointed, with a loud engine pushing it that looks like three regular outboards stacked on top of each other. Rodney can really zip about in that thing. He's a thin ugly fellow with a scraggly black beard and big slanted eyes above his crooked nose. He's from here, of course, and he won't let me forget his lawful nativity. Much higher up the scale than me, he claims, for what am I but some itinerant, an alien washed up from nowhere, tolerated by the locals? If I didn't happen to be an old codger, and lame, Rodney says, he would drown me like he does his kittens. Hop, into the sack, weighed down with a good boulder, and away with the mess. But being what I am, sort of human in a way, he puts up with my presence for a while, provided I don't trespass on his bit of the shore, crossing the high-tide line, for then he'll have to shoot me, with the deer rifle he now uses for poaching. Rodney has a vegetable garden, too, even though he doesn't care for greens. The garden is a trap for deer so that he can shoot them from his shack, preferably at night, after he has frozen them with a flashlight.

There are reasons for me not to like Rodney too much. He shot my friend, the killer whale that used to come here some summers ago. Killer whales are a rare sight on this coast, but they do pop up from time to time. They're supposed to be wicked animals that will push your boat over and gobble you up when you're thrashing about, weighed down by your boots and your oilskins. Maybe they do that, but my friend didn't do it to me. He used to float alongside my dory, which he could have tipped with a single flap of his great triangular tail. He would roll over on his side, all thirty feet of him, and grin lazily from the corner of his huge curved mouth. I could see his big gleaming teeth and mirror my face in his calm humorous eye, and I would sing to him. I haven't got a good loud voice, but I would hum away, making up a few words here and there, and he'd lift a flipper in appreciation and snort if my song wasn't long enough for his liking. Every day that killer whale came to me; I swear he was waiting for me out in the bay, for as soon as I'd splash my oars, I'd see his six-foot fin cut through the waves, and a moment later his black and white head, always with that welcoming grin.

Now we don't have any electricity down here, and kerosene isn't as cheap as it used to be, so maybe Rodney was right when he said that he shot the whale because he needed the blubber. Blubber makes good fuel, Rodney says. Me, I think he was wrong, for he never got the blubber anyway. When he'd shot the whale, zipping past it in the powerboat, and got the animal between the eyes with his deer rifle, the whale just sank. I never saw its vast body wash up. Perhaps it didn't die straightaway and could make it to the depths of the ocean, to perish in peace.

He's a thief, too, Rodney is. He'll steal anything he can get his hands on—to begin with, his welfare. There's nothing wrong with Rodney's back, but he's stuffed a lot of complaints into it, enough so that the doctors pay attention. He collects his check and his food stamps, and he gets his supplies for free. There's a town, some fifty miles further along, and they employ special people there to give money to the poor, and counselors to listen to pathetic homemade tales, and there's a society that distributes gifts on holidays. Rodney even gets his firewood every year, brought by young religious men on a truck; they stack it right where Rodney points—no fee.

"Me against the world," Rodney says, "for the world owes me a living. I never asked to be born, but here I am and my hands are out." He'll be drinking when he talks like that, guzzling my Sunday bourbon on my porch, and he'll point his long finger at me. "You some sort of Kraut?"

I say I'm Dutch. The Dutch fought the Krauts during the war; I fought a bit myself until they caught me and put me in a camp. They were going to kill me, but then the Americans came. "Saved you, did we?" Rodney will say, and fill up his glass again. "So you owe us now, right? So how come you're living off the fat of this land, you with the crummy legs?" He'll raise his glass and I'll raise mine.

Rodney lost his wife. He still had her when I settled in my cabin; I got to talk to her at times and liked her fine. She would talk to Rodney, about his ways, and he would leer at her, and he was still leering when she was found at the bottom of a cliff. "Never watched where she was going," Rodney said to the sheriff, who took the corpse away. The couple had a dog, who was fond of Rodney's wife and unhappy when she was gone. The dog would howl at night and keep Rodney awake, but the dog happened to fall off the cliff, too. Same cliff. Maybe I should have reported the coincidence to the authorities, but it wasn't much more than a coincidence and, as Rodney says, accidents will happen. Look at me, I fell down a telephone post, nobody pushed *me*, right? It was a brand-new strap that snapped when it shouldn't have; a small event, quite beyond my control.

No, I never went to the sheriff and I've never stood up to Rodney. There's just the two of us on Moose Bay. He's the bad guy who'll tip his garbage into the bay and I'm the in-between guy who's silly enough to pick it up. We also have a good guy, who lives at the end of the north peninsula, at the tip, facing the ocean. Michael, his name is, Michael the lob-sterman. A giant of a man, Michael is, with a golden beard and flashing teeth. I can see his smile when his lobster boat enters the bay. The boat is one of these old-fashioned jobs, sturdy and white and square, puttering along at a steady ten knots in every sort of weather. Michael's got a big winch on it, for hauling up the heavy traps, and I can see him taking the lobsters out and putting the bait in and throwing them back. Michael has some thousand traps, all along the coast, but his best fishing is here in Moose Bay. Over the years we've got to know each other, and I sometimes go out with him, much farther than the dory can take me. Then we see the old squaws flock in, the diver ducks that look as if they've flown in from a Chinese painting, with their thin, curved tailfeathers and delicately-drawn wings and necks. Or we watch the big whales, snorting and spouting, and the haze on the horizon where the sun dips, causing indefinably soft colors, or we just smell the clear air together, coming to cool the forests in summer. Michael knows Rodney, too, but he isn't the gossipy kind. He'll frown when he sees the powerboat lurking in Moose Bay and gnaw his pipe before he turns away. When Michael doesn't stop at my dock, he'll wave and make some gesture, in lieu of conversation—maybe he'll hold his hands close together to show me how far he could see when he cut through the fog, or he'll point at a bird flying over us, a heron in slow flight, or a jay, hurrying from shore to shore, gawking and screeching, and I'll know what he means.

This Michael is a good guy; I knew it the first time I saw his silhouette on the lobster boat, and I've heard good stories about him, too. A knight in shining armor who has saved people about to drown in storms, or marooned and sick on the islands. A giant and a genius, for he's built his own boat, and his gear—even his house, a big sprawling structure, out of driftwood on pegged beams. And he'll fight when he has to, for it isn't always cozy here. He'll be out in six-foot waves, and I've seen him when the bay is frozen up, excepting the channel, where the current rages, with icicles on his beard and snow driving against his bow—but he'll still haul up his traps.

I heard he was out in the last war, too, flying an airplane low above the jungle, and he still flies now, on Sundays, for the National Guard.

Rodney got worse. I don't know what devil lives in that man, but the fiend must have been thrown out of the lowest hells. Rodney likes new games and he thought it would be fun to chase me a bit. My dory sits pretty low in the water, but there are enough good days here and I can get out quite a bit. When I do, Rodney will wait for me, hidden behind the big rocks east of my cove, and he'll suddenly appear, revving his engine, trailing a high wake. When his curly waves hit me, I have to bail for my life, and as soon as I'm done, the fear will be back, for he'll be after me again.

I didn't quite know what to do then. Get a bigger boat? But then he would think of something else. There are enough games he can play. He knows my fondness for the seals; he could get them one by one, as target practice. There's my vegetable garden, too, close to the track; he could back his truck into it and get my cats as an afterthought, flattening them into the gravel, for they're slow these days, careless with old age. The fear grabbed me by the throat at night, as I watched my ceiling, remembering his dislike of my cabin and thinking how easily it would burn, being made of old cedar with a roof of shingles. I knew it was him who took the battery out of my truck, making me hitchhike to town for a new one. He was also sucking my gas, but I keep a drum of energy near the house. Oh, I'm vulnerable here all right, with the sheriff coming down only once a year. Suppose I talk to the law, suppose the law talks to Rodney, suppose *I* fall down that cliff, too?

I began to dream again, like I had done before, when I was still climbing the telephone posts like a demented monkey. I was bored then, hopelessly bored, and now I was hopelessly afraid. Hadn't I dreamed my way out once before? Tricks can be repeated.

My dream gained strength; it had to, for Rodney was getting rougher. His powerboat kept less distance, went faster. I couldn't see myself sticking to the land. I need to get out on the bay, to listen to the waves lapping the rocks, to hear the seals blow when they clear their nostrils, to hear the kingfishers and the squirrels whirr in the trees on shore, to spot the little ringnecked ducks, busily investigating the shallows, peering eagerly out of their tufted heads. There are the quiet herons stalking the mud flats and the ospreys whirling slowly; there are eagles, even, diving and splashing when the alewives run from the brooks. Would I have to putter about in the vegetable patch all the time, leaning on a crutch while pushing a hoe with my free hand?

I dreamed up a bay free of Rodney. There was a strange edge to the dream—some kind of quality there that I couldn't quite see, but it was splendid, a great sight and part of my imagination although I couldn't quite make it out.

One day, fishing off my dock, I saw Michael's lobster boat nosing into the cove: I waved and smiled, and he waved back, but he didn't smile.

He moored the boat and jumped onto the jetty, light as a great cat, touching my arm. We walked up to my porch and I made some strong coffee.

"There's a thief," Michael said, "stealing my lobsters. He used to take a few, few enough to ignore maybe, but now he's taking too many."

"Oho," I said, holding my mug. Michael wouldn't be referring to me. Me? Steal lobsters? How could I ever haul up a trap? The channel is deep in the bay. A hundred feet of cable and a heavy trap at the end of it—never. I would need a winch, like Rodney has on his powerboat.

Besides, doesn't Michael leave me a lobster every now and then? Lying on my dock in the morning, its claws neatly tied with a bit of yellow string?

"Any idea?" he asked.

"Same as yours," I said, "but he's hard to catch. The powerboat is fast. He nips out of the bay before he does his work, to make sure you aren't around."

"Might get the warden," Michael said, "and then he might go to jail, and come out again, and do something bad."

I agreed. "Hard to prove, it would be," I said. "A house burns down, yours or mine. An accident, maybe."

Michael left. I stayed on the porch, dreaming away, expending some power. A little power goes a long way in a dream.

It happened the next day, a Sunday, it was. I was walking to the shore, for it was low tide and I wanted to see the seals on their rocks. It came about early, just after sunrise. I heard an airplane. A lot of airplanes come by here. There's the regular commuter plane from the town to the big city, and the little ones the tourists fly in summer, and the flying club. There are also big planes, dirtying up the sky, high up; some of them are Russians, they say; the National Guard has to be about, to push them back. The big planes rumble, but this sound was different, light but deadly, far away still. I couldn't see the plane, but when I did, it was coming silently, ahead of its own sound—it was that fast. Then it slowed down, surveying the bay.

I've seen fighter planes during World War II, Germans and Englishmen flew them, propeller jobs that would spin around each other above the small Dutch lakes, until one of the planes came down, trailing smoke. Jet planes I only saw later, here in America. They looked dangerous enough, even while they gamboled about, and I felt happy watching them, for I was in the States and they were protecting me from the bad guys lurking in the East.

This airplane was a much-advanced version of what I had seen in the late forties. Much longer, it was, and sleek and quiet as it lost height, aiming for the channel. A baby-blue killer, with twin rudders sticking up elegantly far behind the large gleaming canopy up front, reflecting the low sunlight. I guessed her to be seventy feet long, easily the size of the splendid yachts of the rich summer people, but there was no pleasure in her; she was all functional, programmed for swift pursuit and destruction only. I grinned when I saw her American stars, set in circles, with a striped bar sticking out at each side. When she was closer, I thought I could see the pilot, all wrapped up in his tight suit and helmet, the living brain controlling this deadly, superfast vessel of the sky.

I saw that the plane was armed, with white missiles attached to its slender streamlined belly. I had read about those missiles. Costly little mothers, they are. Too costly to fire at Rodney's boat, busily stealing away right in front of my cove. Wouldn't the pilot have to explain the loss of one of his slick rockets? He'd surely be in terrible trouble if he returned to base incomplete.

Rodney was thinking the same way, for he was jumping up and down in his powerboat, grinning and sticking two fingers at the airplane hovering above the bay.

Then the plane roared and shot away, picking up speed at an incredible rate. I was mightily impressed and grateful, visualizing the enemy confronted with such force, banking, diving, rising again at speeds much faster than sound.

The plane had gone and I was alone again, with Rodney misbehaving in the bay, taking the lobsters out as fast as he could—one trap shooting up after another, yanked by his nastily whining little winch.

The plane came back, silently, with the roar of its twin engines well behind it. It came in low, twenty-five feet above the short, choppy waves. Rodney, unaware, busy, didn't even glance over his shoulder. I was leaning on the railing of my porch, gaping stupidly. Was the good guy going to ram the bad guy? Would they go down together? This had to be the great sight I had been dreaming up. Perhaps I should feel guilty?

Seconds, it took, maybe less than one second. Is there still time at five thousand miles an hour?

Then there was the flame, just after the plane passed the powerboat. A tremendous cloud of fire, billowing, deep orange with fiery red tongues, blotting out the other shore, frayed with black smoke at the edges. The flame shot out of the rear of the plane and hung sizzling around Rodney's boat. The boat must have dissolved instantly, for I never found any debris. Fried to a cinder. Did Rodney's body whizz away inside that hellish fire? It must have, bones, teeth, and all.

I didn't see where the plane went. There are low hills at the end of the bay, so it must have zoomed up immediately once the afterburners spat out the huge flame.

Michael smiled sadly when he visited me a few days later and we were having coffee on my porch again.

"You saw it happen?"

"Oh, yes," I said. "A great sight indeed."

"Did he leave any animals that need taking care of?"

"Just the cat," I said. The cat was on my porch, a big marmalade tom that had settled in already.

Time has passed again since then. The bay is quiet now. We're having a crisp autumn and I'm enjoying the cool days, rowing about on the bay, watching the geese gather, honking majestically as they get ready to go south.

A TALE WITH AN END

Cows the size of elephants, that's my work. I'm a biochemist by trade, and extraordinarily intelligent (that's not what I say; that's what my professors said), and I've been working on genetics some thirty years now. My present project is the manufacture of cow embryos in which the genes have been manipulated so that the adult creatures may have the size of elephants. Will that be good? You shouldn't ask me. I'm a mere scholar, stumbling along the specialist's path. Other geniuses have computed that the elephantine size will be optimal in all respects, leading to an excellent relation: so many kilograms of meat per square meter of grass. I disbelieve their equations. However, the Europeans are almost ready to launch their supercattle babies and we Americans have to pass them before the finish. If you ask me, all this will come to naught. Can you imagine what will happen once our mastodons thunder across our ranches? They'll break their legs, sink out of sight, shatter all fences, wander across the interstates. Buffalo Bill didn't exterminate the bison for no reason. What we should do is wait and import a few of the freaks from Europe, just to see what's what. If there is something there, we can always clone the samples. Do I have to waste my good time on this lunatic project? Let's not complain too loudly, for there may be a knock on the door. The Free World came, as you may still remember, to a full stop in 1996. Then the Emergency became official and the Man took over. Since then we do as Our Father in Washington tells us to. If O.F. wants cows the size of elephants, why not? We'll fill the order as promptly as we can.

To be overcome by stress is still permitted and I succumbed, like so many others. My analyst, who isn't right in the head, asked if I could handle a sailboat. Sure, as a kid I owned a dory. He filled in the slip and sent me to Bar Harbor. The last generation of advanced therapists concluded that my kind of craziness will be cured on the water. My shrink uses a computer that has been programmed along the latest lines. You feed the symptoms into its silicone chips and the flashing robot spits out instructions, immediately, of course, for its brain is instant. In my case it strongly recommended sailing, in some plastic tub, poured and dried overnight, in a mold that copies some ancient model. "Plenty of nature and all by yourself," said my analyst, who isn't right in the head. Whenever he goes mad himself, his computer tells him to sit on a thirty-foot post for a day and a night. The good doctor has horrible facial nervous tics, his neck is all loose, and his teeth chatter when he talks. I should never have called on him; I have no faith in science—just look where our intelligence has taken us to.

I got whisked to Bar Harbor and the boat was waiting. I was given a map, instructions (pull on the jib when going through the wind—beware the boom because it may knock you out—bail when the vessel ships water), and a two-way communicator. The marina's manager removed half its chips. I could listen to O.F., but he didn't care for any comments. Near-total solitude was part of the therapy.

"Bye," said the manager, and I took off. The sheets were tight, so were the sails; oil-tipped waves knocked against the bow, dead birds rustled along the sides, the bowsprit pierced the dirty fog, but it was high tide and I didn't think much could go wrong. Plenty of dried food was stored below, and I had some treated water in a tank. When you dissolve the powder in the fluid, you can swallow the mixture and stay alive. I steered to starboard, to where the map said the islands were. I had been there before, before my wife left and when the sun still shone. Strange, isn't it? That wasn't so long ago. It all did go so quickly: the overpopulation, the massive acid rain, the laser beams from the stratosphere that burned the Middle and Far East, the end of the rain forests, the overall death of original wildlife, the endless multiplication of rats— it did add up. And now we'll have cows the size of elephants to trample the last grass. I began to get excited again.

My boat tried to skim along the swelling sea. The sun, what do you know, became visible for a while. A couple of gulls, ever-surviving eaters of whatever is dead, planed above my wake. We shouldn't underestimate life; I did think that for a minute, and some vague hope stirred. Nature persists; something still moves. I thought of my university's experiments; we must have gained somewhere. But what have we come up with? Sure, the fighting apes do well—they make them on the floor below mine. The apes are delivered to the Ministry of Defense. The Communist Consolidated Republic and the Europeans have them, too, but ours are somewhat healthier. But that tale will end, too; all the blustering baboons can handle is automatic arms. They'll kill each other by the millions, and their rotting corpses won't improve the landscape.

I sailed most of the day and anchored that evening on a semifluid site that, according to the map, would be close to Isle au Haut. The island showed as a crumbling purplish dark strip, touched by blood-red light. I saw a few scraggly trees, so they still had trees out there, and some square low buildings, rooted in the tarred ledge.

The ferry passed close by, blowing a hoarse horn, and I saw human silhouettes leaning on the railing. There was a big man on the bridge wearing a bowler hat and sucking a cigar. I waved, but he shook a fist and pointed toward Bar Harbor. I obviously shouldn't be anchored where I was. I tried to remember what I had heard about Isle au Haut. What had been whispered in the university's corridors? Was the island supposed to be a penal colony nowadays? Most of the rumors usually pass me by: a person who is creating cows the size of elephants has no time to waste on gossip. My work has been so diligent that I'm listed in the new *Who's Who*. I carry the emblem of the green dagger in my lapel buttonhole, symbol of aggressive fertility. Really, what nonsense it all is—aggressively, my cows will change grass into mud, but the dagger does have some value. It obtains entry into the best federal restaurants, and if I want to watch sports, I can sit in a reserved seat. "O.F. is proud of you," the Second Secretary said when he issued me the button. I got it when I was still working on the fighting apes, because of my viable combination of obedient and courageous genes. If I don't hurry up on the giant cows, I'll lose the dagger again.

It was getting darker and the ferry passed once more. The captain hadn't changed his tune. His horn croaked and his fist shook, but I didn't feel like lifting my heavy chain and looked the other way. The ferry stopped and the captain lowered a dinghy.

"How're you doing?" I asked when he hoisted his bulk into my boat. The bowler hat seemed glued to his fleshy ears.

"Are you deaf or just retarded?" the captain roared. "I represent authority here; I'm a lieutenant with the Reserve Police. When I say git, it's git." His jacket moved (he wore a three-piece suit), and I saw a laser gun strapped to his belt. Never foulmouth the Police; since the Emergency they've been doing quite well. Crime is down all over the country. I smiled subserviently and was about to ask where he wanted me to park when the captain saw my green dagger button. The bowler hat flew off his bald head. "I'm sorry, sir. Are you here for a special purpose? If I can be of help, please say so at once." He even tried to smile. "I mistook you for a trespasser." He bowed a little. "It's this damn fog; makes it hard to see. Washington sent you, sir?"

I like to be sirred. Courtesy went out when the Emergency came up and swept away the democracy, but then O.F. created rank. Even the staff of state stores grovel when we flash our buttons. The green dagger smooths the routine, and we're the few who can still travel. It works everywhere except in Washington. I've stopped wearing the emblem when I report to the hub. Everyone who moves about in the Man's shadow wears it out there. Maybe I still like to be special.

"I'm a biochemist," I said.

The captain dropped an eyelid. "Right, I get it. The shark project, yes"—he pulled the eyelid up again—"*sir!*"

Sharks the size of whales, I thought, but I only grinned. When you deal with the Police, even if the power seems to behave, you mind your manners. Dagger bearers may be outside the law, but you never know and I'm too busy to risk any trouble.

Sharks are everywhere now, even in the rivers, far inland, and the sea, as I had noticed when I left Bar Harbor, is positively alive with them. One shoal followed me from the moment I left the shore, first showing their sharp, triangular steel-gray fins and later even their pointed snouts. The captain had to go again and they swam alongside his dory, pushing his oars playfully. The official didn't like that much. "Git, boys! Beat it!" They obeyed at once and streaked back to my boat. I heard their sandpaper skin rubbing against my hull. The ferry plowed on. There were no passengers on deck, but I did see shadows moving about in the cabins below.

That night I slept a little and dreamed about the past. I helped my wife wash up. We talked to each other, softly and pleasurably. I arranged the cups on the brass hooks screwed into the shelf so that they could dangle in parallel patterns, all with their handles to the left, and warned her so that she wouldn't hurt her head when I opened the cupboard above the sink. We got along well until she became chairperson of an important feminist group. She works with Rat Extermination now, and keeps drawing up her lip so that her sharp upper teeth show. It seems she was pulled up for correction some time ago; she was charged with treating male rats only— I believe they inject the animals with infectious germs.

In the morning my boat was solidly stuck. I had anchored too close to Isle au Haut, and low tide had sucked me into evil-smelling mud. I was closer to the island than I expected, and while I dissolved and stirred my breakfast, I saw people wandering toward me, clumsily jumping from rock to rock. They hardly returned my greeting but ambled about the boat, mumbling and grinning. They seemed bored after a few minutes and set back for the shore.

I waited for the tide to change and hoisted my sails. There was a stiff breeze and the wind pushed me toward the island, especially after I tangled the jib sheet so that I couldn't turn against the wind anymore. The wind strengthened even further and within minutes my boat was grinding on rocks, mushing large yellow slugs that were tearing at the seaweed. I dropped the sails and clambered ashore.

"What's up?" a cop asked. "You got a permit?"

I pleaded innocent and pointed at my lopsided boat.

"Only makes it worse, buster . . ." but he saw my dagger and saluted correctly. "Sorry, sir. I'll take you to the chief. Be so kind as to follow me." On the way he pointed out the sights. "Those are our barracks, sir, and that building over there is the central kitchen for our charges. The building behind there has all the latest video games."

"Who are you jailing here?"

"Jail?" He seemed genuinely surprised. "This is no jail, sir. They come by themselves, don't they? And they're free to do as they like. The ferry will take them back if they want to go home. I took a whole batch aboard just an hour ago."

He pointed at some young men who were combing their hair on a balcony. "Most of them want to stay anyway. They won't get such a good deal anywhere else, sir. *Everything goes and no rules.* That's on the big sign the chief had put up in our port."

The chief carried the green dagger, too, and welcomed me with a smile and a hug. "Washed ashore? How unfortunate, but we'll make sure that your vacation won't be spoiled. I'll have your boat pulled free, and if she's damaged, we'll fetch another from Bar Harbor. You'll be my guest meanwhile, I hope?"

The common dagger makes for a strong bond. "What's going on out here?" I asked after coffee and pie. "I've been told that Isle au Haut is some penal colony."

The chief looked sad. "Is that really what they say?" He was a tall, handsome man, resplendent in the full-dress uniform with gold braid that staff officers are wearing now. He took me by the arm and we marched together through the door, opened smartly by a cop standing at attention. "I'll show you what goes on here. Penal colony indeed. Some sort of heaven, old buddy— that sounds better, don't you think?"

I understood a little more. The human shapes, clustered in the town's alleys, were all engaged in smoking, sniffing, or injecting. The latter-day islanders would all be users, and not just insane, as I had thought earlier.

"Right," the chief said. "Patients in need of care, you might say, for dependence on dangerous drugs is a type of disease. Hopeless, unfortunately. Most of them are on heroin and the others will get there soon; whoever slides into opium derivates becomes a terminal case at once."

"Any therapy?"

My suggestion made the chief laugh briefly. "No, no, those

times are gone. Another dreadful democratic mistake, one of the many that led us into the Emergency. We turned around a long time ago and you won't catch us looking back."

I looked about. A young but fairly flabby woman dressed in a dirty sheet that she had tried to knot around her body approached us with mincing, unsure steps. "But surely you do make some effort?" I heard myself ask a little timidly. I watched the woman trip and stumble. "That lady might be helped."

"Nah," the chief said. "All she wants is more of something stronger. We'll give her all she craves."

Three ragged men sat on a bench, seemingly engaged in deep conversation. I stopped to hear what they might be saying. "For the fishshsh," the man in the middle said. His mouth was dry and he had trouble pushing the words off his tongue. The others nodded in complete agreement. While I watched, the speaker slid off the bench. I put out a hand to help him back on his seat, but the chief pulled me along. "Leave him be, old sport. He's a tale with an end. The cart will be here in a moment and my men will pick up the body. I think we should improve our selection again. That bum should have been taken out at arrival."

"Out of what?"

The chief shrugged his wide shoulders.

"You mean you do away with them?"

"Sure," the chief said. "But usually we'll grant them the time of their lives first. And when they do go, they have no idea what's happening. *Freedom forever*—that's one of our slogans. We don't like force; the patients' desires are granted at once."

"But how does this work?" I asked. "Where do these wrecks come from?"

The chief had linked his arm with mine and addressed me cheerfully. "From the big cities, mostly. We've been at it for years now. Haven't you noticed how safe your environment has become?"

"I hardly go outside," I said, and told him about my work and life, that I live on campus and that our security works fine.

"You can forget about security," the chief said happily. "All the street trouble is caused by junkies. Statistics are quite clear in our field and our hypothesis has been proved again and again. Crime is on its way out." He caressed his dagger button and smiled at me. "When they raised me to the Dagger Order, last year in Washington, I had to lecture, to all the police chiefs of our big cities. A standing ovation, I got, old buddy. They knew what we do for them here."

"You dragged all the junkies from the streets and collected them on Isle au Haut?" I asked unbelievingly. "How? By rounding them up? Nobody resisted?"

The chief squeezed my arm. "Now, now, colleague, the ideas of the new order have progressed immensely. Terror doesn't work; we've known that for a while. I took a course on Stalin and Hitler, and recent history in the East proved it again. As soon as you apply pressure, reaction pushes back, and all struggle is plain painful. Our Father is known for his love and compassion. Look, there comes our new load."

I looked. The ferry was vaguely visible in the fog. The chief waved and the captain lifted his bowler hat. "All passengers got on of their own free will." The chief's hand clasped mine. He wiggled three fingers on his other hand. "That means thirty per trip and the ferry goes three times a day; that's less than a hundred a day, a mere trickle, and still going down. There were more when we started."

"And how do the junkies know where to go?"

The fog thickened all of a sudden, and I brought out my handkerchief to protect my face; the foul air can be quite smelly. The chief was coughing. "How're you guys doing with the antipollution?" he asked when he could breathe again. "The papers keep saying there's some headway, but I can't say I've noticed that we're gaining at all."

I said that I was with a different department and that the media are hardly credible since Washington put a stop on all the negative news.

The chief winked. "But what does my professor think himself?"

I watched my step. Our Father's love and compassion have failed to convince me so far. How come all complaining colleagues have disappeared from my university? What I believe is mine alone. *I* believe that the point of no return was reached years before the Emergency was declared. We were too late. I've conducted enough scientific experiments to know that there's always a final point from where there's no going back. Maybe the universe goes on forever, but our planet is finite. At a given moment our end was reached; we couldn't go on expecting life to balance pollution. Certainly, once we take our own species away, the planet will recuperate, but even so, not from one day to another. Once our fouling presence is removed, a new balance will come about and change again, steadily reaching upward. Evolution will set out in a new direction. We might even follow the new line, just a few of us, say two or three million, thinly spread over the earth's surface. Our reproduction will have to be severely limited so that our numbers won't increase again, and all sinners will have to be killed, to be replaced by their own illegal offspring. I can just see myself presenting that proposal to Washington! "Our Father, the only way out is to do away with ourselves." All present efforts are getting us nowhere; even wars won't help. If you don't believe me, watch what's happening in the East. Two billion killed, but recent probes saw new populations crawling about among the ruins, like evil vermin.

"We're doing fine, chief," I said politely. "We're on the right path." He giggled doubtfully and I thought a little flattering might be in order. "Thanks to folks like yourself. If you can take care of all New England's junkies on one small island, you're heading the reformation Our Father is pushing through."

"We've cleaned up New York, too," the chief said modestly, "and I've set up Key West to take care of the South." He slapped my shoulder. "Do you know that the Japanese who've taken over the new western prefectures have been out here to see if they can copy us, too?"

"Splendid," I said. I punched him gently above the gun belt. "But now how does this really work? You're getting a hundred a day, you said. How come they're not all over each other? Some forty thousand a year. Do you send them back when they're in order again?"

"In order?" We passed a few hunched-up individuals crowding a soda-pop dispenser. "They'll never be in order."

"How many do you have here now?"

"The flowing average? Five hundred, I guess, but what hangs out in town is the worst part of the total. The with-it persons are doing some work. They only work when they want to, of course. House servants, beach cleaners—you would be surprised if you saw what drifts in every day. If we don't take care of all the dirt, it would swallow us in a week."

I hadn't seen a chimney anywhere, or a building that might house a cremation oven. "So the suckers arrive voluntarily, right? Someone tells them that Isle au Haut is the place?"

"We tell them, the Police," the chief said. "The method is simple. Junkies commit crimes to get cash to buy dope. You know that the Police couldn't do much before the Emergency was declared. The jails overflowed and the bastards kept walking about. Demand causes supply and the supply always trickled in. When we arrest a mugger or burglar now, we fill him up with his favorite drug, right at the station, hand out a free bus ticket, and tell him there's more out here."

"But when they find out that there's no return?"

"Ha-ha."

"Pardon?"

"Simple too," the chief said. "We select a suitable specimen every now and then and take him to the special settlement in the north of the island, straight from the ferry. The settlement is our top-level heaven: gardens, swimming pools, beautiful people, whatever you like. Say the person wants to go back, to visit friends or relatives—that's fine, too. A powerboat drops him off and he can take some dope out. There's no limit to what we do to serve."

"Okay." I had to admit that the setup was ideal. "He'll use the dope and will tell his mates where to go for more. Brings them in, right? In droves?"

"Exactly, old buddy. The system knows no flaw. Our propaganda spreads nicely. With compassion and love we clean up the cities."

"But . . ."

"Yes?"

"Look here," I said. "If you want your population steady, you have to get rid of a hundred a day. What happens to them?"

"They do die, you know."

"Of old age?"

"Right," the chief said. "Their old age is young. They aren't too healthy."

"So a few die, of disease, or self-inflicted starvation maybe, but no hundred a day."

"OD," the chief said enthusiastically.

"Beg pardon?"

"Overdose, colleague. They do it themselves. Remember the gentleman who fell off his seat just now? The dancing girl? They'll be all done this very day, without any interference on our part."

"You do give them a hand."

The chief shook his head slowly. "To give a hand is overstating the situation. We don't feed them poison—our dope is grade-A fancy—but the specimens are greedy. Heroin addicts require more every day or they can't reach the level they've reached before. Our funding is limited and I can't pay for weighing gear. All we have plenty of is dope, and they've got to figure out their doses themselves."

"You've *got* to give them a hand," I said stubbornly. "Overdosing can never be normal procedure. Surely, your patients have some experience."

"Okay, we do give them a bit of a hand."

"How?" I asked. "By suddenly supplying them with extra-strong junk?"

"For instance—dirty needles help, too. We do have a hospital, but the only medication is more of the same." The chief grinned helpfully. "*More of the same.* Another of our slogans."

"Risky," I said. "Imagine someone gets away, from this side of the island, not the northern tip that you just mentioned. The escapee will tell his friends that this is a terminal resort. Nobody likes death; they'll prefer living on in their accustomed habitat."

"Escapees?" the chief asked. "You sure you know something about the psychology of an addict? All he wants is dope, and dope is available here. When they want to go away, we escort them to the ferry. The ferry supplies dope, too, and the captain's quality is what we call *zero zero*. The captain is a trusted cooperator; he will be cruising around until it's all quiet in his cabins."

"Hmm," I said. "I have been asking some dumb questions."

"Not at all," the chief said. "The situation is somewhat special and to you it's a bit new. Our solution is only partly propagated." He smiled contentedly. "A method without fail, old buddy, that came to us from Washington's brain box. Thought out by eggheads like yourself, equipped by computers expertly programmed. I'm only a practical employee, following orders as best I can. So now it's elephants with udders, is it? Will science ever fail to save our skin? Nothing impedes us now that you guys have figured it all out."

I agreed wholeheartedly. We're surrounded by Nothing and ready to tumble in.

My boat turned out to be severely damaged, and I had to wait until the Police picked up a replacement in Bar Harbor. That night I stayed in the chief's ample cottage, and we were served by lovely, albeit dreamy, ladies. Dinner was excellent and we feasted on tender steak and tasty vegetables.

"Sea-produced," the chief said. "The vegetables are boiled-up weeds."

"Was that your idea?"

"I only studied criminology and management," the chief said. "I combine the talents of others. One of the patients that stepped off the ferry turned out to be a marine biologist, same trade as yours. You know"—the chief heaped up my plate with something that looked like lettuce but tasted like asparagus—

"I've been lucky. When they come in, we make an immediate selection. When the sea scientist arrived, I almost sent him the wrong way. That would have been a really bad decision and I would never have known. You know how we do that? Selecting, I mean?"

"Not by force, I trust."

The chief wobbled an eyebrow. "Never. No, we just indicate the way. I, or another—depends who is on duty—stands on the pier and points left or right. There are some fences, but we don't yell or show weapons. The fencing is high; once they're on their way, there's an end to their choice."

"Aha," I said. I was seeing the scene. The commander in his French uniform (Our Father is from New Orleans and likes foreign ways; the Police wear kepis now, just like the French Foreign Legion), pointing with his swagger stick.

"Yes, that marine biologist was nearly lost down the drain. It does take some doing to keep him going, but we keep him on his toes. His first project was seaweeds; I never cared for these new dried foods."

"Aren't the seaweeds polluted, too?" I asked. "That slimy goo I saw floating around my boat didn't seem fit for consumption."

The chief cut me more steak. "There are some exceptions and the fellow found them for me. What do you think of this meat?"

"Absolutely delicious."

"Shark steak." The chief laughed loudly. "The fortuitous and beneficial combination of two inmates, the biologist and a cook." He patted his button. "My favorite project and claim to obtaining oak leaves under the daggers. Sharks thrive on all disasters—aren't they doing well?"

"I did notice quite a few when I came out," I admitted.

"Sharks are survivors, but even they are running out of food. When I took charge of the island, I saw them eating each other in the surf."

"They don't anymore, I'm sure," I said, and ate more steak. "Tasty, very."

"Well prepared." The chief's knife slid through the meat. "Took some work to get the fishy taste out. So you see, we're all doing something, us knights of the green dagger. You with your lumbering cows and I with the sharks."

"And what do your sharks eat?" I asked stupidly.

No, I didn't see the sharks feeding. I've got weak nerves and was on vacation. My new boat arrived the next day and I sailed the Bay of Maine for another week. If I did perhaps notice anything, it was from far away. The ferry stopped halfway from the island, and I saw the sharks beat the sea while the captain off-loaded his cargo. I also saw some dump trucks, lowering their beds at the shores of Isle au Haut. A hundred corpses a day won't be unwelcome to our torpedo-shaped friends, but will the quantity do? I'm wondering about that. The moralistic aspect is well outside my scope, and we do acknowledge the Emergency that cures crime with crime. Viewing the matter scientifically (from the point that considers the greatest common good) the experiment is worthwhile, but what's forty thousand in an overpopulation of some six billion? Isn't the number rather a negligible drop in a worldwide ocean of goopy slop? I do like the principle of the beneficial circle. The sharks eat us and we eat the sharks. It would be easier if we could eat ourselves, but I doubt that even the most brittle eggheads among our Washingtonian supply of applied psychologists could ever break the taboo against cannibalism.

Ah, well, I'm back in my laboratory and cutting up some genes. The first embryos have already been placed in ordinary cows' wombs, and next spring we may expect our deformed babies. I refuse to consider the effects of my cause. One of the female giants is sure to lie down and have herself fertilized by some normal bull. We're only aiming for female mastodons and are programming them to be well behaved, but once oversize bulls start roaming about, free to bring about all sorts of havoc, the end is in sight. I keep having a feeling that they may breed in what used to be Philadelphia, or one of the other areas that we've given up for lost. Enormous weeds are reputed to grow out there; we couldn't even get at the beasts from the new polycopters—oh my, oh my. Am I worrying again? What do I care, anyway? A tale with an end, after us the deluge, of slimy waves that are mostly rotting foam.

Meanwhile, we have the plague, I hear, erupting in all locations at once. The papers ignore the news, but people still whisper to each other. It's a new-fangled microbe, and even our strongest antibiotics are food for its growth. The disease follows a sudden, so far untraceable, destruction of our immune system. I had been thinking for a while that some virulent killing virus would be next. As the pollution can't be stopped, in spite of our best scientific efforts, we will face sicknesses that won't fit any imaginable models. The scourge resembles medieval bubonic plague—large pustules appear all over the skin—and once they break, death occurs within minutes. The first symptom is an itch. I've felt a little itchy myself lately, but when I scratch, the irritation goes away. No such luck for me, I'll be around to see the end.

JACOB SANDERS' FINAL SOLUTION

(N)otes in an exercise book, found in a house once occupied by the German army, May 1945.)

It's chilly again, after a couple of fine hot days. Inside the house it's cold, too, but that can't be, for our superb home is well insulated and centrally heated with steam, generated in the basement. My brother Elias connected the system to a powerful whistle that he attached to a wall on the first floor. Once the pressure becomes dangerous, the whistle shrieks and we all run to the cellar to see how Father, Professor Sanders, shovels burning coal into buckets. The pressure goes down, the shrieking subsides, and we can all go back to bed. Nothing bad can happen to us, for we are very intelligent. My other brother studies, just like Elias, physics and mathematics. His name is Benjamin and he was supposed to be the last born, but I happened to come along, labeled "stomach cancer" at first. Later I was an intestinal disorder, causing smelly gas, but later again I turned out to be a baby. My name is Jacob.

I'm in grammar school now, and fifteen years old. Everybody says I'm bright, too. Yes, in our family the talents have been distributed well, provided my mother is counted out. She has been ill, in bed, moaning a lot, ever since my birth, and I was raised by maids, German maids; there have been times that I spoke better German than Dutch. The maids aren't just raising me; they also cook—that's why I got so chubby. But the fat has been melting lately, first because I began to exercise a little and more recently because I've been unwell.

We live in Rotterdam, on an avenue called the Duke's Wall, in a tall house topped by a turret, a useless structure until I broke the boards that my father had nailed across the door. From the turret, through another little door, I can reach the roof. Under the turret is a small room. There are two other rooms in the loft, with plywood walls—that's where maids number one and number two sleep, but for a month now we have employed a third maid: the Rumanian one who calls herself Elly Walach. She claims to be nineteen years old. I think she is very antique.

Elly now sleeps in the little room below the turret, and I live in the room below hers. The first night that I knew her to be so close, I imagined I could hear her clothes rustle when she undressed, but that couldn't be true. Our mansion is built solidly; all floors are covered with thick Oriental rugs, for Father is rich. He makes a lot of money and inherited from Granddad, the diamond dealer. Mother is affluent, too. We have quite a car and the furniture is ancient French. Our winters are spent in an Alpine Swiss village with snow up to the gutters and steaming grits for dinner. I dislike both snow and grits. We summer in our own cottage on the Italian Riviera. It's better there, for I can take walks by myself and don't have to play fatiguing games. The journey out, and back, is pleasurable, too. The boys at school are jealous of our Rolls and call it a garbage chariot, but the car is comfortable. A touch of splendor can't harm anyway. Most days I'm driven to school, and I make the chauffeur get out first, open my door, and touch his cap. Maybe that's not so good, in view of all the poverty in the world, but I like to exaggerate. Moreover, I'm convinced of the illusionary nature of our wealth. The year is 1939. Hitler yells through our radio. I've read his literary works. I do sometimes believe that I'm the only genius of the family, for I have no hope for the future. Hitler is going to kill all Jews; the fact faces us, no matter from which angle we choose to look at it. Europe will be German—I don't think he will be able to reach much farther. America is too strong, even for the booted death squads with the swastika bloodying their black uniforms. We have to get to America, but Dad, Elias, and clever Ben underestimate reality. They keep telling me that it'll all be fine in the end and even ignore Uncle Max's testimony. Uncle Max slipped out of Germany, and his family— our aunt and cousins—are in some camp by now, if they're anywhere at all. Uncle Max wasn't home when the police car came for them. That took place in Aachen.

Aachen is so close that the streetcar cuts through Dutch territory for a few yards. Uncle Max used public transport to make his getaway. He got off, without luggage but with his memories, on the Dutch side and came to us. He now lives in a boarding house, in Rotterdam's inner city, at our expense, and reads Goethe in German. He is too old and ill to continue his escape, and every time I visit, he gives me the same advice: "Get out of here, Jacob, get to New York." But what shall I do in America? I don't know anyone out there. I can see it now, me with my steamed-up round spectacles, dragging my fat body through all those numbered streets. I could take some cash; if necessary I could steal the money from Dad's wallet.

He usually carries a thousand guilders in notes. That's a few hundred dollars, enough for the passage. As a minor—and I'm undersized as well—I'll attract attention and the police will send me back. No, death awaits me, as soon as it has strengthened enough; it's getting plenty of exercise in Germany now. The war has started already; I'm really amazed that this small country is still free.

I no longer argue with Dad. He teaches economics and gets all wound up about intrigues at the university and the attitude of his students. My brothers are after their master's and Ph.D.'s; they want to equal Dad and be qualified at a ridiculously early age. I read literature in Latin and understand analytical geometry, ahead of time, for I'm only supposed to get the credit next year. Intelligence relates to the capacity to adapt to new circumstances. The new circumstances are flexing their muscles behind the frontier, but we look the other way and do anything but adjust to a changing environment. We continue our silly routine, and I would be desperate if Elly Walach had not been suddenly introduced to my world. Her legs are long and slender, her torso is supple, her breasts are firm and tilted, and she has small delicate hands and a moist dainty mouth. Elly's nose is straight and her eyes are large and beautifully slanted. Her hair is long and raven black. That color I take from mythology. I have no idea how black ravens are; there aren't any in the Rotterdam zoo. But Elly's hair is blacker than mine and shines, as if alive with fire. Her teeth are good, too, the teeth of a predator with canines that are longer and sharper than the others. Elly isn't tall; she's about my size, so the teeth are fairly small, too, but razor-sharp. I have to stop for a moment now. I'm tired and ill; I've been in bed for weeks. I've been scratching the scabs on my neck again. The pages of this notebook are smeared with blood. I'll dream for a while; real sleep is beyond me now. I sort of float while vague thoughts take sudden shape. I see much of what Uncle Max has been telling me about. Storm Troopers march through the street where Uncle owned his store. They force their way in and destroy the stock and furnishings. The dog-faced soldiers, or policemen, or whatever they call themselves, growl and bark at the clerks and salesladies. They take my aunt and my cousins, even the smallest one. Esther is three years old, if she's still alive. Uncle Max is old, the children are from his second marriage. He's quiet now; he no longer cares. He reads Goethe in the cheap bed of the room Dad rented for him, and when the Germans come here, too, he'll swallow a pill and fly away, just like me, a little later, when I'm done with these notes. But Uncle Max will fly away for good, and so far I've always managed to come back.

I took my nap. The doctor made his brief visit. He really comes only to maintain my mother's eternal complaint, the psychosomatic disorders that stop short of death. Mother's symptoms differ every week; it's her back now and she rests under a half barrel that contains some heating elements. The doctor professes intense interest in Mother's conglomeration of diseases. I think half his income is paid by Father. My treatment probably doesn't even show on the bill. Doc pounds my chest, glances at my tongue, and makes me piss in miniature bottles. So far, he hasn't noticed the wounds near my throat. I'm cultivating a cough and wear a scarf. The wounds are rather small. Elly's canines are sharp and her tongue licks softly.

The doctor is a quack. Surely, he should be aware of my weakened condition. But I shouldn't be ungrateful.

He also prescribes a tranquilizer, juice of valerian. Valerian dulls the nerves that conduct fear. I do suffer from fear—that part of his diagnosis is correct. I'm frightened of the black-shirted rabble marching toward us from the other side of the border, and I'm afraid of Elly Walach, too.

Isn't it ridiculous that I have to put up with fear? We are wealthy folks; doesn't money equal energy? Besides, Dad, Elias, Ben, and I are supposed to be geniuses. Dad's friend, Professor Polak, a psychologist, tested our IQs. We scored incredibly high. Intelligence added to stored energy—what more could we ask for? But here we are, little mice squeaking in a trap; worse, we don't even know we're trapped. Yes, sure, I know, but I happen to be the youngest and most helpless of us all. Should I empty Dad's wallet and leave the country? Several vessels leave for America each week and my passport is stored in the Napoleonic chest. The chest is locked, but one swing of a hatchet and I'm equipped with all the papers I need. I could become a newspaper boy in New York. In a few years I'd be old enough to help battle the Germans, defend good against evil. I'm just lying here instead and allowing my life force to be sucked away.

Elly Walach is a vampire. I suspected that at once, the first time I saw her in the corridor downstairs, trying to hold on to her dissolving cardboard suitcase. She said she was a fugitive, an orphan from Bucharest, picked up by the Red Cross and forwarded to Holland a few years ago, institutionalized here and taught how to be a servant. Don't make me laugh. The poor, pathetic little thing; as if those large, dark, alert eyes didn't betray her despicable nature. Why would she have selected me? Doesn't Aryan blood taste better? Rumanians are anti-Semites—I heard that somewhere—and it would be our own fault, for the Jews were used by the Rumanian gentry to collect their farmers' rents. We would have abused the population, urged on by counts and dukes; that's why the Rumanians hate us so. I know nothing about all that history. My father is an economics professor and I'm a diligent grammar school pupil. In my innocence I might say that the fault lay with the Rumanian lords, with criminals like Archduke Vlad of Walachia, the fifteenth-century vampire, degenerate owner of a mountain castle. Each night he flew out, in his atrocious form of a bat, and satisfied his perverted lust, crouching near the beds of his tenants' beautiful wives and attractive daughters. Vampires prefer the blood of the opposite sex. Elly Walach would rather suck me than girls. She has to be a great-great-granddaughter of Vlad of Walachia. Her first name is no good either. Elly—Elizabeth. Elizabeth Báthory lived during the seventeenth century and was a Hungarian countess. I overheard Elly on the telephone the other day, whispering to a friend. She wasn't speaking Rumanian. Rumanian I would recognize, for the language derives from Latin. I found all sorts of information in father's library. Countess Báthory was, if possible, even more wicked and cruel than the archduke of Walachia. Too lazy to fly away at night, she had her victims brought to her bedroom. The countess seduced the poor young fellows with her dazzling beauty. Elly is lovely, too.

A buzzer protrudes from the wall above my bed. The buzzer is a capsule made out of Bakelite and holds a button. The Bakelite is creamy white, cracked a little in places. I painted the button pink myself. When I press the buzzer once, maid number one appears, but the terrible apparition whom we employ these days doesn't like to be called and snarls before she slams the door. She speaks a guttural German she learned in Prussia and has her own radio so that she can hear the Nazi news. Why we keep that dragon in the house is quite beyond me. She'll be the first to denounce us when her countrymen arrive and will kick us into the police van herself. When I press the buzzer twice, Anne comes; Anne is maid number two. Anne is pleasant but stupid and doesn't smell very nice. Three touches of the buzzer and Elly stands next to my bed. Would the young gentleman care for a cup of tea? Her Dutch is rather exotic—she sings our words. I'm very fond of Elly.

There's a book on sex, hidden on the top shelf of one of my father's bookcases. I've read the chapter on puberty so often that I know it by heart. Adolescents are supposed to suffer from intense sexual fantasies that force them to masturbate incessantly. I hate handling myself. A novel translated from Italian says that some fathers take their sons to brothels. Dad would never do that; I doubt whether he ever visits such establishments himself—he's far too busy with his theories on state-controlled economies. But that's the way it should be, really. Dad takes son to the lovely ladies. A few visits might do away with my compulsive and solitary occupation. I've seen monkeys at it, in the zoo, all by themselves on a board in their cages. Yank, yank, yank. Two or three drops to show for all the expended energy. Can't they get the monkeys suitable mates?

Our mathematics teacher at grammar school, a short, square female with a belt around her hips, peering at us through fogged-up spectacles, claims that my sense of logic is impeccable. She likes to give me equations that should be beyond my training. I usually solve the problems, and if I can't see the answers immediately, I formulate questions that, properly thought through, will lead to solutions.

This is the problem:

The Germans are on their way—there's no stopping them; the evil they perpetrate at home will be repeated here. I'm Jewish, so my number is up. Not only that I will be killed—the suffering leading up to extermination will be unbearable. They'll beat, kick, humiliate me; there'll be no end to the harassment. They'll probably do everything that I can imagine they will do. A type like Hitler is as cunning as I am myself. He can look deeply into my soul, as deeply as I can look into his. I understand exactly what motivates his activity. All right. Once they've done everything they can think of, they'll slaughter me at the end. I should escape, but I'm too much of a coward, too lazy if you like. I think I'm still too young to take individual action. Dad has to protect me, but Dad does nothing: he walks on the rugs in his study, bites the stem of his pipe, and worries about aspects of future socialism. Dad will never leave for America. Elias and Ben also prefer theory to practice. Mother groans under her electrical heaters. I'm lost. How do I save myself? And how do I save myself with maximal pleasure?

Uncle Max is lost, too. He's stretched out on the couch of an upstairs room in Erasmus Alley and enjoys his Goethe. Uncle Max is not as helpless as we are. He believes in free will. "Jacob," he says, "listen to me well. You were born; you can't be blamed for suddenly being here. You stood in your crib, rattled the bars, filled your pants, and cried a lot. You couldn't escape then, but now you certainly can. This time you're free. When life no longer suits you, when you feel that your part of the planet is being poisoned, well, my boy, say good-bye to the mess."

One of the boys in my class hung himself. He was bright enough—all the teachers liked him; his parents are wealthy—they live in a villa on the shore of a lake. That boy—Frits was his name—was good at sports, too. The summer before he died, he won prizes with his sailboat. A good-looking fellow, tall, wide-shouldered, curly hair—all the girls were in love with Frits. Only son, so no jealousy at home. Not Jewish. Even so, isn't that strange? It makes one think. Our history teacher, a pleasant chap who makes old stuff worth looking at, said that Frits committed suicide "because of idealistic convictions." In other words, Frits didn't like it here. I think that's great. I also think that's courageous. Compared to Frits, I'm a weakling; I'll get out because I'm scared. If we could live in America—and why couldn't we? all Dad has to do is weaken his socialist ideas a bit and they'll give him a job, but he doesn't want to do that because his German is better than his English, dear God, does he prefer to go to Berlin?—if we could live in America, I would be happy. In America I could get a driver's license when I'm sixteen and I'd ask Dad to buy me a sports car. Without fear I could have a very good time indeed.

Here I'm troubled by fears, but string myself up? No. As far as that's concerned—I'm discussing methods now—I'm cleverer than Frits. I'll solve my problem differently, obtain my liberty in a more spectacular manner. I'll have to, for I do want to have just a wee bit of pride in myself. Self-respect needs to be satisfied, too.

Can you follow me, readers of the last pages of my paper?

I should really be able to catch the whole issue in one mathematical formula. *The pleasure of reaching liberty increases in proportion to the subtlety of the method applied.* That's my hypothesis and I intend to provide the proof.

That Elly Walach is a vampire was no more than a vague suspicion during the first days and nights that she lived in our house. Maids numbers one and two regularly fill the bird feeder in our rear garden; it hangs from a wire stretched between two trees. I always like watching the birds peck at their food. I sit on the stairs that connect the back porch with the garden. I eat raisins from a brown paper bag, and I watch the sparrows and the starlings, the lone thrush, and almost feel happy. One evening I was on the stairs again and saw a bat. The little animal flapped about, then screeched and fell. I didn't understand immediately what had happened, but a little later I could reconstruct the event. Behind our house are some cheap high buildings with small apartments. A boy must have shot the bat with a BB gun from one of the balconies. I picked up the little corpse and took it inside. Bats don't look pretty close up. What god can design such horrible apparitions? I saw a pushed-up flat nose between bulging, evil eyes and misshapen ears. The bat's mouth hung open, stilled in that final squeak of death. Its sparkling white teeth contrasted with the sweet pink of the moist inner cheeks and bright red tongue. Especially its canines frightened me—they were that sharp, that efficiently precise; they appeared as small instruments of torture. But that's no more than the fantasy of fear. Elly Walach's teeth hardly hurt. Sometimes I don't even feel her bite.

Suspicions are no good by themselves; the scientific mind keeps on prodding and isn't satisfied until solid proof is produced.

I already explained that there's a turret topping our mansion and that I had taken off some boards. Before Elly arrived, I used to spend many hours in there, feeling both safe and crafty, for nobody knew where I had hidden myself. Through the window up front I could see the high school on the other side of the avenue, and the statue of some old codger being kept company by two maidens hacked out of stone, with their blouses slipping off their shoulders. The bosoms of those ladies are something to behold. Street boys sometimes aim for the nipples with pebbles, and a cop with a helmet, riding a bicycle with polished handlebars, chases them off. I can see them sneak back from my hermitage in the turret. There's a back door, too, leading to a deck. The architectural meaning of the construction has never been clear to me—but there are riddles that even I do not attempt to answer. I sit there and think; the summer wind caresses my bulging cheeks.

In order to catch Elly at the execution of her devilry I hid in the loft, after everyone had gone to bed. It was so quiet that I could hear my own breathing, and listen to the thumping of my heart.

And, right, there she came from her room, in a tight black frock. Before climbing the stairs to the turret, she paused for a moment, making sure she was alone. I held my breath, the blood thumping in my ears. When Elly stepped on the first stair, I saw her wings, thin but strong, connecting her arms with her back. They were folded still, of course, but later, when I had mustered enough strength to follow her, I saw the wings in their full span. Elly stood, with raised arms, on the small deck behind the turret, and I clutched the flimsy staircase, my eyes just above the threshold of the door. She flew away. That part of her performance didn't particularly impress me; bats are a little clumsy when they're in flight. They flutter rather than soar, but do manage to stay aloft.

That night I didn't sleep. I sat on my bed and read the chapter on vampires in my father's encyclopedia.

Encyclopedias tell a lot of nonsense, but I only notice that truth when I'm fairly familiar with a particular subject. According to the learned nitwit who hides between the initials Dr. I. v. S. (Ignorant von Stupidstein?), a vampire has no shadow. That isn't so. Elly does throw a shadow. A few weeks ago, before I got too weak to leave my bed, we were in the street together. It was a sunny day's three o'clock. I looked behind us and saw our shadows. Mine was pitch black and clearly outlined; hers was grayish and not too sharp, but she did have a shadow.

Something else that isn't true; supposedly you can keep vampires away by wearing garlic. Well, I tried that experiment. It's quite a business making holes in garlic cloves, but finally I had a garland to wear around my neck. That evening Elly came, as usual, and she giggled at my effort. "Now what did you do, you silly boy?" And *schleef*, she sank her teeth into my neck, and she was sucking my blood, smacking her lips with pleasure, her nose pressing against my earlobe. I caressed her back and buttocks meanwhile; she doesn't like that, but she was too busy to push my hands away.

And then that balderdash about vampires not being able to face the light of day. Elly can't play maid in the dark, can she now? I hope Dr. von S. will read these notes. When vampires are in their human shape, they're just like him and me; it's only when they become giant bats that they stay out of the sun.

Ignorant also states that you can get rid of a vampire by sticking a metal rod through its heart. A remarkable piece of advice. Even Hitler would croak if you slide a poker through his chest. The silliness of that bit of wisdom irritated me, but it did give me an idea. The first evening after I could prove that Elly really was what I thought all along, I went to her room and took Elias' sword with me. Elias is with the Student Guard and has a uniform and a sword. Or would the weapon be called a saber? Whatever the right term may be, it's sharp, it gleams, and it's usable.

I knocked on her door and she said, "Come in." She even gave me a chair. She got back into bed and smiled at my sword.

"You want to do away with me?"

"Yes," I said, "because you don't happen to be just another maid; you're a vampire and I exterminate vampires."

She said she wasn't a vampire, but I told her I had seen her on the roof. I reminded her of her ancestors, Archduke Vlad of Walachia and Countess Elizabeth Báthory. She cried a little to prove her innocence, but I asked her why her teeth are pointed.

She got out of bed and knelt down on the linoleum of her poor quarters. It was quite exciting. I could look down her blouse. "Please, darling Jacob, don't tell anyone."

Why should I tell anyone? Am I ever taken seriously? For more than a year I have been pointing accusingly at the East, but my family keeps believing that Hitler is really quite a nice sort of chap and that the German Jews are taken to vacation camps where the work is quite acceptable and the food rather tasty: pea soup, perhaps, and pineapple with whipped cream on top to follow. It's a pity that my father is an atheist and even ignores the Jewish faith. If I had been raised religiously, I could scream "ay-wai-wai" now. Jews are good at complaints— even their wailing is part of the discipline. To wail is good; it releases tension but, alas, I cannot join in. I do have the intelligence of my race, however.

Elly admitted that she was a vampire and her confession provided me with power. I could now control evil. It's impossible to make a deal with Hitler; he wants our total extermination. Vampires like to suck blood; they're not so much into killing. I like sex. My ancestors were merchants; I know how to go about the exchange of services.

Elly said she didn't care so much for sex—well, okay. I really dislike bloodsucking. Nothing for nothing, right? How about undressing, right now, without too much hurry; I actually ordered her to do that, and got hiccups as I voiced the command—I also trembled and sweated a lot.

"And afterward I can suck your blood?" she asked. I think she was as thrilled as I was. Her voice was hoarse and her hands changed into claws, the claws of a bat.

"Sure," I whispered, "but next time taking your clothes off won't be enough. I'll want a lot more."

She told me sex was a waste of time. I wanted to know if this was her first erotic adventure. She said it wasn't. As a technical detail the information was welcome, but I chose to ignore the emotional implications. Elly was mine, just as I would be hers when her lips pressed against my neck and her teeth broke my skin. Whatever she had done before had nothing to do with me. She wasn't a virgin; maybe that would facilitate my first attempts.

That's the way the affair started. Her side of it was simple enough: all she wanted was my blood. She insists that I lie down, she bends down over me, I unbutton my pajama jacket, her teeth sink in. After a while she'll lie in my arms and let me stroke her body. My desires are more complicated. She's the only woman I'll ever know, so she has to be many women for me. I make her wear different clothes (she doesn't have too many herself, but my mother is her size; Mother's wardrobes supply me with an endless choice). Sometimes Elly enters my room like a grand lady sweeping into a ballroom; she'll wear dresses that touch the floor and high-heeled golden shoes. It'll all have to come off again. I also make her wear underwear of black lace or dress up as a schoolgirl, with a dark skirt and a white blouse, pigtails and all. Whatever I can think of, she'll have to do, and so she does—she's quite obedient. The illustrated instructions in my father's sex book are helpful, too. I found a series of forty-nine different postures, modeled by Japanese. Most of the postures are variations on a few themes, but some of the more perverse possibilities are both educative and exciting.

Ouch, my neck smarts. The doctor is due this afternoon and Elly will visit me tonight. I've got six pillows propped against my back and need all my willpower to keep pushing this pen. According to the radio, the international situation is degenerating. Uncle Max, who visited me yesterday—nice old chap, he's quite weak himself—listened to an address in which some crazed demon from Berlin discussed the Final Solution of the Jewish Problem. The SS officer minced his words somewhat, but that we'll all be smashed is hardly doubtful. Does smashing hurt? I dislike all pain. Uncle Max wanted to know if I was in pain. He's a dear old man and that's precisely why I won't trust him. If I were to tell Uncle Max what's really going on with me, he would probably warn my parents. And then to think that I'm only doing what he himself advised. I prefer to escape through death, like he plans to do himself. With one's family one must always be careful: they tell you what to do, but when you do it you're in trouble.

Elly brought tea and a piece of cake. In a minute she'll be back again with a bowl of egg-drop soup. When she plays nurse, I don't mention our intimate connection; the tenderness is for between midnight and 1 A.M. Last night she told me that she feels weird because with me she doesn't have to be a bat. When she sucks me, she does change a little, however; when I feel her back, I notice that the wings begin to form and her eyes bulge somewhat and her nose flattens—a few minutes afterward she looks human again.

When she gets too greedy, she makes me sick to my stomach. Dr. I. v. S. claims that a vampire's victim will become a vampire himself in due course, but that can't be true either. Whatever happens, I will never suck anybody's blood. I once had dinner at a friend's house and saw his mother cutting up some bloody sausage. I had to excuse myself and threw up in the toilet.

"Do you love me?" Elly asks sometimes, against her own will, emotionally weakened because of my kissing and fondling. I prefer not to answer. My feelings for her are all mixed up. I don't know much about love between a man and a woman. My mother never spent any time on me, and the flirting and fumbling at school passes me by completely. We have some good-looking fellows in our class and they monopolize the situation. I can peck a girl's cheek in the cinema maybe (if I provide the tickets) and I did kiss a bit at birthday parties. I've read widely on the subject, but an affair like Elly's and mine hasn't been reported on, as far as I know. I'm Elly's victim, but she is also mine. We keep each other going, but I'm afraid I'm now nearing the end. I'm getting too weak. Sometimes my soul floats away; some days ago I was flying about in the street. The experience frightened me and I was glad to get back into my body.

Tonight . . .

Tonight? I believe it's day again, Sunday perhaps. Yesterday I couldn't write anymore. Elly came and sucked. First she had embraced me for a while and looked at me, with her large moist eyes, the eyes of a daughter of Archduke Vlad of Walachia, but also the eyes of the Hungarian countess, the lady of the despicable orgies in her burgh on the moors. I felt how Elly's gaze pulled me in, far into a faraway landscape, and further still, to where the earth dissolves into the empty universe. I was both within and without her being and finally I wasn't anywhere at all. I understood how everything does fit together, outside the limitation of our usual perception. I must remember this, I thought, pumping away stupidly, because it seemed that I had penetrated the ultimate mystery, but now I only recall that I did think I knew something. Terrible, to be faced by incomplete recollections. I'm myself again, but then I was looking at the temporary form of one Jacob Sanders, from a point a long way from here.

It was good-bye to ignorance, as I'm saying good-bye now to an existence. I'm leaving this stained notebook behind. Up till now I've been hiding it carefully, but now I'll let it slide onto the floor. I will finish this sentence, put away my pen, push the notebook off the blanket. Then I will wait a while. When I get bored, I won't even have to close my eyes, because they stay open when you die.

THE
YOGA YO-YO

Archie is a friend of a friend. When he put me up that night, in his loft in the Village, New York City, I noticed the little altar displaying an orange plastic yo-yo on a piece of brocade, half a foot square. Incense smoldered in a sand-filled copper bowl. I tried to explain the yo-yo, but I was wrong, of course— partly, anyway. I was right in assuming that Archie venerated the yo-yo as a manifestation of whatever gives meaning to life, I was wrong in seeing it as a female torso. I was also wrong in comparing it to the Easter Island statues.

I arrived in time for dinner and invited him

out. We had some cocktails and I mentioned the yo-yo. Archie is tall and thin, with a nervous twitch in his cheek, large eyes, and fluttering lashes. He is shy. But we got on well and the cocktails helped.

The yo-yo, like many good tales, started in a bar, in Manhattan. A singles bar. Archie had gone there to find what he could find, or, rather, I think he wanted to be found, for he is shy. He was found at the bar, by a rich girl called Lorraine. A beauty, Archie says. Tall, dark-haired, blue-eyed, well-dressed. She had had a good deal to drink and talked a lot, but she wasn't drunk. She introduced herself and Archie said he was Archie, a sub-editor at a lesser-known publishing firm, recently fired. That suited her, she liked writers, she said. And as she was rich, she liked sponsoring writers. Archie said he wasn't exactly a writer and right now he wasn't anything really, for he had just been fired, but she wasn't listening. She said she was rich because her father had sold a million cowskins, in Texas, but also in Africa. He had died a year before, halfway between two farms, on a sand road, of a heart attack. Her mother had died earlier, in a hotel in California, of an overdose. The money was now with some silver-haired gentlemen on the fortieth floor of a white building on Fifth Avenue, and she was getting 9 percent in a check every three months, which was good. And she was paying a lot of taxes, which was bad.

Archie had another drink and told her that he would be getting tax back, because he was on unemployment now, but she wasn't listening.

Archie got worried. He swallowed his drink and waved for another and pressed his thigh against Lorraine's thigh. She stopped talking for a few seconds and smiled. She didn't move away from him.

"We can go to my apartment."

"Fine," Archie said.

"But finish your drink first; we have time. I live by myself; we have all night."

"Fine."

"Ever been to India?"

No, Archie said, he had never been to India. He had been to Mexico City and Vancouver.

"That's all *here*. You've never been out of America?"

No.

Then she told him about the guru and the ashram. It was a long story, and he had another two drinks while he nodded and said hmm-hmm in a half-eager, half-patient way every now and then. It seemed that Lorraine was a Hindu, converted some years back when she was still at college. She had spent time in U.S. ashrams until she had taken the plunge and gone to India. She had been to the Indian ashram twice now and would go again.

"Really?"

"Yes. Tomorrow. Please come with me."

"No money."

"I'll pay."

Archie had had enough by then. He didn't want to drink anymore and he didn't want to listen anymore. He wanted to go home. He asked for the check, but the bartender gave it to Lorraine and Lorraine paid. They left the bar together.

"Just a few blocks, we can walk."

She walked fine, her hand rested on his arm but didn't weigh him down. She didn't steer him either. He got to her apartment building by his own free will.

The man in the lobby was black and wore a uniform and a gun. The lobby was made of marble. There was an Oriental rug in the elevator. The apartment had a sun porch filled with eight-foot palm trees. She took him to the bathroom and turned the taps and sprinkled bubble powder and stripped. He stripped, too. He got excited, but she restrained him and they had a good time. Then they had a better time on the big double bed in the room next to the bathroom. Then he fell asleep.

When he woke up, she was making breakfast, and he had another bath and shaved with a female razor that he found on a shelf. They ate an omelette filled with herbs, and there was lots of toast and fresh orange juice and strong coffee. She was talking about India again, slowly, in a low pleasant voice. The plane would leave in the afternoon.

"Do you have a valid passport?"

"Yes."

"There are no strings. If you don't like it, you can go back. I'll buy you a return ticket. You don't have to feel grateful, I don't like going there alone. It's a pleasant, quiet place. You can have a rest. A month maybe, two months; there is no time in India."

She left the room. He ate the rest of the omelette. Well, why not? She came back and he said he would go, thank you very much, very nice of you.

She bent down and kissed him.

They went to his apartment together; he packed a zipper bag and got his credit card and money. She checked his passport. His passport was okay. He could get a few hundred dollars on the credit card and he had a few hundred dollars in cash.

"You don't have to take any money."

He slipped the credit card and bills into his wallet.

They got to Kennedy and the plane was delayed. They had lunch. He wanted a drink.

"Perhaps not. Hindus don't drink, really."

"Okay."

He tried to understand the movie, but his earphones didn't work. He ate, then he slept. There was a lot of space outside the window and clouds underneath. He woke up a few times to look at the space and the clouds. Then they were at New Delhi and Lorraine made him sniff the air when they deplaned. She said the fragrance was exotic. He thought the place stank and that the people were too noisy. She hired a taxi, a rusted-through '59 Ford. The driver killed some chickens on the way, swerving so that he could hit them full on. Some blood splattered onto the windshield. The driver laughed. The trip took over three hours.

The ashram was an acre or two, closed in by a high wall

with plaster peeling off it. Some thin trees trailed dusty leaves, and half a dozen buildings were scattered around a well where a stuttering truck engine pumped water once in a while, to fill a tank resting on four-by-fours. A fat little man came running to welcome Lorraine. He was the assistant guru; Archie didn't catch his name. The assistant guru spoke English, in a high voice, spitting out sentences consisting of nouns and verbs only. He ushered them to a small house and waved at the door, then he took off again.

A tube was clamped to the wall and ended in a tap. Lorraine stood under the lukewarm trickle while Archie cleaned up. He picked up used sanitary napkins and dropped them in a bucket. He also found two plastic syringes, and there was a sweet smell—hashish, he thought—mixed with perfume. The bed had a thin mattress; the little night table had an irregular pattern of burn marks. Lorraine came in and unpacked her aluminum suitcases and Archie tried the shower. He swayed so that the trickle could find different spots on his back. There was a barred window and he saw some ducks, high on their legs and with short, tightly folded wings. They reminded him of clerks, strutting up and down with their hands on their backs. The ducks went away and three roosters appeared and crowed nervously. The thin, pitiful screeching annoyed him and he shouted through the bars. They shut up, and then started up again.

"You like it here?" Lorraine stood in the open door that connected the bathroom with the bedroom.

"Sure."

"Take your time, I'm going to the kitchen at the other end of the compound. They serve rice and vegetables; we can eat here. You don't mind being a vegetarian for a bit, do you?"

"No."

He was asleep when she came back and refused to wake up. She was annoyed when he did wake up, the next morning. He said he was sorry, he had felt very tired. He said he still felt very tired.

"That's all right, Booby, you'll get over being tired. You'll get over a lot of things—hindrances, we call them. You will learn to meditate here, to breathe."

She began to call him Booby. He tried to tell her that his name was Archie. She also gave him a meditation lesson. The assistant guru sent cushions. Archie had to fold his legs and sit up straight. He was told to concentrate on his breathing. The posture didn't bother him too much, but he got bored after a few minutes. Lorraine sat next to him. They both sat quietly for half an hour. She made tea and they sat for another half hour. She said they would sit for three hours that day, but he refused and walked about the yard. One of the roosters attacked his shin and he kicked it. An elderly British lady wagged a finger and invited him into her room. She gave him tea with a lot of milk and sugar and told him about love and goodness and how the small ego dissolves and becomes like a drop in the ocean.

"What ocean?"

"The divine ocean. The All."

"Really?"

"Oh, yes."

When he came back, Lorraine wouldn't speak to him. The British lady had given him a book on yoga, and he read it for an hour and fell asleep.

The next day the guru arrived. The guru was a stately old man with a flowing white beard. He asked them over to his house and explained that the ashram had some difficulties. More guests were expected, more buildings would have to be constructed. Money was needed. Lorraine wrote out a check. They were invited for communal meditation that night and Archie tried to refuse, but Lorraine interrupted his protest and called him Booby again.

The ceremony was impressive. The guru and the assistant guru sang and several young men played drums and guitars. There was a short sermon, about love and goodness, and then they sat quietly for two hours, with a short interval after every half hour. Archie's leg itched and he scratched it, and Lorraine's elbow shot out and hit him on the arm.

There were several British ladies, and they took a liking to Archie. Whenever he refused to meditate with Lorraine, they would catch him and preach. The roosters kept on crowing and the one rooster kept on attacking his shins. He would stumble over the ducks. He didn't like the rice and the vegetables. Lorraine wouldn't let him smoke in the bedroom. The truck engine broke down and they didn't have water for a few days. After two weeks he said he would leave.

"No."

"Yes. I am sorry. Would you give me my return ticket, please?"

"No."

He sat down on the bed and lit a cigarette. She took it out of his mouth, dropped it on the floor, and stood on it. He packed his zipper bag and walked to the door. She ran ahead and blocked the door. He pushed her gently.

"Please stay."

"No, I'm sorry, Lorraine. This isn't my scene."

"Where do you want to go? Stay another month and we can go back together."

He pushed harder and reached the yard. He walked quickly and she ran after him. She was crying. "Please, Booby."

He shivered and walked on. A rooster came and he kicked it. He had reached the gate. It was almost dark. The yo-yo lay in the road outside the gate and he picked it up. Lorraine was hanging on to his arm. He tried to make a joke. "Look, a yoga yo-yo. I'll take it with me."

"Just another month, please!"

"Let go of my arm."

He could feel her nails in his flesh and moved close to her, then stepped back suddenly. He yanked his arm free and ran. She fell, sobbing, but he didn't stop. After a while he began to walk. He walked all night and reached New Delhi in the morning. A bank gave him three hundred dollars on his credit card. There was enough to buy a ticket home. He meant to go home then but changed his mind in the bus to the airport. He got off the bus and found the railway station and bought a cheap ticket north, to the end of the line.

The journey took days, for the train was slow and there were passengers everywhere, even on the roof. They shared their lice. He bought food in the stations, but it didn't agree with him and he had to throw up and contracted diarrhea. At one of the stations he was still behind a tree when the train left, but his ticket was valid for the next train. When he came to the end of the trip, he was in a pleasant, quiet town. Mountains rose just behind it and the evenings and nights were cold. He found a hotel room and bought an army coat and a sweater in the street market. For a week he walked about, playing with the yo-yo. The toy shot up and down with a quiet hiss that soothed his mind. The people of the town accepted the silent white man and smiled at him or greeted him with folded hands. He read the yoga book the British lady had given him and read it again. Then he left it on a rock. Some of it he could understand, but he didn't agree with the love and goodness. He saw the starving dogs and the mutilated beggars. He also saw the mountains that didn't care, and the pale blue evening sky.

One afternoon he wandered outside the town and found a field and a Buddha statue in the field. The statue was old, overgrown with moss and lichen. He stood and made the yo-yo hiss, and a man in a patched red robe came up to him and bowed. The man said that his name was Yeshe and that he was a Tibetan monk, a refugee who had lived in a camp for some years and learned English and now lived here, in a shrine.

"Please come, I will show you."

Archie liked Yeshe. Yeshe was a small man, with orange-brown skin and a shaven head. He had a low forehead and large, dark slanting eyes. He carried a wooden bowl. He explained that he had begged for his food in town and had been given a meal and some money and was on his way home now.

"Do you like the Buddha?" Yeshe asked.

"Hmm?"

"The statue you were looking at. The Buddha."

"I didn't know he was the Buddha," Archie said.

"Oh, yes. Oh, yes. He is the Buddha and I am a Buddhist monk." But the shrine was Hindu. It had contained an altar and a statue once, but they had disappeared. Yeshe had built walls out of old boards and flattened cans and used a soapbox for an altar and a flowerpot for an incense burner. He had two army mattresses and offered one to his guest. They sat and drank tea. Yeshe accepted a cigarette. There was also a stove, made with bricks and fueled with leaves and twigs.

"Sometimes I eat two meals—one I beg and one I cook. When I have money, like today."

"You're a holy man."

Yeshe giggled. "Yes. So they think. In Lhasa I was important, a *trappa*, an ordained monk. I worked in the office and bought supplies. Here I am a holy man."

"You like that?"

"Like. Dislike. Words."

Archie went back to the hotel and checked out. Yeshe had invited him to stay in the shrine. Why not? It would be cheaper, and some company wouldn't hurt.

His routine hardly changed. He walked around the landscape, and when the landscape became too quiet, he would walk through the town. He visited the street market and bought another mattress. He meant to use one as a meditation cushion, but it took a while before he joined Yeshe, who liked to sit in the early morning and in the evening. Archie never sat long; he would get up and go outside and smoke and come back and drink tea. Yeshe didn't seem to mind. He sang before and after his meditations, starting with a ho-ho-ho in the back of his throat. The chant was never loud and caused pleasant vibrations.

He came back to the shrine one afternoon and found that it had been robbed. The thieves had left nothing except the soapbox, and they had broken the flowerpot. Yeshe came home a little later. He shook his head. Then he smiled.

They were cold that night. Archie went to town the next morning and bought mattresses, cooking pots, some food, an oil lamp, and a copper bowl. He also wanted to buy a brass Buddha statue, but the vendor wanted thirty dollars, claiming it was an antique. He also bought incense.

He told Yeshe about the statue and Yeshe said it didn't matter. Then he asked to see the yo-yo.

"This thing, what is it?"

"A toy. I found it."

"It is important to you. What do you think when you make it go up and down?"

"Nothing."

Yeshe was speaking a little louder. "Nothing?"

"Yes."

"That's good. Think of nothing. Some teachers say, 'Think of something, concentrate on something.' That's good, too, but to think of nothing is better."

Archie laughed. "Yoga yo-yo."

"What?"

"Its name."

"Name? I forget name. Name not important. I'll put it here on altar; later you take it again. Yes?"

"Yes."

Time passed and Archie became ill. It was the same illness he had had in the train, but this time it didn't pass. Archie became so ill that he began to float through the shrine and no longer recognized Yeshe, who made him drink tea and dried his body. A doctor came, an old man with a kind face, and his antibiotics finally stopped the fever, but the doctor said that the illness would come back and kill Archie. "If you want to live, you must go."

"Yes," Yeshe said, "he will go."

Archie left a few days later and Yeshe saw him off on the

train. By that time Archie had stayed three months and his money was almost gone. It was completely gone when he reached New Delhi. He was dirty then and his clothes were torn. The guards at the embassy wouldn't let him enter the gate and shouted and pushed him back into the street. He nodded and smiled. The fever had come back. He considered the possibility of lying down somewhere, but a plane flew over and made him change the thought. He walked to the airport. When he got there, several busloads of Americans arrived, and he slipped past the building and saw a plane and shuffled toward it. The yo-yo shot up and down, but he no longer thought of nothing. There was a word in his mind, just one word. *Home.* He thought *home* as the yo-yo came up and he thought *home* as the yo-yo shot down. The tourist crowd reached him, and he smelled the bathed bodies and the crisp clothes. He also smelled his own stench and nearly vomited, but the word was more important. *Home.*

It couldn't be done, of course, but that didn't matter. He reached the stairs leading up to the plane. He was on the stairs. Somebody slipped and fell. The crowd no longer flowed but broke. He must have slipped through, but he never knew how. He was still mumbling "home," but then the plane was in the air and he was served coffee and orange juice.

It took me a while to take it all in. I sipped my drink and looked into Archie's large luminous eyes.

"Wow," I said when the drink was down, "so that yo-yo got you home, right?"

"Yes."

"And now you burn incense for it. It must be valuable to you."

He laughed. "Not really. It's just a toy, you know. I'll keep it as long as it will stay with me."

I couldn't think of anything more to say, so I said "wow" again.

"Yes," Archie said.

THE
ℜEW DISCIPLE

Master Tofu lives on the eastern slope of Mount Hyee, a little west of the fishing village, Sakamoto, at Lake Biwa, in a cabin at the end of a winding path. The emperor appointed Tofu as a Living National Treasure. That title is given only to true artists who have reached their goals. There's a painter on the northern island of Oshima who's a Living Treasure. He only draws cormorants, on flat stones that he finds on the beach. The emperor acknowledges that the painter understands the essence of the cormorant.

Master Tofu makes vases and teabowls. He uses

the local clay and burns twigs under his oven. His tools consist of a few blunt knives and a wheel. He built his cabin himself, and his disciple lives near him in an even smaller cabin. Master and disciple spend months turning pots and then place them in the oven. When the oven is full, the master goes for a walk. He sits on the rocks and watches the blue shine of the large lake down below. He sits in the sunshine or in the cold light of the moon and mumbles or hums. The wild animals pass close by, birds chirp near his ears, a butterfly rests on his hand. Then the master will become quiet himself, and once nothing disturbs him and his soul is as pure as empty space, he will return to the oven and light the fire. The flames roar up and lick at the closely fitted bricks, and the master sits on a stool and waits. When the fire dies and the ashes stop glowing, Tofu will pry open the oven to check whether his vases and bowls have withstood the ordeal. Most of the pots he will break up, but usually a few remain.

Every item that carries his seal is worth a fortune, and Master Tofu will go to the art dealers in town and exchange his creations for bank notes. He looks like a kind old man. His clear eyes glitter between the wrinkles of his funny apple face. He doesn't walk easily and supports his spare little frame on a gnarled stick. When he has collected his money—he twists the notes in tight rolls that he secures with elastic bands—he will walk to the pleasure quarter and start the evening with a bowl of tofu soup. Tofu is a jelly made out of soybeans. It's supposed to be healthy, has little taste, can be bought everywhere, and isn't expensive. Rumor has it that the master was born in a noble family, but he lives like a poor hermit and gave himself that silly name. Perhaps he wants to show his modesty in that way. Except for tofu soup, he usually eats only fruits and the roots of plants that grow around his cabin, but when he's in town, he'll drink rice wine and then wander about the streets where the prostitutes hang out. After a couple of days and nights of partying, Tofu goes back to baking pots, walking, and sitting quietly.

Some ten years ago the experts requested the emperor to

appoint Tofu as a Living National Treasure, because the master's art is so pure and simple and contains a touch of ungraspable refinement. The true artist tries to break through the frontiers of human restriction, and Master Tofu must have been successful, for his pots cannot be caught within definitions. It goes without saying that young potters like to learn from him. It seems, however, that Tofu does not want to teach, and hides whenever someone shows up. Only Turu has managed to penetrate Master Tofu's defenses, but he had to camp for weeks near the master's property and wait patiently until the old man finally deigned to show himself.

"What can I teach you?" asked Master Tofu. "Making good pots is ridiculously easy. You take some clay, form a vase or a bowl, put it in the oven, and wait until the fire is done. That's all there is to my simple craft. Don't think; make your hands surround the emptiness. Empty within, empty without. What else is a pot but a line in space? Do you have to bother me to hear what you know already?"

Turu stayed. "You have to pass on your skill so that your knowledge can be shared by whomever comes after you."

"I don't have to do anything," said Tofu, "but if you think that I'm wrong, I'll order you to weed my garden."

Turu did everything the master told him to do. He collected twigs for the oven, did the laundry, swept the floor, carried clay, cooked potfuls of tofu, and tried to imitate the master's ways. Turu also made vases and bowls and put them in the oven. At times his pots looked a little better than at other times, but they never in any way resembled what Tofu was doing. "No, no," Tofu said. "You've got to quit thinking. Allow the shape to come out by itself."

"Yes, but," Turu said.

"Yes, but," Tofu said, and broke all Turu's vases and bowls with his stick.

Turu bowed angrily and walked to the city, but came back the next day. He tugged on the master's sleeve. "What now?" asked Tofu.

"We've got to leave here," said Turu.

Master Tofu sighed.

"I do know," Turu said, "that you never have to do anything at all, but this time the obligation will save your own existence. If our very lives are threatened, do you think we should defend ourselves?"

"Are our lives being threatened?" Master Tofu asked.

Turu lit a cigarette and bent his head to the side. "Yes. Don't you know that we now have neighbors?"

"I do," Tofu said. "Two strapping young fellows. They built a cabin on the other side of the brook."

"I met them," Turu said. "Just now, on the path. I know who they are. They are no good."

"Who is good?" Tofu asked.

"Not me," Turu said. "That's what you're always saying. I do everything wrong, in the wrong way. But our new neighbors do everything wrong in just the right way. They're terrorists from the capital."

Master Tofu kept quiet.

"Listen," said Turu. "You have no idea of what goes on in the world. They're against the existing order and want to destroy civilization, so that a new society can arise from the ruins. They blow up trains and kill ministers of state. They're afraid of nobody and nothing. There are all sorts of terrorists, and the most terrible are disciplined intellectuals. I think that these two belong to the worst kind."

"Exceptional people?" asked Master Tofu. "I hope you're right. Muddlers I know aplenty. I believe I'm a terrorist myself, of the very worst kind, but unfortunately, I have neither time nor inclination to cause any trouble."

Turu closed his eyes and shook his head. "These fellows are werewolves who'll do all the evil they can envision. We've got to leave at once. I'm not even sure that it's not too late already. Their photographs are on the front page of the *Kyoto Times*. I recognized them at once, and I'm sure they noticed."

"So what?" asked Tofu.

Turu began to sweat. "Have you gone crazy, Master Tofu? Am I really addressing a senile old codger? They asked me whether you happened to be the famous Living National Treasure. Everybody knows that you're stashing a fair supply of cash. Please, think of a plan so that we can escape. We're almost out of time."

"Bah," said Master Tofu, and lit a cigarette, too. He blew the smoke into Turu's face. "Turu," said Master Tofu, "you behave like a fool. I can't teach you anything. For years you've been scurrying around my feet, but your head is filled with clay, and I can't get it out for you. Maybe you learned something here, but you won't notice until you've broken away from me. You have to understand your own wisdom, which is no different from my own. You've got to go."

"Where can I go?" asked Turu. "They'll wait for me and cut me down. They have binoculars and are watching us right now."

"I'll distract their attention," said Master Tofu. "In the meantime, you'll sneak out of the rear window and crawl through the bushes, climb the mountain, and make your escape down the western slope."

"Yes, but," said Turu.

Master Tofu picked up his stick.

"What difference does it make," asked Turu, "whether I'm murdered on the eastern path or break my neck falling off the western cliffs?"

"If you stay here, I'll crack your skull," said Master Tofu.

Turu grabbed an axe. "Don't try to fight me, old fool." He trembled with fear and rage.

"Choose," Master Tofu said. "My stick is deadly."

Turu attacked the master. Master Tofu sat on his stool. Turu's axe flashed. The metal protector at the end of Tofu's stick kept warding off the axe's blade. Every flash of the axe coincided with a sweep of the stick. The fight went on until Turu came to the end of his strength.

"Well?" asked Tofu.

"I'll go," Turu said.

Tofu went outside and danced on the field outside his cabin. He sang and waved his arms. While Tofu danced, Turu slid through the rear window and crawled through the bushes. He reached the forest and sat on a rock. "I have to make a choice," Turu thought. "I can climb the mountain and try to get away via the steep cliffs on the other side, but then I'm almost sure to fall to my death. If I go down this side, the terrorists will see me and cut me off. They're tall and strong, and one is armed with bow and arrows, and the other with a sword. If I go back, Tofu will go for me with his stick. It's time to face the truth. Tofu is no master at all. The terrorists want to rob him. What is that to me? I'll offer them my services, and get a third of the loot."

The more Turu thought about his plan, the better he liked it. Wasn't it true that he had given up everything to become a master's disciple, and had gotten nowhere after years of strenuous labor? Wasn't it equally true that he owed nothing to a society foolish enough to appoint unspectacular potters to the rank of Living National Treasure? "The ignorant people," Turu thought, "have supplied Tofu with a lot of money because they thought that he was a great man. I'll take some of that cash myself, so that I'll be equipped to make a proper beginning."

The two men now living on the land west of Tofu's were called Sakai and Yasudo. They were both honor students of Tokyo University's Department of Philosophy. Sakai had practiced sword-fighting for some ten years, and Yasudo was a formidable exponent of the art of archery. They had become close friends because they both believed in the "opposite direction." "Only Nothing is of value," they were always saying to each other, "and therefore we have to reach that Nothing." Sakai had graduated with an exhaustive study of "The Essence of Duality," and Yasudo was approved by the university's authorities because of his brilliant comments on "The Untruth of Good." The professors who only practiced theory were much surprised when the two young doctors claimed credit for a devastating fire in downtown Tokyo, the disastrous

211

derailing of one of Japan's famous "bullet trains," and the subsequent brutal murder of a minister of state.

Sakai and Yasudo were now resting on Mount Hyee, the holy mountain that protects the temple city of Kyoto, Japan's spiritual heart. Hyee is also known as the Mountain of Rumination, and its landscape resembles those of ancient paintings—impenetrable forests reach up to razor-sharp cliffs shrouded in lofty mists. There the human spirit sheds all that holds it down and floats over fields covered with fragrant herbs. The thinker learns to listen, like the clever fox whose ears turn around to catch the slightest rustle, in secret meditations that reach for and connect with the empty base of all.

Sakai lowered his field glasses. "Amazing. That old man limps somewhat, but his dance is impressive. One would think that he might try to compensate for his useless leg, but he exaggerates its lameness, so that the defect becomes the theme of what he's trying to express. What do you think he knows?"

"My guess'll be as bad as yours," said Yasudo, "but we're having a visitor, the fellow who scared so easily when we met him on the path today. There he is, under the gnarled pine tree." He picked up an arrow and lifted his bow.

Sakai touched his friend's arm. "Wait a little; maybe his information is of some value."

Sakai concentrated again on Master Tofu, who had just finished his imitation of a wounded rabbit and now became a heron, standing silently on one leg, staring into clear water, beak withdrawn shyly, ready to spear a fish. "Quite an amusing fellow," Sakai said softly. "Now why was it, again, we wanted to kill him?"

"In order to combine the necessary with the pleasurable," Yasudo said. "A Living National Treasure represents the best of our present society. When we do away with him, we'll advertise our effort, and Tofu's stash will enable us to continue our performance."

Turu approached and bowed.

"Hello," said Yasudo. "Formulate as clearly and succinctly as you can what brings you here."

Turu told his tale.

"Right," Sakai said, "from the frying pan into the fire. Tofu tried to teach you the mystery of form, and obviously you failed to grasp his teaching. With us you're worse off, for we teach the art of how to do away with form."

Turu laughed. "I've been well trained in that particular field. Whatever I made was broken by Tofu's stick. I'm ready for revenge."

"Good," Yasudo said. "You say Tofu managed to collect some solid capital. You know him well, and the arrangement at his house must be familiar to you. Go down and make him give up his money, then return and give it all to us."

"That doesn't sound so good," Turu said. "I'll be of use to you, and you'd better be of use to me. Nothing is for free."

"Nothing is for free, indeed," Sakai said. "Wait until dark and then complete your mission. Don't try to get away, for it'll be easy for us to hunt you down."

Yasudo smiled. "Why do you hesitate? Your choices are already made. By coming here, you surrender to our power. Maybe we'll accept you, in time, as our comrade, but first you'll have to prove yourself."

"Good evening," Turu said.

Master Tofu woke up.

"Listen," Turu said. "I'm no longer your property, for I've broken my chain. Your stick may have parried an axe, but I'm now carrying a sword. See this magnificent weapon? My new masters stole it from Tokyo's Imperial Museum. It once belonged to Prince Yozo, and was forged by Tokoro. Whoever holds this sword is invincible. If you use your stick, I'll cut off your head."

"My stick is in the corner," Tofu said. "I don't need a stick when I'm asleep."

"Stop chatting," Turu said. "I've come for your money. If you give it to me, I may save your life."

"You don't mind if I don't get up?" Tofu asked. "My money is in that vase."

"I hope you're not joking now," Turu said as he squatted and put the vase on the floor. His right hand held on to the sword as his left hand approached the vase's neck, which was wide at the top.

"Just a minute now," Tofu said. "I know you're all-powerful since you've become the friend of great spirits, and your sword, which once conquered the country and was made by a master forger, does frighten me a lot. Even so, I do think I should advise you. Are you sure you want to put your hand into that vase? I made it when I was still struggling with my own demons, and it could be that one of them sneaked into it. It's night now, and even demons have to rest. Perhaps he'll be upset when you disturb his sleep."

"For years you have used me as a slave," Turu snarled. "I thought that I could learn from you, without ever realizing that I was being abused. Now shut your trap, for when I lose my temper, you'll surely lose your head."

Turu put his hand in the vase and then pulled it out, yelling with fear and pain. A writhing viper dropped to the floor.

"Simpleton," said Tofu. "Did you really learn that little about forms and shapes? The money was at the bottom of the vase, and because its neck is too narrow below to admit your hand, you should have smashed the vase."

Turu rolled about on the floor. The snake's poisonous teeth had bitten deeply, and Turu's arm was swelling already.

"Help me," begged Turu.

"The poison is fast," Tofu said, "and in your blood, on its way to your heart. The viper is the demon that is born from greed. Each spot on its skin is a golden coin."

"I'm dying," yelled Turu.

"Take a deep breath," said Tofu, "and relax your muscles. It'll stop your fear. To die is an interesting experience, but fearfulness will spoil it for you."

Turu beat the floor with his fists and began to whimper. His eyes bulged, his face turned purple, his jaws cramped open, and spittle dribbled down his chin.

"The clouds keep passing the moon," Yasudo said, "and I can't see what's happening out there, but I do believe that Master Tofu is preparing a burning pile. And now he's dragging a body. He's lifting it onto the branches and lighting the fire. I'm afraid our new disciple has left us already."

"Would *you* like to go now?" Sakai asked.

"Now what?" Master Tofu asked. "If you're after the money, I keep it in that vase. I don't mind if I'm to lose my life, but I detest being woken up all the time."

Yasudo studied the vase. He thought aloud. "The money is in the vase, but if one reaches for it, something unpleasant evidently results. Besides, the vase's neck is too narrow below. In order to get at the money, I'll have to break the vase."

"Splendid," Master Tofu said. "Your logic is impeccable, but my teacher used to say that a little straight thinking does no more than produce a little answer."

"Was your teacher right?" Yasudo asked, while he fitted an arrow to his bow.

"Well," Master Tofu said, "right or wrong, who'll make the ultimate decision? A little of both, it all depends on how you look at the problem."

"Get up," Yasudo said, "find a hammer, and smash that vase."

"May I warn you?" Tofu asked.

"Please do," Yasudo said. "Although I really never care for advice."

"Go away," Master Tofu said. "That vase contains only money. A lot of it, I do admit, and free to you, but you're still a young man, and it may be better if you make your own."

Yasudo aimed his arrow at Master Tofu's heart. "You're not

telling me that I shouldn't steal, I hope. What is possession? What difference can there be between what's yours and mine? I'm ordering you to break that vase."

"As you like," grumbled Master Tofu. "All I'm trying to do is catch some sleep, and everyone barges in as if my humble abode were the Central Railway Station. Why should you involve me in your mistaken routine?"

"Our paths cross each other," Yasudo said, "and we'll both have to accept the consequences of this meeting. Are you about to do as I say, or do I have to release this deadly arrow?"

Master Tofu got up, grabbed a hammer, and smashed the vase. The viper fell out and so did the money. Yasudo tried to watch the viper and Master Tofu at the same time. The viper slid toward Tofu, and Tofu bowed his head. The snake turned in a flash and went for Yasudo. The arrow hit the spot where the viper's head had been half a second ago.

"Ouch," Yasudo said.

"I'm sorry to see that you're now dying," said Master Tofu.

"I didn't pay sufficient attention," Yasudo said. He stretched out on the floorboards, and crossed his hands on his chest. He took a deep breath and closed his eyes. The viper had bitten him on the leg, and the poison rushed up toward his heart.

Now look at that, Sakai thought. The performance is about to repeat itself. Master Tofu has plenty of firewood. I'm sure he'll leave enough to dispose of my body when the time comes. Isn't Yasudo burning brightly? Now how could he have lost that unequal battle? He's the best bowman I've ever met. He recognizes the danger of a situation long before a crisis occurs, and there I see his body, consumed by hellish flames.

"Once more?" Master Tofu asked. "Three is a strange number indeed. I have often been successful at the third try. What can I do for you?"

"I'm unarmed," Sakai said. "Your former disciple brought you my sword, but I'm physically stronger than you and excel at karate."

"Are you threatening me?" Tofu asked from his bed.

"I'm not sure yet," Sakai said. "Frankly, I'm not even sure of the purpose of this visit. I've been watching you today. First you danced, then you burned the corpses of your own disciple and my friend. It seemed to me that you were quite contained in the midst of all activity, even when you were prancing about, showing me some of the aspects of your being."

"You like to chat," Tofu said. "But I prefer to sleep at this time. How about coming to see me in the morning?"

"There's some money on the floor," Sakai said.

Tofu groaned and sat up. "It's all yours, provided you leave my home. That money has been causing trouble all night. I should never have kept it. You know, when I make money, I always get drunk, and once I'm drunk I like to play with the ladies, but there's always more of the stuff than I can possibly spend."

"And there's a snake, too," Sakai said. "He looks unhappy."

"That's because he lived in a vase," Tofu said, "and I smashed his home."

"Why do you call yourself Tofu?" Sakai asked. "Hermits go for fancy names. Master Cranebird, for instance, or Master Unicorn. Tofu is a colorless jelly that never hardens, it just becomes somewhat spongy. Are you colorless and spongy?"

"Yes," Tofu said. "Would you please take the money and leave me alone?"

Sakai shook his head. He got up, found a vase, and inserted the money. He put the vase in front of the viper. The viper slid into its neck. Sakai placed the vase on a shelf, found a broom, and swept the shards into a neat little heap.

"Will you be leaving now?" Tofu asked.

"No," said Sakai. "Will you take me as your disciple?"

Tofu kept quiet. Sakai continued sweeping.

"You walked the wrong way," Tofu said, "but never mind;

it hardly matters how we define what has been brought about. The suffering that you caused will have to be put right sometime, however."

"As you say," Sakai said.

"And there's nothing I can teach you; all that the mind needs to grasp is already present within the mind."

"That I haven't grasped yet," Sakai said.

Tofu sighed. "You'll find some bedding in that cupboard over there. Let's go to sleep. Tomorrow you have to weed the vegetable garden."